G000141712

If the World Hates You

By

AB Lawson

Published 2021

ISBN 9798731220545

Dedication

To Pat

iv

Acknowledgements

With sincere thanks to those who read the book before publication and gave very helpful feedback, especially Alex and Margaret.

To Bruce, who gave his usual honest and direct comments in the early stages of development.

To Debbie who kindly printed out the first copy.

If the World Hates You

Chapter 1

70CE

Jacob caught his shoulder on the wall corner as he fled into the next street. Behind him he knew the Romans had broken through. He hit his arm on the side of an abandoned cart, dropped his broken sword and winced with pain. In this street the sound of the clashes and screams behind him were dulled slightly. What should he do? This street was deserted: it was given to heat haze and the smell of donkey piss. There was a pile of straw on the other side of the street a few paces up on the opposite side. He chose to hide. On running across the road it was not just straw but dung. He jumped headlong by the wall side of the heap where the level was lower and scrambled to cover himself in straw and drying excrement. He struggled to control his breathlessness and his heartbeat raced.

He paused.

1

He could see a little of the street through the craze of straw around his head. Flies returned to their activity in the dung. There were the sounds of Roman soldiers at the corner he had rounded. They had seen the broken sword. Orders were shouted.

Further up the street a door opened and a child giggled. He ran out with what looked like a rag toy. He had taken it from his little brother who was crying in the house. It was a game to run away from his mother who was bearing down on him to restore it to its rightful owner. The screams of the mother, however, were not about the toy. She was three paces behind him.

The sword hit the child just above the ear and took off the top of his skull. The white wall was sprayed with blood and brains shot randomly across the ground. The child laid crumpled and still in a similar shape to the toy. The mother stopped in shocked silence. She held her hands against her stomach and fell to her knees. She could not sob. She could not reach the depth of that place where it should start. Her forehead touched the ground. She made a noise that, had Jacob not seen its source could have been the long quiet bray of an ass. She had lost her child.

2

The soldier's shadow passed over her. He slipped and stumbled in some of the gore and cursed. The woman was ignored. He only had orders to kill males that day.

84CE

"You having a vision again?" Jacob came to the present at Marcus' question. He was conscious of his nose running and tears dripping from his chin. At least the tears had not splashed onto the papyrus.

"It cannot be a vision from the Lord." He felt Marcus needed explanation. "It was that child again. I keep reliving that awful time. Why did they have to kill the children?" The voice was almost controlled.

"I wasn't in the Jerusalem campaign. I was building roads and shithouses on the route to Eboracum.[1]" Marcus paused. "They warn all the others not to mess with Caesar's boys I suppose. I am thankful I found my place in engineering or I would have had to live with more of your sort of memories."

---

[1] York, UK

"God did not save any of his children." Jacob cleaned his face and wiped his nose.

"It strikes me, Jacob that God does not save many of his children in your history. All the boys in Egypt and only Moses won through. Then there were those poor Egyptian first born little buggers who perished as the slaves walked on water across the sea." Jacob did not correct his catechumen because he liked the oversimplified image. "And what about the Canaanite babies having their heads dashed against a stone?" Jacob had no answer.

"I came into this faith because of the sense of one God rather than the fiction of a bunch of weirdoes on a hill interfering at a whim with human life. I find a message of Love and respect in Jesus as Lord. The biggest miracle is that Jesus could come out of this cesspit history of violence of yours with a message of Love. The second biggest is that we have got to where we are despite the infighting, arguing and disputes amongst ourselves since."

Jacob was still subdued and pensive. Marcus looked to stimulate a response from him.

"You never told me how you broke that sword."

4

"I should never have been given one. I'm a scribe not a fighter. Everyone was given a basic training but it was not really an army: it was a rabble. They had been used to fighting each other in mad chaos until the Romans were past Jericho. Once the Romans broke through in force they formed up waiting for a counter attack. It was like an iron wall with the shields with swords hacking from between them. I was in the first attack and without a clue what to do in the face of a shield wall. There were hundreds of men behind me all screaming as they ran onto the shields. The Jew in front of me got a sword through his guts and he just looked confused when I thought he would scream. I thought if I swung down hard on the top of a shield it would knock it down enough to let me stab the man behind it. The sword broke instead, but the broken bit flew on and hit the soldier behind the shield where he didn't have armour and blood went everywhere. When he fell the Jews beside me ran into the gap and attacked the Romans to the side of him. I found enough space to dodge between the Jews who were behind me holding up the broken sword so they knew I was not running like a coward. When I looked back our attack was like a butterfly against a brick. I could see Romans walking over bodies as the wall advanced. I just kept running." Jacob sighed." I still feel like I have to justify myself"

5

"The memories stay with you." Marcus was visualising something. "The only real fighting I did was against one of the tribes on the road to Eboracum. One half of the tribe was against the Romans and the leader's wife led the other half of the tribe that wanted us there. I didn't rate marriage much after that." Marcus had made the same joke several times before on social occasions and looked for Jacob's smile. Jacob made the token smile, but welcomed the levity.

"You might have fanaticism on one side," Marcus was serious again, "but there is nothing like the threat of decimation to concentrate the mind on defeating it. You don't buckle. I got to live with the death of strange enemies, but found it hard work to execute your own. With young soldiers they didn't only salute. They farted." Jacob looked puzzled and wasn't sure whether this was another joke. It wasn't. Marcus saw the puzzled look. "They were likely to shit themselves."

"Are you feeling better now?" Jacob nodded with resolution. This old soldier deliberation had occurred several times, and the friendship had deepened as a result. "How are you doing with that script? If you are finished do you want to come back to eat with me? You'll be losing the light soon. I'm trying some of the new wine tonight."

6

"Thank-you Marcus. Let's find Chloe to say thanks and farewell."

The hostess and church house owner was supervising servants somewhere across the courtyard from the scribes' room she had given over permanently to church use. The warm evening sunshine slanted across the roof and lit the rosemary on the opposite corner of the atrium. Martha, one of the maids was sitting beside it grinding herbs for the evening meal. Both men smiled as they passed her. She returned the smile with the hint of a bow. Martha had been a slave until Chloe's conversion to The Way several years before. She had been Chloe's mother's slave before that. All Chloe's slaves were given their freedom, but all elected to stay in the household. They joined the faith and were baptised before Jacob had arrived. Jacob settled in the town as a Deacon and he was very humbled by this household of prayer. That midweek morning started with prayers just after Jacob had arrived at the house and Martha had prayed for the emperor in the open session in a tone of voice that caused everyone to turn to her. Jacob intended to ask her if she knew something he didn't, but now was not the time. They moved into the tiled passageway into the cooler interior

7

"You are leaving?" Chloe moved between the busy women to reach up to give the men a holy kiss. She had the smallest stature in the room but the greatest confidence. She was a beautiful widow nearing the end of childbearing age, but there was not a hint of sexuality in her embraces, which were frequent and given to most of her guests. She had to reach high to put her arms around Marcus' neck, and he stooped to accommodate the affection. The embrace was redolent of a father about to pick up his ten-year-old daughter. She then turned to Jacob.

"You have had that sadness again." She held Jacob in her embrace for several moments in silence. "You must learn to forgive yourself. If the Lord has forgiven you, who are you not to?" Jacob was leaning to receive the embrace and she kissed him on the cheek. "Will you be here tomorrow?"

"I may have letters to write for Gaius. If I can I will. I have almost completed another copy of Mark's good news. If not, I will see you on the Lord's Day."

The chorus of farewells echoed behind them as they left the mosaic entrance porch and into the channelled stone street. The heat still radiated from the afternoon baked stones, now in early shadow

8

from the homes opposite. Slaves had begun to run evening errands. Shops in the trading district a few streets away would be re-opening.

****

"How do you get on with Gaius?"

"With iron discipline." Jacob had struggled to live up to the maxim he taught as a deacon: whatever you are in life, be the best you can at it. That way you might win hearts by admiration of your living of the faith. If you are a slave, be a good slave. If you are a master, be a good master. If you are a wife, be a good wife. If you are a tradesman be the best you can at your trade, and be the fairest trader in the marketplace.

"Yes he is a smarmy bastard."

"You pray for him as well then."

Marcus laughed. "The Lord was honest in his conversation. I still believe in confronting bullies, especially arrogant ones."

"You have the size and experience for it, and you are not his scribe."

"He is a just a magistrate with aspirations of Roman rank. He is already above his station in my view. He sucks up to me because I was in the Praetorian Guard and my father has influential friends. I am pleased to be away from the politics of Rome and don't take easily to upstarts trying to recreate them here. He's taken on Roman religion just because he thinks it will advance his position. He is greedy, fat and I suspect he takes bribes."

They walked on in silence for a few paces.

"Mind you I don't shout about influence. If it hadn't been for my father forgiving me after ten years for leaving home and joining the army I would still be supervising slaves carving the curved bits of stone arches for military buildings. He got me into the Praetorian Guard so I could come back to Rome. Then that enabled me to retire earlier. He is

10

still angry with me though. He wants me around in Rome to plot to make me emperor, and I want to run a vineyard. I am happy and he is not. He even arranged a marriage for me."

"You are married?"

"Octavia didn't want to leave Rome so I let her stay. I did my duty and we have a son, Livius. My father has a grandson so he is a little satisfied. I make some provision for them but my father is still the provider really. I can't live with his bullying and manipulation so I came here. I can't stand plotting and power struggles and he lives only for them. No doubt he had a hand somewhere in the new Emperor's appointment."

"What do you know about the Emperor?"

"Domitian? You were fighting his brother in the Jewish War. I never met him but I knew about him through the Praetorian Guard. By the way, how come you didn't end up in Masada? The rest of the Jerusalem Jewish forces did. How the Romans missed the escape route from Jerusalem I'll never know."

11

Jacob began summoning difficult memories and replied after several paces.

"I spent most of that night hiding in doorways, sliding around in blood and falling over bodies. The Temple on fire gave me enough light to see the Romans before they saw me. I moved with wailing women the following day and one of them let me use some of her clothes as we carried bodies out. Once away I kept away from roads and headed north near the Jordan. I had no idea where the rest of the Jews went or where I was going to go. I did not eat for days. Stupid: after all that horror, I was going through all sorts of guilt about ritual uncleanness for the blood and the bodies I had touched, and there was no temple left for atonement sacrifices. Then I came across a group of Christ's followers in the wilderness. Or rather they came across me. I was praying for death and I think I had passed out. They had seen it all coming and left the city weeks before. They had no intention of fighting. Something the Lord said about those living by the sword will die by the sword." Jacob suddenly became animated. "That is another saying of the Lord's that Mark did not have!"

"You will never have all his sayings if he didn't have a scribe with him."

12

They crossed the road and walked through some date palms in an open space between houses. They were moving into another row of villas. Marcus was still thinking about Martha's prayer that morning. "Is there anything to fear about Domitian?" Jacob asked.

"Any emperor is only awesome because soldiers obey his irrational orders. There is something to fear about all emperors. Power usually goes to their brains and they get mad with it. My fear is this proclivity of theirs to call themselves gods. They have everyone call their dead predecessors gods, but none of them ever came back to be godly. They really come as often as Zeus or Jupiter and all his weird family on the hill. I know what's behind it. If you want to hold onto power, you get everyone to swear allegiance or burn a pinch of incense and place the Emperor alongside your god in your priorities. You don't want to disobey your god and you don't want to be on the end of a treason charge."

"You must have worshipped in the army before you joined us."

"I like The Way because there is a God who is interested in me and everyone else and not just in having parties on a holy mountain

13

or changing into bulls to seduce maidens. I was always a thinker and wanted to cut through the crap. If God gave us a mind he does not want us to believe stupid things, and that goes for The Way as well. I have a few more questions for you when we get chance for a chat without interruption for an hour." They moved from earthy ground back to a Roman-made chariot road with its high kerb. "I can't see emperors as gods because I once met one.

The two men stepped off the high kerb and crossed the road. They rounded the corner into Marcus' street. The sun had only an arc of brightness left and there was coolness in the new found shade.

"I cannot accept a given statement I cannot question. If it is not a faith I can question it is not worth holding it."

"You should not be testing the Lord."

"I don't think that is testing the Lord. I think that is growing closer to the Lord. Questions are a sort of searching. I don't take kindly to preachers bullying me. Welcome to my home Jacob."

Marcus turned into his own villa entrance. Jacob had an impression of purple flowers and evergreen foliage before he was in a

14

courtyard not unlike that of Chloe. They passed a small statue of Pan in a square pool.

"Which god is that?" Jacob could not hide his consternation.

"The god of the previous house owner. I thought it was rather well carved so I left it there. Like the psalmist said: something about 'eyes and see not, ears and hear not.' No-one here worships it. Judith nags me about getting rid of it."

"But what is that saying about your commitment to The Way?"

"Judith's nagging?"

"Joker to the end!."

"As I see it, Paul was not bothered about people of The Way eating meat offered to gods unless it weakened the faith of those who ate it. You see other gods all over the town and in everyone else's homes, but you still love only The Lord. I still only love The Lord. Why worry about that lovely carving?"

Marcus became distracted. "Smell that food!"

15

"Has that been offered to gods?"

Marcus stopped for some while with abject laughter, ultimately wiping tears from his eyes. The laughter was infectious and Jacob joined in. Judith appeared from the neighbouring room.

"We have a guest. Welcome home Master. Welcome Jacob." Judith bowed, but was smiling as she entered the presence of the laughing pair. Here she was a slave among free men in her master's house.

"I invited Jacob on a whim. I trust we have enough."

"We have, master. The vegetables are not cooked yet."

"Please bring us two cups of the new wine." Judith bowed again and left the room. Both men watched her leave. "I would give her her freedom if I did not fear her leaving. I paid over the odds for her three years ago. I could sense her intelligence and maturity. I got in a bidding war with Fortunatus. I hated the thought that this woman would become one of his prostitutes. She was already bearing with stoicism the loss of her son who had been sold ahead of her when that rat started probing her body. Now, for the first time in my life I am happy to come

16

home. I totally rely on her here. You know it was she who brought me to the faith?"

"I didn't but I can understand that now. Judith was my catechumen as well. She was among the first group I prepared."

"She had a wonderful peace to her. She had a bearing of dignity. She talked about her prayer life when I asked her what they did there. When she asked permission to go to Chloe's house I was curious. I suppose I am less open to people about my new found faith because I was in Rome as a youth when Nero did his worst."

"How did you know about Paul and the food offered to gods?"

"I was talking to Onesimus at the last agape feast. He invited me to look at his copies of Paul's letters that week. He is most proud of his originals. He had tears in his eyes when he showed me that short one to his old master. [2]He let me spend an afternoon reading through them all. He doesn't seem to know where one letter ends and another begins. I think it has been his life's work to put them all together. He's a lovely old man."

---

[2] Philemon

17

"Onesimus is a deep character. Don't be fooled by the doddery old image. He has a depth of wisdom we couldn't tap. Not many achieve an experience like his that started with slavery. And knowing Paul gives him a kudos not many of us could ever match."

The wine arrived.

"I prefer earthenware don't you? Lead leaves a metallic taste. I only have one silver cup that was a gift from my father when I returned to Rome. Besides, I saw the conditions in the land of the Celts where the lead is mined. A health to all of us!"

"A health to all of us." They drank. "Thank you Marcus. This is very generous." They paused again as Judith left the room after her bow.

"I wish I could give all of them their freedom but how do you run an economy? How do you run a vineyard without slaves?"

"The original model for the Way was that we all held everything in common and all shared the produce. We can't do that when slaves of faith are owned by people not of the Way. They have nothing material to bring to us."

18

"I can't see a sustainable organisation that only relies on the total wealth being brought in and used up. Once it is used up you need more converts with even more wealth to keep everyone already in the church. You would need to retain all the property and work it to sustain everyone. I have a sympathy with that man Mark describes who turned away sadly because the Lord asked him to sell all he had. I would be sad as well. And then I would be totally dependant on the church instead of bringing a sacrifice to the church as I do now. And what would I do with no vineyard to run? Surely the Father as Creator made us in His image to be creative. I am trying to be creative making wine. I know they use my wine in the Remembrance after we leave for more catechism each Lord's Day. I couldn't do that if I had sold the vineyard. Others drink it at Saturnalia in the Bacchanalian feast. Should I be worried? When I give, The Way is receiving money for wine sold to worshippers of other gods."

Jacob was sipping his wine. He saw the logic of the food offered to gods so did not engage the issue of profits from wine sold for their celebration. "It would be good if the entire world's wealth was owned by everyone in common and worked by everyone for the common good of everyone."

19

"Yes it would be good. There are wonderful ideas that fall down because we all have a tendency to be greedy and want a bit more than the rest. Sin will always get in the way. How many emperors or his promoted friends are going to join the Way, do you think? I suspect the true faith will always be a subversive minority until the world is so full of the faithful that they overflow the old system like a bursting wine bottle. Isn't that what the Lord meant by being yeast in the dough, or whatever it was in that other scroll you use apart from Mark? [3]I can't keep calling it that. Who wrote it?"

"We don't know. It was a scroll of his sayings that has been put together some years ago. I think you are right. The Lord always stayed in the homes of those who supported him without them always becoming disciples. We hold a church at Chloe's house but she has not given it to the church. We have to support some full time Apostles though."

"Why? As I see it Paul was always a tentmaker. Once you get full timers you get people like emperors with power that enjoy the power and the status and have a motive only to keep it. That is exactly what I see the Pharisees doing and what The Lord challenged. Not all

---

[3] Q

20

elders will be like Onesimus. I have a great respect for you Jacob, but I wonder if you are hankering for the old days back in the secure scribe's status with attendant privilege. Now you have to do a real job while living a faith."

"No. There is a freedom now I never had in Jerusalem. Most of my scribe's work there was repetitive copying. I spent more time counting words than writing them. Now at least there is something I can feel is being created as I write it. The atmosphere was oppressive under a pharisaic system. I couldn't go back to it. Besides, I rely on church members supporting me." Jacob held up his wine cup with a smile as a visual aid. "I could not live on what I get from Gaius after I give Fortunatus his rent." Both men sipped again.

"You did go back to Jerusalem didn't you?"

"Three years later I went back to see if anyone of my family survived. I think my father died in the temple fire. I don't know of any others. Lots of prisoners became slaves and I wonder if we will meet again. I saved my scrolls though, thank the Lord."

"You had a wife?"

21

"I was betrothed. I have no idea what happened to Ruth. I think I am still being faithful even after all these years."

"How did the scrolls survive?"

"I built a false wall across an alcove in my house. If you have toiled for years writing scrolls you don't want Romans using them as kindle. There must be thousands of scrolls hidden by our scribes from Jerusalem to Masada."

In the darkening room the oil lamp cast a warm glow. Noises of plates on surfaces were coming from the next room. There was a reflection from the lamp glinting on a vessel on a shelf opposite Jacob. "What is that?"

Marcus craned over his shoulder. "Oh that! It is a piece of which I am so proud. A friend and colleague bought it for me in the south of Persia when we were together on a brief posting. It is the only place on earth that makes them." He rose to pick up the vessel. It was a beautifully curved gold vase a hands length tall and a both-hands girth diameter. It was sealed at the top with a sandalwood lid. Marcus twisted the lid and held the jar to his nose. Jacob joined him and Marcus wafted the jar gently. The aroma was sweet and new to Jacob.

22

"What is it?"

"The locals called it myrrh. It is an ointment scented with sandalwood dried sap: incense I suppose. The jar is pure beaten gold. I told Judith that she has to anoint my body with it before I am buried."

Judith arrived to inform the men that the food was ready and was aware of the scent in the air. "Are you ready to be buried now Master?" The twinkle was still in her eyes as she told them of the food being ready after the laughter had subsided.

"Lamb shoulder," said Judith as the men entered.

"We'll serve ourselves Judith. More wine, please." Marcus had finished his first cup. Jacob had only sipped his a few times. Judith went to fill a jug. She was used to Marcus entertaining.

"Please say some thanks to the Lord for our fellowship and meal." Marcus asked and Jacob obliged with a brief prayer in Hebrew.

"Please translate."

"'I will give to the LORD the thanks due to his righteousness, and sing praise to the name of the LORD, the Most High.' It is from the

23

Psalms. I was going to translate it. We used to say it at home in my childhood."

"You are quite a linguist. How many languages do you know?"

"Hebrew, Aramaic, Greek and Latin."

"Fancy speaking a dead language! Do you speak it with anyone now?"

"Not since I stopped attending a synagogue. It's useful to know the original language. I'm not happy with some parts of the Septuagint.[4] That's the Greek copy of the scriptures we normally read. I still have some of the prophet scriptures I copied in Jerusalem. We had to learn some Hebrew as a right of passage. I stuck with it to be a Scribe. I was copying it for some years. Excuse me sitting upright Marcus. Food sticks between my mouth and my stomach if I am reclining to eat. It might stick anyway so excuse me if things get uncomfortable. It started happening after I left Jerusalem."

"I will sit up as well then."

---

[4] A Greek translation of the original Hebrew named after the seventy elders who did the translation.

24

The first few minutes of the meal were in silence. Both were hungry.

Marcus began after his plate was half empty. "The scriptures are full of crying: Abraham after the death of Sarah. David and his men were quite a crying group after Ziklag."[5]

Jacob did not really want to open up the subject of his earlier tears. "I've never had a reader like you of all my catechumens."

"I have the time, and I give thanks for the access. No. I was thinking about you earlier and thinking back to the times I have wept. The ointment jar brings it back to me. I was very close to the man who bought me it. He must have spent a year's wages on it. What a sacrifice! The army throws men together in close comradeship. You learn to rely on each other. I note the scripture that talks of men not lying with each other, but I also note David's love for Jonathon when he died. 'Greatly beloved were you to me; your love to me was wonderful, passing the love of women.'"

---

[5] 1 Samuel 30

25

Marcus was pensive for some moments, and there was the hint of a wavering in his voice. "I wish I'd had that verse when Quintus died."

"Did he die in battle?"

"No. We laughed when he fell off his horse amongst thorns. He didn't seem hurt beyond a few scratches and hurt pride. There was no pressure from any enemy. We were going north to inspect a new barracks in Eboracum. The thorns must have been poison. Within a week he was in high fever and was in constant cramp. I wept inconsolably. I have never been able to love since, not like that. The greatest soldier ever known used to lie with men, so they said: Alexander. I am thinking of using that as my baptismal name. Judith chose her Baptism name wisely and I was happy to accept the change. I don't think I could have gone through life with the name of Waterpot. More wine?"

"Thank-you. But I have to be alert tomorrow with Gaius."

"Yet Onesimus kept his name. Who wants to be called 'Useful'?"

26

"That little letter from Paul to his master says it all. Paul plays on the name of useful, as useful to me and useful to you. There is something about the power given to someone who gives the name. It was important from creation. God changed the name of those he chose like Abraham. The Lord changed the names of some of the Apostles: like Peter. Paul was changed from Saul. It says a lot to have your name changed." It seemed the end of a teaching sentence so both sipped their wine a little.

Marcus broke the silence. "You know Gaius is not a Roman, despite the name. He married a Roman widow. He chose to be called that in addition to his Greek name. I think he was called Amyntas. His father was a freed slave who inherited his former master's small estate. He has a chip on his shoulder. He treats his slaves like dirt. He's one of the few round here who keeps his slaves naked in the house. You think he would sympathise given his background."

"How do you know his background?"

"The soldiers know my past and they talk to me. I entertained the procurator here as well. We knew each other before we joined the army. He is going back to Rome soon. His successor might bring news from Rome for us. If ever you think Gaius is bullying you, let me know."

"Thank-you Marcus. I think he does not go too far with me because his Latin is appalling and I make him sound credible in his letters and legal papers. He relies on me somewhat." Jacob's body language was of being about to rise and leave.

"I think Judith has something sweet to finish our meal. She does wonderful things with curds and fruit."

"Thank-you. That sounds tasty. My diet on my own is a bit basic."

Judith appeared moments later to clear the plates and returned with the bowls of blended figs and yoghurt. She made her customary bow and disappeared to her kitchen duties. Jacob watched her retreating. Marcus was right. She was attractive with a confident bearing. Jacob found a stirring within himself that he was used to resisting. He tried to put fantasy out of his mind. He had no idea as to the protocol of a relationship with a slave of another man, and both of whom were of his congregation and both of whom for which he was

Deacon. He could never afford to buy Judith as a slave, and it was perfectly clear that Marcus would not sell her even if he could.

The evening ended with farewells and prayerful blessings on each other, with a manly hug and slaps on the back. Judith was called by Marcus for a farewell. She kept her eyes down and Jacob laid his hand on her head and prayed for her to be blessed. He thanked her for her service, something slaves seldom received and she bowed again. Jacob again tried to avert the stirring feelings of earlier and avoided staying too long on the moment, sensitive to betraying his emotion to his friends, an emotion so new and strange after so long.

Once on the street, and alone walking across the town to his own rooms on a second floor in the more plebeian centre he was struck by the clearness of the sky and brightness of stars. There was a crescent moon and two bright planets nearby. He had remembered stories of these planets in conjunction making a spectacular sight, but tonight was not that night. The cicada chorus was incessant. Jacob had a new feeling in his being that he had not felt since the other world of hopes before Jerusalem had fallen. He could not place why, because not that much, if anything, had changed. Now the rigid sense of duty that had carried him through was enhanced by something more positive: a sense

29

of wellbeing and achievement among friends. He offered it to the Lord in prayer. It seemed easier to do that with the heavens spread above him.

He reached his tenement building where at the outside entrance doorway was his upstairs neighbour of two weeks. He had seen her on several occasions but apart from courteous greetings there had been no conversation. She was alone in her home most of the time but did not appear to crave company. She was a pretty girl in late teens but she bore a face that held staring eyes and hard experience. As he reached her he noted even in the gloom a rather haunted look of anxiety and distant thought. Slightly startled as he approached the door she appeared to have a realisation and bared a breast. He was being solicited by a prostitute. Jacob was shocked and gasped, not because he had not seen prostitutes or indeed solicited by them but because he was not expecting one outside his own shared doorway and by his neighbour. "You want to help a girl be happy?" he thought he heard her say. This was not a normal place to meet prostitutes. Perhaps the girl was on her way to the market square to ply her trade and chanced upon Jacob. Jacob had not experienced coitus in his life despite his age. The fact that he had not was not because of his ability to do so, he believed, but because there was holiness to his body that should be given to a
30

promised one. He thought he could never detach himself from Ruth despite the remoteness of ever seeing her again. He could not, despite the fantasies that came up from a healthy libido, bring himself to engage in casual sex, and certainly not on the sort of contractual basis currently on offer to him.

At the same time his natural compassion for the girl did not allow him to condemn or reject her. "I am your downstairs neighbour, Jacob." he said. "Can I just be your friend when you are not working?" He felt a little silly and still felt he was rejecting her. She was in the sort of material need he could not meet without massive compromise to his own well-being. He perceived her real need as one that could not be answered while she was trapped in her present life conditions. If the Lord had an answer it did not occur to Jacob despite his prayer for one. Another conversational response was demanded. "I will pray for you!"

He sensed deep despair in the girl but there was also hostility. She was dismissive. There was anger and shrillness even though it was in a quiet voice. "No god ever answered any prayer for me." Before he could formulate a response the girl had walked away. His earlier "I will pray for you" suddenly felt like a cliché.

31

Chapter 2

The morning produced a fresh wind from the sea in Jacob's face as he walked to his room in the Magistrate's buildings on the edge of the market square. Stallholders from the surrounding villages were setting up their wares of meat and vegetables alongside the stalls displaying freshly caught fish. To his right a few feet away there was a disturbance and the loud scream of fear in an adolescent voice. The breaking voice between the child's falsetto and the youthful tenor were shouted, "I was not running away! I was just finding my amulet." In the middle of five men was a restrained and struggling youth who had no capacity to move more than a little, met with equal force by his captors. Each was holding a limb, and the youth was borne completely face up. The fire that had hitherto been griddling the fish of some fishermen stallholders' breakfast after their night's work had become a source of heat for a branding iron.

"You don't have property you little runt. You are property!" roared the bulky man nearest the fire. He had a fistful of the boy's hair in his

32

left hand, while the right grasped the end of the heating branding iron. The lad's voice was hoarse with the previous ten minutes of panic. He moved from shouting to begging in sobs. There was no sympathy, except in Jacob's churning emotions, but Jacob had no authority and still less confidence to intervene. He could not move on. He had to watch. His only resource was prayer for the lad, and for mercy from his captors. There was none. The youth's screams rose as the branding iron came out of the hot embers. The business end was glowing red. The screams for mercy became screams of pain. The branding iron and the lad's forehead were in contact for about five seconds, and the cries changed to a wheeze. The youth's larynx could no longer sustain the shout. The smell of burning flesh pervaded the surrounding air. Now there were only sobs of defeat and hurt from him.

"Put him down!"

The lad sprawled on his back, but his natural movement to roll into a foetal position and sob was arrested by a kick in the leg from the holder of the branding iron. "Get back to your master!"

The slave rose and ran blindly away from the square, his constant childish crying diminishing as he returned down the street along which

Jacob had walked. The captors were moving on to a new agenda, and the brander with a vague look of satisfaction on his face saw Jacob looking on. He nodded. Jacob, with no other response to give, nodded back, and he continued towards his work, berating himself for his lack of action, even though no apparent action to intervene was open to him.

He still felt disturbed as he turned to mount the stairs. Two of Gaius' leather clad armed men stood talking by the door and they acknowledged Jacob.

"Morning scribe."

"Morning." And he passed through the open door. He moved to his writing table in the inner room moments before Gaius entered. There was no ceremony. "I need three letters writing. The first is to the procurator." Jacob caught a slightly nauseating whiff of garlic and tooth decay as the magistrate passed him. Gaius had produced some vellum for this first letter and his dictation was an unctuous tribute to the procurator's service, now that his recall to Rome had been announced. The others were reports on judgements he had been making in cases he had been hearing in land disputes.

"I need you to go to these people and sign and you must sign to witness their signature or mark." Jacob made brief notes in clay before producing the final manuscripts. Shortly Gaius would be gone leaving Jacob to produce the documents, and he preferred to be away from his employer as soon as possible. Gaius had no other pressing engagements so stayed. Jacob had built a routine of listening with dignity without answer unless he was asked a specific question. He seldom gave away his feelings to Gaius if possible. Gaius spoke in short sentences with long pauses between them.

"I have just bought another slave." "She is a Jew." "You are a Jew aren't you?"

"I was born of a Jewish family yes."

"What does that mean? You are a Jew then."

"I am not practising the Jewish religion."

"Well done giving that up. I prefer to have a choice of gods. It must be so boring having only one." Jacob was not sure whether his silences were seen as respectful of an employer speaking to a listening employee or of dumb insolence. If it irritated Gaius he did not mind. He

35

preferred the ambiguity as it kept a defence for him. Gaius moved to stand near the desk to Jacob's side, too close to comfort, but that is the effect Gaius wanted.

"The slave was taken in Jerusalem after the revolt. You can't tell the ages of these women but I would say she is about twenty."

The slight flutter in Jacob's stomach abated. He was concerned that it was someone he knew. He knew very few children in Jerusalem. It certainly was not his betrothed Ruth who would be about twenty eight by now if she survived.

"Were you at Jerusalem?" Jacob could not be honest as he might be identified with the revolt and therefore be a suspected rebel. At the same time he could not be seen as hesitant.

"I left before the troubles."

"Good job or you would be dead and not my scribe." It was the first hint of a compliment ever received from Gaius who seemed to treat all but Romans with a sort of disdain. Jacob was wary as a result and tried to keep his mental guard up. He knew he was Gaius' better in language and writing and Gaius would hate to feel inferior "You are not married are you?"

"No Sir."

"I could see you with a wife like this girl. I haven't decided on a name for her yet or what she will be doing. You don't bet on a horse until you see how it runs." Jacob remembered Marcus' comment about Gaius' slaves being kept naked in the house. He was also conscious of a possible attempt to be belittled.

"Some owners let their slaves get too familiar. I like my slaves to know their place."

There was a pause. Jacob sensed the climax of the line of discourse and suspected Gaius had been rehearsing this to himself for some time.

"Slaves only know their places when they have a fresh memory of having something pushed up their arses." Jacob hoped his distaste didn't show. He wished he was of a rank to ask if that was Gaius' view when he was a slave himself before his father's manumission. His mind drifted back to the youth suffering that morning. He kept the same

37

silence. His eyes were intent on the vellum and he started putting his writing materials ready. Gaius, however, had not finished.

"Are you not married because you prefer boys?" Jacob remained unprovoked.

"No Sir." He had no wish to open up the reasons for his marital status, and he was certainly not going to display embarrassment at the insolent intrusion. He behaved as if the conversation was over and began to write. Gaius was behind him. The silence was longer this time. His scribal experience gave him great confidence in his work, and he was alert for the slap on the back that came from Gaius. It pretended a farewell from a comradely boss, but Jacob suspected it was an attempt to spoil his first page. It would be a large loss to have to replace the vellum out of his meagre fee. Gaius left.

38

Chapter 3

It fell to Jacob as a deacon to visit the needy of the congregation. That afternoon he called on Urbanus and Phoebe, an elderly couple near the centre of the town. They owned one of the few green open spaces with its olive trees flanked by tradesmen's homes and shops. The tenement building known as "The Island," in which Jacob lived backed on to it. Urbanus suffered from gangrene and weeping sores on his legs while Phoebe was arthritic. Neither left home as a result. They had had a large family and the grandchildren frequently visited, and when in season harvested their olives to provide their limited income. Urbanus' sons had long realised that the olive grove could barely provide a living income for one family, so they had learned other trades.

"Welcome young Jacob!" said the old man as he entered with a "Peace be on the house!" A wrinkled open smile showed his one remaining tooth in the bottom of his mouth. The room had an open wall onto the olive grove. "How is everyone? I do miss you all. Have some olives" Jacob was struck by a strange stillness in the room but refrained from remarking on it.

"Thank-you brother." Jacob chewed the flesh from a juicy green olive and threw the bare stone out into the grass of the grove. "We are gaining in strength praise the Lord. How are you both?"

"Very much the same Jacob. Much pain and little sleep. We are having some worries with your landlord badgering us to sell the olive grove to him."

"What does Fortunatus want with an olive grove?"

"He doesn't. I think he wants to build another island, and get the rent from another forty hovels. It will probably be a whorehouse. This land belonged in my family for as long as anyone remembers. I always see the grandchildren of the family running around in it."

"He has his answer then."

"He won't take no for an answer. I've had his thugs round intimidating me. Thirty years ago I would have thrown them out. I need my boys here when they come again but I get no warning. If we had a decent magistrate he would put a stop to it but Gaius and Fortunatus are corrupt. You can't tell the difference between Gaius' so-called police and Fortunatus' robbers."

"He still can't have it if you won't sell it."

"You read about Naboth's vineyard? Gaius makes the law up as he goes along to suit his own interests." Jacob avoided the temptation to criticise his employer. "I wanted to give this land to the church as long as it stays an olive grove. My sons know that is my wish as well."

"Bless you for that." The conversation moved on to Urbanus' family and then the prayer and pastoral support Jacob was there to supply but he left the house with a sadness that this old couple should suffer from the greed of men who have enough and more than enough, but should impose suffering on others in their acquisitiveness.

Jacob spent the rest of the good daylight in Chloe's scribes' room copying Mark's Good News. As he completed the copy it struck him again that Mark's document was either not really finished or Mark had finished with a grammatical howler.

"Who finishes a document with the word 'but'?" he thought to himself. He made a mental note to discuss it with Onesimus when he got the chance."

Chloe entered and invited him to a simple meal that was shared amongst the women of her household after their afternoon of sewing garments for their market stall. He was hoping to find a moment with Martha to satisfy his curiosity about her prayer the morning some days earlier but she ate apart from the main group. Sitting beside Chloe he wondered if Martha had opened up her reasons to her. When two of the adjacently sitting women went to clear dishes Jacob posed his question.

"Yes, she did tell me." Chloe replied. "Martha dreamt that the emperor raped her." Jacob's incredulity must have shown on his face. He felt a mixture of pity for Martha for such a fantasy and disgust that anyone should consider such an act on an old woman, even in a dream. In his confusion he asked himself if the dream was the dream some sort of message? Dreams were portents in the earliest scriptures. He also felt relieved he had not asked Martha himself. Chloe must have seen through his considerations.

42

"Martha was not always an old woman. She was sold away from her mother as a seven-year old. The reason she sits all the time is because her legs were broken after she ran away from her second owners for the third time. As a child she was bought as a plaything for the growing sons of her owner. She was habitually raped, brutalised and sodomised. My mother found her crawling down the street past our home one early morning like a worm. Mother was only a few years older than Martha then. She brought her into this house and hid her. Martha has never left this house since. My grandparents were complicit in hiding a runaway slave, so apart from the compassion in keeping her they were breaking the law in either giving a runaway slave sanctuary or stealing a slave. Martha has never walked since. She is doubly incontinent. Together we clean her up during the day when we need to. She sits alone most of the time by her choice, not ours. She was once very pretty, and if she had her legs again would have been very attractive for an emperor. If only the Lord would come and tell her to stand!" There was a prayerful pause.

"She says that the evil visited on her is also the blessing that the Lord has called her to a life of prayer. The evil one cannot win when you ask how the Lord can use the evil for His purpose."

43

Jacob was reduced to silence for some time. Saying anything would have been like throwing a cup of water into a stormy sea. It had all been said for him. He yearned for Judgment Day all the more. Final victory for the Lord was long overdue. The verse of the psalm crowded his mind, "How long must I bear pain in my soul, and have despair in my heart? How long must my enemy triumph over me? How long, O Lord? Will you forget me forever?"

"I have a prostitute living upstairs from me." Chloe put an expression of feigned shock in response to Jacob's news that made Jacob smile again.

"Don't be tempted to go upstairs then." It was light hearted again. Then more seriously, "We will pray for her and you. She will be going through a living hell in her life and you have a problem if you want to help her. She needs a woman to talk to." Chloe stood up and picked up objects from the table.

"Finish your food." She said, like a mother, and kissed him on his head from above him as she passed. Jacob realised he had not eaten for some minutes and alone at the table finished his meal. He could not

44

resist a tear running down his cheek at the emotion realised by Chloe's affection.

Jacob approached his tenement, The Island, as the dying deep red sunset was cushioned in the indigo of the encroaching night sky and the planets he had seen that week were shining. The girl from upstairs was not at the door tonight. His room was in the gloom of far gone dusk. He seldom needed light as he possessed so little he could feel for what he had to use. He only possessed a leather bucket, an earthenware dish, two changes of clothes and a disused stretcher from a former departed worshipper on which he slept. Family noises in the tenement homes around were the norm at this time. All had completed their allotted work but some of the children were not asleep.

In the midst of the family noise a piercing scream sounded. He aurally located it immediately to the girl upstairs, whose name he had not yet discovered. There was a second scream, clearly of pain. It became a continuous howl with pinnacles of volume. Jacob made for his door and stumbled up the darkening brick staircase to his neighbour's room. The howls continued. He arrived as others were opening doors on the same dark corridor. The door enclosing the screams gave little privacy and swung without any security as he

45

pushed. Three men from the group that branded the youth earlier that day were restraining the girl. Her bedding was on the floor. She was on her back on it, or the little of her back that could touch the bedding. Two of her assailants held a foot each and were pushing them behind her head, her legs splayed. Her shift had ridden up to her waist. Jacob could see from the dim light of a lamp her bare buttocks pointing vertically in profile. The third assailant was lashing a several stranded leather whip on her buttocks and genitals from the foot of the bed. The sobs and howls continued. The whip hand stopped.

"This bed is not for sleeping it's for fucking! Now get back to work you lazy whore. We paid good money for you. Let her go." It was the same voice that had shouted "Get back to your master" and "Put him down" that morning. The men had not seen Jacob at the door as they were intent on their violence, and were titillated by it. Suddenly they realised their violence had a witness. Jacob was in the room holding the door and heard shuffles behind of neighbours curious to know the source of the racket and peering past him.

"Are you a customer?" Jacob was asked aggressively by the whip holder. Jacob did not feel intimidated.

46

"I heard a neighbour in trouble."

"So you did! You can go home again then unless you have brought money. It's none of your business. Her master owns her, he owns this room, this bed, and he probably owns yours."

Jacob ignored him. He looked to the girl who was now sitting squat on the floor having pulled her dress down. "Talk to me when you have time" he said gently.

This was a provocation to the whip handler who was shaping up to stride the four paces to Jacob intending to strike him. "We tell her who she talks to and it's only customers." On the second pace his foot caught on some bedding and he stumbled forward. He tried to move his second foot to regain balance but it also caught something and he began his fall. Jacob intended leaving before his assailant reached him to weave and avoid blows in the dark cramped corridor behind him. He allowed the door to swing back. As the aggressor fell forward he stretched out his hands to the floor to cushion the shock of falling. Before his hands reached the floor an alignment of the aggressor's feet, spine, head, door edge and door posthole occurred. Behind Jacob he heard the crack of head on door followed by the dull thump of the

47

unconscious thug crumpling on the floor behind the now closed door. He would have been badly hurt. Jacob returned to his room as the chaos in the room upstairs resolved itself. He knew with some foreboding however, that there was unfinished business that might visit him any time soon. They knew where he lived. These were Fortunatus' men so they would know where he worked as well. Whether Fortunatus' "nest mate" Gaius was any protection was not guaranteed but he would not want his scribe's hands damaged. Jacob smiled to himself as he appreciated the image given him by Urbanus that morning.

He heard stumbling and shuffling some time later as the men passed his door. He waited expecting forced entry and confrontation, but none happened. He could not sleep for a long time because there was still a possibility of reprisals that night. Eventually his mind turned to the girl upstairs. He wanted to express concern but his motive might be misunderstood. Then he relived the earlier confrontation and felt that the aggressor had been served right by his accident after two very violent episodes that day and attempting a third on Jacob himself. Jacob had not deliberately moved the door to the strategic point of collision with the falling man. He was simply avoiding a blow from him and let the door go. Whether the witnesses would see it that way remained to be seen.

48

Then it dawned that maybe the Lord does work in mysterious ways. He prayed for those he had met that day. Shortly after that, with morale returning Jacob slept. Perhaps, as his mother once told him, if you go to sleep while you are praying, you go to sleep in the arms of God.

He was in the temple. For the first time he entered the court of the priests. His father was occupied, as he always was, with cutting throats of animals and offering sacrifices. Jacob was not allowed near the Holy of Holies any more than he was allowed to enter the court of the priests but there was a compelling force moving him there. He was in terror. He was the closest to the veil when a brilliant light shone behind the veil and brilliant fire blasted from within through its surrounding edges. The light was painful to his eyes. No-one was with him of the group in the court earlier. A voice that hurt his ears thundered, "The Lord is leaving His Temple!" Jacob tried to scream for mercy, "Lord do not leave me!" but only a wheeze came from his lungs. He tried to scream again and the same. The heat from the veil was hurting him and he turned to run but his legs would not move. Then he woke up. His anxiety was overwhelming. What could this mean? It was daylight.

49

Chapter 4

Jacob picked up his bucket and left the building to walk to the aqueduct's first trough where it divided to three channels to other parts of the town. Slaves and wives were gathering with their water pots for the household supply. Sitting by the approach was the blind beggar that everyone called Zach. "I hear you Jacob" he said. "I hear a man's footsteps when you come. Jacob dropped a small coin in Zach's bowl. Any conversation with the blind man on the ground was cut short.

"Was it your prayers?" The barefooted girl from upstairs had run up quietly behind him. The pouring water drowned out the noise of her footsteps.

"What is your name?"

"Doria. That is the name my father gave me. It is not what those pigs call me."

The women by the water were chattering and their voices could be heard above the foaming water in the trough. Their body language indicated they were talking about the new arrival with Jacob.

"We never really know the power of prayer, Doria" replied Jacob, "but we like to believe The Lord knows and loves us whatever is happening. We do expect a big Judgement Day soon. Occasionally little judgements seem to come early."

Their arrival in the group by the water trough seemed to quieten the women. "Peace to you sisters!" Jacob's was a familiar face at the water supply. He received smiles but there was a mixed response that seemed to stem from Doria's presence. The group was dispersing with their water containers, mostly on their heads. Very soon Doria and Jacob were the only ones at the trough.

"The beast got a judgement when he hit that door. He stayed out for ages and then was very dizzy as his monkeys helped him home." Doria filled her bowl and Jacob filled his bucket. They left the trough and were passing the beggar.

"Bless you Zach." The man on the ground raised his hand. Jacob and Doria continued their walk home.

"Which God do you pray to?"

51

"I follow The Way. Jesus the Christ the Son of God came to us and now prays for us."

"Can I come with you to your temple? I don't know the temples here."

"We have no temple. Our temple is our own body. We try to pray in it constantly. Together we meet in a house on the first day of the week and then together the people are the temple. Our temple is where the people of The Way are."

"Why is it called The Way?"

"Because it is a way of life and is not meant to be a religion. We mean the whole world to belong to it in a life of love and care for one another where we are all brothers and sisters in Christ. Do you want to come with me in a few minutes after I'm ready? You must meet some of my sisters in the faith. We are going to pray together when I get there. They might tend some of your wounds as well"

She thought briefly. "Yes. I'll come. Fortunatus' men never come after me in the mornings. They know that those wanting prostitutes are not going to be here at this time. Why couldn't I have a

52

god who gave me to a rich woman to arrange her flowers? Or better still to be a free woman married with slaves of my own? I want a god like that."

"God loves slaves as much as free people. He loves poor more than rich and he loves women as much as men."

Doria and Jacob met again after their ablutions to go to Chloe's house. Doria was almost skipping like a child alongside Jacob. For the first time in her life that she could remember since being a tiny child, there was someone she could be with who was not likely to abuse her. She felt innocent again, but having the secret dread that she could still be abused at any time when this unreal moment had passed. Her eyes were constantly looking out for her owner's enforcers.

Chloe's women were about to begin prayers as Jacob and Doria entered.

"Peace to you sisters. This is my neighbour from upstairs."

The prayers finished, Jacob left to visit Urbanus again. He had an intuition. He was right. On arrival through the olive grove, Phoebe and her sons were together in the room in which they had met the day

53

before. Urbanus had died. There were no tears. There was a silence in the house broken only by the rustle of material as affection was shared between family members. It was that silence the day before that had given the intuition to Jacob to call. It was a stillness that was not just the absence of noise. It was almost, he felt, as if there was a presence from heaven. Jacob joined in with the hugs and embraces. He refrained from more that a touch on the arms to the arthritic Phoebe. "Bless you Phoebe!"

"He died peacefully in his sleep."

"He sleeps in the Lord until the great awakening." Jacob could not resist the tears of empathy in his eyes.

"We want to bury him this afternoon. He always wanted to go in the olive grove beside his father." Linus the eldest had spoken from behind the group.

"Please will you pray with us as we bury him?" Phoebe asked.

"Of course. I will tell others of the church." Jacob remained for some time as the family remembered significant moments of Urbanus' life with him. The sons then left to begin the process of

54

digging in the selected site for burial. Jacob arranged to return and left for Chloe's house. Her women would spread the word to build the congregation in the olive grove that afternoon. Doria had gone after finding at least one source of support in her life.

He left Chloe's house as the heat of the morning had reached its peak. Crossing the main thoroughfare to return to the Island he stood back to avoid collision with a troop of about ten marching soldiers.

"Halt!" The troop halted as one. "You'll do. Carry this!" Jacob was commandeered to carry the senior soldier's pack. It was sweaty against his back. Thankfully there was not far to go to the barracks so he would not be challenging himself to offer his services for an extra mile. "By the right, March!" Jacob went ahead of the marching group, well able to manage his burden. Some three hundred double paces brought them to the courtyard of the barracks. Adrenaline had energised the carrying of the burden, and he walked briskly with a measure of thanks that he was not a soldier. "Halt! You can put that down now son. Well done." There was a sense that this had been spoken many times in the same tone. Jacob had not spoken a word at any of this imposition. His mind was churning at the proximity to Roman soldiers again, colleagues of those he had once fought. Soldiers were often seen in the town streets but at a comfortable distance. This was too close for memories. He parted with a smile and a nod. It was a gesture seldom seen by a squad more used to grumbling and grimaces. They were being dismissed to find their new quarters.

Jacob was running through unfamiliar streets away from soldiers. He was in panic. He had lost his sword. There was nowhere to hide. He jumped the wall of an animal pen and couched, regaining his breath. He was alone. The sheep had crowded into the opposite corner of the pen, panicking noisily at Jacob's arrival. Feeling shaken, Jacob realised he had fallen back into his Jerusalem experience. He felt embarrassed, not knowing what he might have said or done during his time of aberration, or who had seen him. Then he became aware that his tunic was wet and clinging from his own urine.

Avoiding contact with others as far as he could, he returned to the Island, washed and changed, prayed and resolved on his next steps.

He returned towards the market square, intent on finding something for his midday meal amongst the stalls. As he walked he was already rehearsing in his mind the pattern of worship for the funeral of Urbanus.

56

Chapter 5

While Jacob was reporting Urbanus' death to Chloe, Marcus sat naked in the bath house beside the equally naked procurator, slaves behind them using shells to scrape dead skin from their sweating backs.

"Gallus, have you seen the price of slaves these days? I can't find men for my farm and the price of pretty things is out of hand. We can't have an economy run on brothels."

Marcus was rubbing his eyes of sweat so did not see the procurator's smirk. "I don't know. It's a sort of economy. My soldiers pay the owners of the prostitutes. The owners pay their taxes. The taxes pay the soldiers."

"And who feeds them all?"

"I was joking, but I take your point. Loosen up."

"Another thing that galls me is the castration of male slaves. When they stop being pretty they are only good for bending over and singing high notes. Through no fault of their own they are too weak or fat to work on a farm."

"I agree. I have good news for you there. Domitian has banned castration from now on. I have it from the new soldiers who have started arriving from Rome. They have marched all the way poor mules. He seems to be cleaning the place up. He had at least one of the Vestal Virgins buried alive because she was unfaithful. I hear that Casca is taking over from me. He is coming by sea. You might remember him from your days in Rome."

"Oh yes. How time flies. I knew his family and remember him being born. I didn't think he would be old enough yet, but of course. I hope he settles soon. Please pass on my regards."

"I'm sure he will want to meet up with you again. I will be having a reception for him and I will be inviting you. I'll send you a messenger when I know the day and time."

"Any regrets leaving here?"

"Not really. I'm sorry there is unfinished business. We still get robberies on the roads. I'm sorry you lost your wine on the way to Thyatira last year. It doesn't matter how many patrols, they never seem to find anything."

58

"Just so you and Casca know I'm not starting an insurrection, I have started training my slaves to use a sword in case of another attack." Gallus paused for thought.

"Slaves with swords could be misunderstood Marcus. You have given me an idea though. Someone is warning the robbers of patrols. I think we need a sting operation. I'll recommend to Casca that he sends a patrol in your worker's clothes next delivery you send on that road."

"Great idea. It would be nice to know who is doing the planning and warning. The robbers must live somewhere round here."

"I have my spies. Nothing so far. I pick up all sorts of news about the residents round here. These men behind me are paid well. Right boys?"

"Yes sir!" chorused the bath house workers.

"The ducting in this place is incredible to experience. There is a room near the fire where you can hear people sitting where we are as if you are in the middle of them. I also have a network that picks up all the gossip from the slaves in town. You might be pleased to know you

59

have the best reputation amongst the slaves. The biggest fear your slaves have is being sold to someone else. Do you think Zack looks a bit well fed for a beggar?"

"Him by the top water trough? Good grief. Is he not blind?"

"He has been blind from birth. He has been begging all his life, and all the locals know him. Remarkable how people assume that blind is also deaf. I have the inside scandal on most of the wealthy families round here. Just because they are powerless does not make slaves any less able to talk. I learn too much really. Your mantra of saying you worship at the temple of the Unknown God in Athens is wearing a bit thin. Be careful who you call Lord when the emperor's ears are being bent."

"I didn't think after my past that I needed to prove my loyalty to Rome."

"Better men than you have had tragic ends despite wonderful records in the name of Rome. Make sure when the time comes you can call Domitian your lord in a temple or there will be serious questions."

"How ridiculous is that? I can say all sorts. I can do all sorts that affirm all sorts of fantastic claims about any Emperor, but he can't send soldiers into my mind to see what I really think and believe."

"It's about appearances Marcus. It is all about keeping the Empire's money flowing around and the wealth coming into Rome while keeping the Emperor at the top of the heap. Any hint of opposition to that will be stamped out. We've seen it all before. The only reason I keep the peace is not about fairness or justice. Who gives a fig for the lives of anyone in a protesting crowd or their call for justice? The peace is only maintained so that the road to Rome is open for the flow of wealth. Blow justice" There was a natural pause in the conversation. The men moved to another room and began drying.

"How long is Gaius going to keep his job? You must know he is corrupt."

"I know all about Gaius and I know about Fortunatus. They sit where we have been sitting. Most of the time they are only thinking up new ways of doing perverted things to pretty slaves if they are not boasting about the things they have already done. The only thing of consequence otherwise is their attempt to build another Island on the olive grove."

"Not another one! Have you seen that thing? You at least credit me with knowing how to build after years as an engineer. That place is a death trap. It's no better than those that burned down in Rome in Nero's time. We can't let them build another. In any case, they don't own the olive grove."

"They are trying to get it by fair means or foul. I'll give Casca a detailed appraisal." The men were now dressed.

"Just a word to the wise Marcus. I pick up some of the gossip doing the circuit in Rome." Gallus spun a coin to the nearest bath house worker with a nod. They took the hint and left. Gallus dropped his voice. "It is time you went to see you wife and family. The gossip is that you are going to be a father again. The gossip is also that you are not going to have a son but a brother." Marcus' expression said it all. "Whoa! Don't attack the messenger. Only a friend could tell you this! I've not told anyone else round here."

Chapter 6

"Jesus is Life. In Him is the resurrection." The family and several of the available congregation stood round the grave in the middle of the olive grove. Jacob then recited the psalm from memory, "The Lord is my shepherd," and those who knew it joined in. Family members had shared their memories of Urbanus in the house, some struggling through the tears. The body was on the floor in its shroud, and the air was pervaded by the smell of gangrene and decay. The sons had worked with a will that morning digging in a space in the grove between trees distant from the house. Carried in and by his shroud borne by the sons, Urbanus' body was, after the short walk, lifted into the waist deep hole. Shrubs and purple convolvulus spread around the area. It was seldom visited. There was a stone plaque nearby on the ground. Upon it was an upturned carved stone cone representing a flame torch that had been extinguished. It was wrapped by the tousled spade leaves and purple flowers. It was the grave of Urbanus' parents. Jacob had earlier recited several psalms, "Lord, I call out to you from this overwhelming sea. Hear me please!" was one of them.

"We return this earthly temple to the ground in the total faith that we will see The Lord together on the Last Day with Urbanus and all the saints and angels in glory. Come Lord Jesus!" Every worshipper present began covering the body. The sons especially worked with a will.

Suckling pigs, reared by one of Urbanus' younger sons had been prepared for all those present afterwards. It was a flavour Jacob had only recently discovered once he accepted the end of his Jewish food restrictions. The afternoon and evening were spent together in affable company in the bittersweet atmosphere of a loving group coping with the fond farewell to a loved one. Most, but not all were of The Way. Jacob returned after the fond farewells to his room in the Island contemplating his lesson to his catechumens the following day.

Chapter 7

Marcus had returned to his house from the bath house in an angry frame of mind. He had long since resolved never to be angry with others over something they could not control. By the time he passed Pan at his entrance he had resolved to go to Rome. There were several items of unfinished business that he had to take care of if he had to spend the months away, not least the managing of his vineyard, farm and leather bottle manufacturing shop and all the slaves who worked for him. He needed a secretary and a negotiator to go with the deliveries of wine to neighbouring towns. Some of the work he could entrust to experienced slaves. Other skills were needed that were not in his present household or workforce. He had a task list in his mind before the midday meal Judith had prepared was set before him.

"Please eat with me Judith." It was a surprise to her to be given that privilege.

"I will get my food." She bowed and left.

"I am in a hurry," he began when she was sitting opposite, "which is why I am asking you to sit with me. I am going to have to go to Rome when I arrange a passage. I need to make arrangements."

65

Marcus started outlining household tasks and routines for his absence. Judith was already experienced in running the household budget. Marcus had a methodical military mind in management. "Are there any questions?"

"Just one master." What followed seemed hard to phrase for her. "You have been wonderful in not forcing a mate on me, and I remember you saying that in the house I would be as a sister to you."

"I remember."
"You said I could choose if I wanted to mate with anyone."

"I remember. You do pick your moments."

"I would like to mate with Jacob."

"Well I'll be blowed! It is beyond my power Judith. I am going to ask Jacob to come here in a couple of days. I am thinking of a proposition for him. I will arrange it so you get some time to talk to him. If he says yes to you he won't be mating with a slave. He will want you for a wife." Marcus thought for a moment. "If he says yes to you I will give you freedom, but only if you agree to stay employed as my housekeeper either living in or coming in from your home with Jacob."

"Thank you master!" Silence in eating continued for some time.

"You dark horse! How long has this been going on?" Judith looked down with modesty and not a little embarrassment.

"Nothing has gone on. I have had…feelings for Jacob since he taught me the faith. He has never known. Only when he laid hands on me in prayer when he came for supper with you it was too strong. I had to ask you."

"Does he know your past?"

"A little of it. He knows I had a baby that was sold just before you took me into you house."

"Hardly a baby. He was about twelve you told me."

"He will always be my baby." Judith looked down again and then a few moments later wiped the silent tear on the back of her hand.

67

"I wish for your sake I knew where he went. I would try to get him for you. If he works anything like you he would be a wonderful asset to any owner." Marcus put his plate down. "Now have you any figs? I will eat them on the road. I have to find the farm men and the vinedressers." Judith went out to find the fruit and gave it to Marcus.

"Thank-you master." Marcus sensed the emotional turmoil she had.

"You are wonderful." He put his arm round the woman's shoulders with a squeeze. "Thank you my sister." Judith followed Marcus to the entrance and watched him striding down the street to the farm outside the town on the north side away from the sea. He still had a military gait with one swinging hand full of figs and the other feeding them to his mouth. Then she turned indoors to her household chores with her mind multi-tasking with the hardest set of words she had ever put together. What on earth would she say to Jacob?

Chapter 8

Early on the Lord's Day worshippers were assembled standing around the largest room, off the courtyard, as all but a few rooms were in Chloe's house. Onesimus entered, attended by Clemens as his deacon that day, and Philip, who was accepted as deputy to the ageing Onesimus. Each was carrying a towel, though there was something about the way they were being carried around the shoulders that suggested they were not going to be used for drying anything. The only person sitting was Martha, who was on a low step marginally outside of the open door from which they entered.

"Peace of the Lord to you all!" he said, looking around the standing crowd, three or four deep by the wall with an open space in the middle of the room. The different classes were clearly differentiated by their clothes with the preponderance of groups, though not totally, of slaves grouped separately from the free. There was an impression of swathes of brown and beige flecked occasionally with the richer hues of the more wealthy. Women stood well integrated with the men. There was a clear joy in the reply from the assembled worshippers though not a uniform response.

69

Onesimus, now from behind a table strewn with scrolls, began an extempore prayer that collected his thoughts. There were words of praise addressed to the Father, for the day, for each other and for Jesus the Christ. There were murmurs of approval echoing around the room. There was a prayer of humility asking the Father to forgive any inadequacies in the worship. His words brought images of awesomeness and power, singularity, depth and universality. He was utterly sincere, feeling, and though there was a sense that these words had been used before, it was no routine set of words. There was an address to the Paraclete. That brought more murmurs of approval. Those present were invoking a living God, and the atmosphere reflected it.

When Onesimus had reached the end of his prayer, there was a silence that was a natural break being used reflectively. Philip picked up one of the scrolls. It was a reading from the ancient Jewish scripture in the Greek language. The atmosphere changed to attentiveness to a person in the room rather than a spirit moving within it. Eyes began to be directed and to focus. Hands and arms returned to sides.

Philip read in a firm and direct tone. In a room of many who had not learned to read, they remembered a prophet announcing that the

70

Spirit of the Father was upon him and he was sent to bring good news to the oppressed. There was a perceptible reaction in the room though not audible. They remembered that the prophet had come from God to the broken hearted bringing freedom for prisoners and their release. The Lord's chosen time had come, God's vengeance was about to happen. There would be the oil of gladness rather than the ashes of grief. There would be an end of despair. One female voice in the room whispered, "Please Father!"

This reading ended, Jacob seamlessly began singing one of the psalms. He had the words before him on a scroll but knew the words by heart from his youth. Some of the congregation of Jewish birth knew the words and joined in. The words they remembered were of the Lord ruling from sea to sea and to the end of the earth. His foes would bow down and enemies lick the dust. Kings would pay tribute with gifts from Tarshish, Sheba and Seba. The needy would be delivered when they called. They would be delivered from oppression and violence. Prayer would be sung and said for ever.

One of the young slaves was weeping. Martha, unseen to most in the room had her eyes closed and was silently and slightly rocking back and forth.

71

The psalm ended, Pudens, a deacon in old age limped to the table and read from one of Paul's letters produced from Onesimus' collection. There is neither slave nor free, male nor female, or Jew or Greek. Some of those hearing this for the first time withheld a temptation to cheer. The female who had breathed "Please Father" held the older woman beside her in an embrace. It was her owner who reciprocated the affection.

Onesimus began a song. Most in the room seemed to know it and joined in. There were a few who were new to the room who wished they could. They could sense that within a few weeks they would know it. It had the feel of being ancient and revered.

Even though the Saviour, the Chosen One was in the form of God it was no crime to be equal to God. He emptied himself came in the form of a slave, taking the likeness of humans, and being found as a human he became utterly humble, obedient to death on the cross. As a result of this action God exalted him to the name above all names and he will be worshipped and exalted in heaven earth, and under the earth. The Saviour, the Anointed One is Lord to the Glory of God the Father above all forms of earthly authority. It was not lost on the singers that the same word for "Lord" was the title of the Emperor. They knew this

72

was a challenge to the order of the day. The song was sung again, and then again. It was a victory song.

Miriam, one of Chloe's household burst into a tirade of oral jabber that the assembled church took as speaking in tongues. Hysteria seemed to take over from the orderly readings that had preceded them, even with the emotional charge that accompanied them. As Miriam called out, the singing stopped mid verse. At the end of her tirade, a prolonged gurgle from Miriam was followed by her falling backwards in a faint. Two of her housemates reached to break her fall, but she would have a bruise later. Onesimus, in a calm firm voice asked if any could interpret the Spirit in that outburst. There was an awed silence that lasted several seconds waiting for an answer.

Outside the door, Martha spoke in a steady voice, "The Lord is a great God. The Emperor will one day worship the Lord Jesus."

It took some time for the room to take in the import of the statement. The stunned silence ended as Clemens moved to the expected next stage of the worship. He picked up one of the scrolls. Some in the room bowed. Some knelt. All but the handful of newcomers could sense this was a climax. This was the spoken word of

73

the Lord Jesus about to be read. Marcus, tall and against the wall since he could see over Judith and the others in front of him knew by its colouration that this was that other document of the sayings of Jesus not contained in Mark's Good News. Other sayings of Jesus were remembered by longer lived faithful having heard them repeated in the worship over the years. Other scraps of manuscript contained other sayings. Given the disputes amongst factions claiming authority for their sect, some of the sayings were having their veracity challenged. None were to challenge what Clemens read on this occasion. It was one of Jesus' parables.

A king was holding a wedding feast for his son. Slaves were sent to call guests to the feast but the guests refused the invitation. Other slaves were sent and the details of the food for the feast and the lavish preparation were given. The slaves were variously maltreated as the original guests rejected the invitation and followed their own agendas. These slaves were then instructed to go into the public places and bring in everyone of whatever status to celebrate the King's son's wedding, while the original guests were verbally condemned.

A prayer of thanks was said for this parable spoken by The Lord.

74

Philip moved into the central open space to give teaching on what had been heard.

"We have one Lord, and we are all his slaves. That Lord who made all things brought us all the creation. He made us like a potter made this cup." Philip indicated an earthenware cup on a small table to the left of Onesimus.

"This cup is not going to argue with me. If I move it, it will move. If I drop it, it will break. The potter had clay that day. He made cups. He made plates. He made the ewers you saw by the Chloe's door. The clay did not argue."

"God the Father made all creation for His purpose. He made all people for His purpose. He made the Patriarchs, He made the Prophets, and He made the Kings for His purpose. He made Israel for His purpose. That purpose was His birth as one of us, His children, all people, loved by Him. And we may not argue just as clay will not argue with the potter."

"His love was so great for us that He came amongst us and took the form of a slave to the Father to fulfil His purpose and that purpose was Love. That Love is shown not in the sentiment of feeling,

75

but in total service. Jesus the Lord died on the cross in that service. That is no mere emotion in the belly but a self giving to pain and death."

"But Our God is a God who will have His purpose fulfilled. That death on the cross was overcome by the power of the Love of the Father. He raised the greatest exposition of love, His Son to a new life. We remember The Son our Lord with us now in our worship and with us always. When we are broken, we too will be raised by that same power at work in us through the Risen Christ in the power of the Spirit."

"Our purpose is to bring all people to His worship, to oneness with each other and oneness in God amongst all people. The pot cannot tell the potter, 'I am greater than other pots.' Only one can say who is greater, and that is the potter who made the pot."

"There is one Lord, and we all answer to one Lord."

"If the potter is not satisfied with any one of his creations, he can take it and remould it. When Israel failed to be the instrument of His purpose, He called others. He has called us. Israel failed to recognise the time of His coming: we have, and we proclaim His purpose to the world."

"In the same way that Israel rejected the Lord's coming, so we expect to suffer the same rejection the Lord did. We are proclaiming the Lord coming again. Like the slaves inviting guests to the Lord's wedding, we are sent to the streets: to people of any rank. The first invited guests, Israel, rejected the call. We must not reject it, and are bound as His slaves to call all others to that Wedding Feast. That feast is the coming together of God with His creation when all things obey His will. Those that do not obey He will remove from creation."

"We see ourselves as the lowest of all so that the Lord may raise us to the greatest in His Kingdom, and not even death can stand in the way of that purpose for us being fulfilled."

"Now I would have thought it self evident that we are here. We can touch each other. Unless we are blind we can see each other."

"When the Lord Jesus was moving in the land of His birth, preaching and healing, he was as here to them as you and I are to each other. No one would have thought that this man only 'seems to be here.' Yet that is what some so called believers are saying. Let us call

77

them 'Docetists' since that is what some of our faith in other churches are calling them. They are saying that since God is Spirit, then Jesus could not have been, as we are, flesh and blood, so must have been some other form of thing. Why, I ask, should God make some other sort of thing when he has already made the thing that we are?" There was laughter in the room.

"There are other groups claiming that the human Jesus was taken over by some divine creature of God. That God could not suffer as we suffer in the flesh. Jesus was as someone possessed by a spirit until that time he was on the cross, and then the divine spirit left Him to cry the words of the psalm, "My God, why have you forsaken me?"

"If that really was the truth, then our forgiveness could not have happened. The sacrifice of God himself for us to answer for all of human sin would not have been real. God in Christ did die for our sins"

"We are forgiven." Philip's emphasis was on 'are'. There was a murmur in the room.

"We are forgiven." There were calls of "Praise the Lord" and "Thank-you Lord."

"We are forgiven." This third repetition by Philip was louder and his arms were open to indicate all present. The congregation spontaneously were saying "Amen Amen" and "Alleluia."

Philip said, "Amen!" and there was a cheer and applause from all present. A chatter and hubbub filled the room.

Onesimus began a brief address to the several newcomers amongst the congregation explaining that the purpose of that presence was obedience to the Lord's command to "remember" Him. The chatter died down as he spoke. It was an explanation all but the newcomers had heard frequently. Jesus was being "remembered", in a word stronger than just a mere thought of something in the past, but in a sense of recalling His living presence. The first part of the worship was "remembering" in His words and in His deeds and in how He fulfilled all the prophecies of scripture. Shortly they would remember in the meal He gave them in the upper room the night before he offered himself on the cross. "This meal is for the baptised," he said, "and I hope that all in a short time would be able to join in as those baptised into The Way." He then dismissed the non-baptised to their further instruction. The separating groups began a spontaneous farewell of embraces and kisses with each other, the majority of verbal farewells being of "Peace be with you."

Chapter 9

Two groups separated on leaving the main room, each with its deacon. Jacob led one group of six to their appointed room. Another deacon, John, led the other with the newcomers to another. Clemens as deacon in the Lord's Supper that day stayed with the main worshipping group of the baptised. Jacob's group included Marcus and two of his young slaves, Abraxas and Aethon, who worked in the bottle making shop. The others were from the household of Bion, a recently baptised Christian who was ordering the conversion of his household. Jacob had a difficult role in teaching his catechumens the concept of atonement to a non-Jewish group. Once the group had settled, and his preamble over, Jacob began.

"Moses", he said, "having led the Israelites out of Egypt into the wilderness came to Sinai. Moses with the Lord on the Mountain gave the Law. He gave what we call the Ten Commandments." Jacob rehearsed the commandments and asked them to repeat them. Only one member of his group could read, so they were repeated several times to enable learning by rote.

"God gave the commandments as a mark of His Covenant."
All but Marcus looked blank. This was a new word. "Covenant is a
legal agreement. We agree a binding arrangement. If I bought a slave, I
would have a legal agreement with the former owner that once the
money has been handed over, he no longer owns that slave and I do.
God delivered the people of Israel from their slavery in Egypt. God has
taken over Israel as His slaves. God set a condition on this freedom
from Egypt. The agreement was, 'I will be your God and you will be
my people.' The mark of you being my people is that you will keep my
law."

"Breaking any of the law is a breach of that agreement and
normally if you break the law, you would be punished. There were a
whole complex set of punishments laid out in the law. These were the
sacrifices that restored a whole relationship with God that had been
broken with the breach of His law." The farm young slaves started to
fidget.

"If a slave disobeyed a master he would be punished." Jacob
spoke sharply. The fidgeters paid attention again. "Once punished, we
would expect of a good master that he would not then keep punishing
him or her for the same offence. Unfortunately people are weak and

82

make mistakes again and again. Consequently the Israelites had to keep making the sacrifices to make good with God again and again. When you have paid for your sin you have atoned. Sin again and you have to atone again."

"The sacrifice in the Temple was always just an animal, and always offered by a sinful man, the High Priest. What we all need is the perfect sacrifice, and that sacrifice, to avoid being corrupted, would have to be by a perfect priest. Only God is perfect, so the only sacrifice is God Himself, and the only priest who could offer that sacrifice without corrupting it would be God Himself."

"God in Jesus offered Himself on the Cross as a sacrifice for your sins and mine. He has set us free from the slavery of sin. We are no longer the slaves of the law or of Israel. We are now sons and daughters of God and equal before Him."

"In the Kingdom of God we are equal before his Love. We are now His children, free, because what the Lord Jesus did for us."

The understanding of being equal to their masters sunk in for the slaves. They were a little discomforted. It seemed a little unreal, like a dream. The young men looked to Marcus. Irene and Talia looked

83

at Athena. Jacob concluded, "This freedom and equality is never to be abused. This status of ours has to be as Jesus showed us: one of service to each other. Whoever is great in God's kingdom is the one who considers himself least in the kingdom. We are given freedom to serve, not rule."

"Paul said, as we heard earlier 'in Christ there is neither slave nor free'. That does not make the slave or the free greater or lesser than the other. We only have the freedom to serve. The Lord lifts us up: not we ourselves or other people: The Lord. We always remain His slaves, and accepting that we become His children. Paul said that we have to think of others as better than ourselves. That is easy to say and hard to do, especially given some of the people we have to deal with."

Hitherto those present for more than a year of Lord's Days teaching previously had been given the stories of Israel's past, and the teachings of Jesus as the new law of how to behave towards each other. They had been learning to pray together. They had learned of the fellowship and mutual care that the followers of The Way had shown over the recent decades, but they heard the tragedy of the loss of some of the saints as martyrs. They knew of the hope of eternal life and the expectation of the coming end of life as it is with the coming, any day,

84

of judgement with Christ in glory with the angels. The group shared some of their personal experiences of knowing Jesus in their lives: how it helped them bear hardship with hope, and witness the care of others of the Way in their lives. The word of Jesus about doing to others as you would have them do to you rang true both for slaves and their owners: all had to live together to their mutual benefit.

The uncertainty of living the faith publicly continued. Marcus mind wandered to the memories of the fire in Rome shortly before he became a soldier and the brutality towards those blamed for it. He was not to know then of the significance and the other side of the story of those executed. He simply believed the official word that circulated.

In due course, the sounds of many voices across the courtyard indicated the end of the worship by the baptised. The group said the Lord's Prayer together and bade farewell. Marcus hung behind the others as they departed. He clearly wanted to talk to Jacob. Jacob, on the other hand, was conscious of a planned meeting of the deacons with Onesimus. Chloe was hosting them and would also be present. All of them were much reliant on her grace in hosting them as well as on the generosity of the benefactors in the sacrificial giving that enabled the

85

full time work of some of the clergy and providing the resources for the scribes to reproduce the scriptures.

"Thank-you for the meal last week Marcus." Jacob was warm in his tone.

"A real pleasure! I hope we can repeat it. I would really welcome some time with you. I wish to make an offer that would be beneficial to you, me and the church but I see you are wanting to leave." Jacob hesitated.

"Are you free if I call on you tomorrow after I finish with Gaius?"

"Thank-you. I will get back from the vineyard in time. I will warn Judith you are coming so she can be better prepared. I hope you are staying to eat again."

"Generous again! Thank-you Marcus. The Lord be with you."

The men parted, Marcus to the front exit and Jacob to the main church room where he was bidden to meet with the ordained men of the church. All were together already. Chloe was organising service of the pre-prepared food. There was warmth of bodies in the vacated worship

86

area. "Come in Jacob!" called Onesimus. It appeared that those in the room for the meeting had already decided an agenda and were following an agreed path.

The splinter conversations died down and all concentrated on Onesimus. "I have been thinking, and everyone I have talked to seems agreed that we ought to put all these scrolls into one scroll. There are sayings of The Lord that are not written yet, and the saints who walked with the Lord are either martyrs in His Name or are so removed in distance from us in His Mission that we may not see them again. We do not want His sayings lost, and we do not want these scrolls to be separated. Jacob is doing wonderful work in reproducing them and furnishing them to other churches, but it does seem right that we should put them into one scroll. Mark did a fine work in giving us his document, but it clearly lacks many of The Lord's sayings and some of His parables and great works of healing."

"In addition we are contending with faction and schisms that are giving false interpretations of His sayings. They are even inventing false ones to further their false notions about The Lord. I don't have to tell you who they are. We occasionally get them shouting their lies in the market place."

87

"Not only that, some of us are arguing with the Jews who talk of the Lord not being one who fulfilled what the scriptures said of Him. That must be dealt with in the new writing."

"What are they contending this time?" asked Jacob.

"There are many things we need to address from all of these factions, but the greatest worry I have is their constant accusation that The Lord came from Nazareth, and the scriptures talk of the Messiah coming from Bethlehem."

"We don't know where the Lord was born." Pudens was the oldest of the group with perhaps the greatest number of anecdotes of the Apostles' interactions with various churches. "We need to look at this in another way. The Lord is God's Messiah, therefore the scriptures told of the Messiah, therefore there are stories we do not remember in the church that fulfilled those scriptures. We need to look at the prophecies and pray for the revelations of the stories we do not now remember." The assembled group looked pensive. Jacob saw the weakness in the argument.

"Surely Pudens and I mean this with the greatest love, it cannot be right to write stories about the Lord if there is no basis in the

88

known events of the time. We might as well be looking at the old scriptures then making it up. That is what you are accusing the schismatic men of doing. Or have they been getting revelations after prayer?" The atmosphere in the room became a little tense.

Philip spoke. "I understand your doubt Jacob, but you have to see that Mark did not write history about the Lord. He wrote the truth about the Lord. He did not simply tell the facts about the Lord: he wrote his beliefs about The Lord. It is all there in the first sentence. 'The good news about Jesus Christ Son of God.' Not exactly beginning with a date and time is it?"

John interrupted before Jacob could reply. "Another omission of Mark is that there are no stories of the Lord when he was seen after the resurrection. It looks as if the Gospel was never finished. Whoever finishes a book with the word 'but'?"

Onesimus called them to order. "This is for detailed meetings later brothers. We need to agree intent. Jacob will you be willing to scribe the document? You are by far our best scribe." All in the room seemed to be nodding or murmuring approval. The enormity of what was being asked dawned on him. The scriptures that rested on the table

89

in worship were highly revered. He was developing the Lord's Word into a single document. At the same time he could foresee contention with others in the room that had a variant vision of the document to be produced. "I am honoured to be asked brothers, but be patient with me."

"We need to meet regularly to agree what is written." Onesimus concluded, "But we must have a first meeting to agree a few things." A time was set and the meeting moved on to other church matters, particularly of the reports of experiences had by the deacons over the week. Jacob on his turn spent some time with his concern about Urbanus, Fortunatus and Gaius.

Chloe was in the room at the end of his story about the assault in Jacob's neighbour's room. The women with whom she shared her home picked up the town's news in the course of a week talking to slaves and others as they moved about the town or at the water trough. She butted in. "Yesterday I was told that Fortunatus' foreman died. He fell against a door and banged his head the day before they say."

After a silence and with superb timing Pudens spoke. "I always thought he was a head banger." He tapped his stick on the floor in rhythm with his laughter.

Chapter 10

"I only have one document today." Gaius was walking aimlessly with his hands behind his back unintentionally stretching his toga over his corpulent belly. He had an awkward air about him and his movement was as if he had a painful rash in his groin, or so Jacob wondered. Maybe Gaius just had too much fat on his thighs. Jacob was seated in his usual place. "I want you to write out a document of agreement to transfer property. Some lines will be left blank to fill in names and specific details later" Jacob nodded though this was an unusual procedure. "When you have completed the document as far as you can I need you to take it to Fortunatus' for his signature and then bring it to my house where the other party to the agreement will be signing it, and I will need you to be a witness then as well. You know where Fortunatus lives?"

"I think so." Gaius began dictating. It was clear from the description of the property that it was the olive grove that was being

91

transferred, and Jacob was surprised that Phoebe and her sons had decided to sell it so quickly after Urbanus' death, and even more so now that Urbanus was buried in it. Maybe the graves were not part of the transfer. They were in a remote and sandy part that was of little use otherwise. Even more puzzling was the hostility to selling they had expressed only days before. Jacob kept his peace. He was here a functionary and it was not his place to question this legal process. He resolved to call on Phoebe when opportunity arose. He was unlikely to get chance to talk to Urbanus' family during the signing at Gaius' house. He was occupied with this document for that morning and he had arranged to be with Marcus that afternoon. A meeting of the steering group for the scripture project was due to follow that.

"And date it with today's date in the 3rd year of the Emperor Domitian," Gaius concluded his dictation. "Before I leave, did you have anything to do with the death of Fortunatus' foreman? It was in your building." Clearly the other men had not recognised Jacob in the gloom, to his relief.

"I heard he tripped and fell against a door upstairs from my rooms."

92

"How did you hear that?"

"Chatter at the water trough." Gaius seemed to be satisfied. Jacob was fearful that if he was placed at the scene he might be implicated through vindictiveness.

"I'll see you at around noon then. I am considering increasing your fee." There was no farewell but Gaius gripped Jacob's shoulder as he passed. Jacob was reminded of the rear of a ploughing ox as Gaius exited. He should have felt elated at an increase in his income but he was overcome more by a sense of foreboding. It was not like Gaius to be generous, and he wondered if undue pressure had been put on Phoebe or her sons. They were vulnerable in their bereavement.

On completion of the deed of transfer Jacob put his materials together with the document ready to take to Fortunatus. He checked the road before leaving. He did not want to be commandeered to carry a soldier's pack again. From his vantage point at the magistrate's building he could see a bireme had docked in the port below. The chances were that troops would be moving from the harbour to the barracks so he resolved to take a circuitous route to avoid the main marching route. As he walked he looked down one of the short side streets to see a procession of soldiers around an oxen drawn cart that appeared to be carrying circular relief bronzes of the sort that were placed on temple walls as shrines as big as a small cartwheel. Jacob had a more concerning sense of foreboding than before. The cult of the Emperor had come to town.

He passed the high walled rear of Fortunatus' villa and along the seldom walked hot dusty side alley. Lizards darted away into wall niches. As he rounded the corner to the front he almost walked into the corner of a delivery cart. It brought back a very painful memory from Jerusalem and he stood quietly in prayer until his anxiety passed. When he looked up there was a youth staring at him. He had left Fortunatus' house to carry another bag of goods from the cart for the household. It was the youth who had been branded. His forehead was blistered, weeping sore, scarred and angry, but a healing process was underway. Jacob could see the vague shape of an "F" in the scar for "Fugitive:" runaway. The youth grasped a large basket of vegetables in both arms and lifted. In the movement there was a glint from his arm.

"I see you found your amulet!"

94

The youth paused before he lifted his load and smiled. "Are you a soothsayer? How did you know I lost it?"

"I saw those bullies branding you and I heard you tell them you had gone to find it. What is your name?"

"They call me Onesimus now. I used to be called Agathon. I deliver things for Fortunatus my master." The youth seemed pleased to have anyone take an interest in him and was effusive. "This is Doris my mule." He said it as if Doris was his best friend, and even his possession. "I must carry this in or they will shout at me."

"Well done Onesimus. You are being useful. If you become like the other Onesimus I know you will be a great man one day." The youth smiled and turned again to lift his next load. "I need to talk to your master."

Jacob followed the youth into the entrance. On hands and knees washing the floor of the porch was an old woman of North African origin, completely naked. "Excuse me sister. I need to walk across your work." The comment and especially the mode of address surprised her. She grinned a white flash of teeth. She knelt up to allow

95

Jacob to pass. She looked emaciated around her ribs and her breasts were almost flat flaps of skin. Jacob returned the smile.

Facing the courtyard of Fortunatus' villa, Jacob waited for the attention of a resident to announce his arrival to the master of the house. Suddenly verbal abuse could be heard being shouted at a slave from within one of the rooms. A naked teenage girl ran out on Jacob's right followed by Fortunatus holding a cane. A welt was already flaring on the top of the girl's thigh. There was defiance set in her face as she ran across to another room. Fortunatus may well have pursued her if he had not seen Jacob from the corner of his left eye. The change in the host's attitude was instantaneous. "Jacob is it? Welcome Scribe. Please come this way."

Jacob passed Fortunatus to enter the room from which the girl had fled. The host was a rather slight man two or three inches shorter than Jacob. "You live in one of my rooms in the Island do you not?"

"Yes Sir."

"You can have one of the ground floor suites at no extra charge if things work out right for me today Scribe. Would you like that?"

"It certainly sounds tempting." Jacob's reservations from his time with Gaius returned. He was pleased with his own response. Falling into temptation now seemed the danger. He sensed a trap but could not identify the pitfall. Maybe he would know when he met the other parties to the transfer. Gaius' offer of a rise in income and Fortunatus' offer of better accommodation were conditional. Neither was known to be liberal with gifts. He would soon have an answer. Jacob prepared the document. He also swatted houseflies that seemed to be taking an interest in him in the close warmth of the airless room.

Fortunatus signed. He used his ring to seal. A deed of transfer usually needed both parties to the agreement present. Jacob duly witnessed the signature and began to collect his things again. "I look forward to a successful enterprise and you will be well rewarded for your part in it." Jacob nodded. Now he was certain his was more than just a scribe's role. Why should he be so rewarded for such a minor functionary piece of work? Now he looked forward more than ever before to the afternoon meeting with Marcus. He was beginning to feel exposed. Fortunatus put a denarius down on the table. "With my compliments, Scribe."

"Thank-you Sir." His income had been supplemented by gratuities on a few occasions but this felt more like a bribe.

"Can I offer you orange juice?"

"No thank you Sir. I need to take this to Gaius now."

"Of course."

Jacob left Fortunatus' house. There were no slaves to be seen in the courtyard this time and the youth's cart and Doris had gone from the front. The heat was beginning to bake the stones on the main roads on that late morning. Jacob adjudged it must be nearing midday as he arrived at Gaius villa. He appreciated the relative cool of the entrance porch shade and floor. The mosaic upon which he stood depicted an attacking dog. It alerted him to a potential canine attack. Thankfully none came. Maybe dogs were loose at night in the courtyard beyond the entrance. A naked prepubescent girl was lifting fallen petals out of the shallow pool beyond the porch. Behind her, rising from the pool stood a female statue but Jacob was not good on the recognition of what for him were foreign gods.

"Please little sister would you let your master know the scribe is here." She splashed out of the pool holding her petals and scampered round the stone pathway leaving her little wet footprints. Jacob stepped back into the shade of the porch and stood on the dog's ears of the mosaic. It was a few minutes before Gaius appeared adjusting his toga on his shoulder and walking with the same wide legged steps he had seen earlier. Gaius offered a humourless smile when he saw Jacob.

"Please may I have the deed?" Jacob reached into his bag. "Thank-you. Please sit in the shade over here. There is some refreshment coming to you." Gaius disappeared with the scroll into a door behind the bench upon which Jacob had settled. There was the sound of rustling scroll behind him from the room and the hum of working bees in the hanging flowers that adorned the cloister of the courtyard. Gaius' voice could be heard in the room but the words were indistinct. Across the courtyard the same girl who had been in the pool on his arrival appeared with earthenware plate and cup. With averted eyes she presented him with a slice of fresh bread in a small pool of virgin olive oil and a cup of orange juice.

"Thank you little sister. What is your name?"

"Adelpha, Sir. Did you see my sister as you came in?" Jacob found himself in a confusing wordplay accidental upon discovering twins in Gaius' household. It was not the same girl as he had thought.

"I did Adelpha. You are very alike." She smiled and left Jacob with his bread and juice. He worked his way through the bread with thanks that the olive oil moistened it. The orange juice moved the last of it that had lodged in his oesophagus as he finished. Gaius came to the door behind him and invited him in. He left his plate and cup on the bench. The only person in the room apart from Gaius was an attractive young woman standing by the wall opposite the door. She was dark haired and naked, possibly the Jewish woman Gaius had referred to some days earlier. She gave the impression that she was not used to being habitually naked in front of everyone and was a little uncertain. Her eyes were averted and she had not looked at Jacob on his entry. The table was against the wall to his right with a stool he assumed was for his use. Upon the table was a bowl of unshelled nuts. There was a long low bench to the left of the entrance. An internal door to the next room was beyond it. There was still no sign of the other signatories. The scroll was spread on the table with two bronze ornaments weighting it open.

"Now how would you like this slave to be a companion in your new accommodation?" It took a few seconds for the import of the offer to register. Jacob wondered if he was feeling a little dizzy. He felt the olive oil and orange juice repeating on him. "I can arrange it." Gaius gestured towards the table. "Can you now please witness the mark of the other party?"

Jacob scanned the document. "Whose mark is this? I did not see them add it so how can I?" Gaius did not answer. Instead he took the bowl of nuts and emptied it behind the bench

"Pick them up," he ordered the girl and handed her the bowl. With a slightly pained look on her face she moved to the bench opposite Jacob. There was no option for her in obeying the command but to bend over and display her naked behind as she rummaged around the far side of the bench. It was an enormous distraction to Jacob's concentration.

"Whose mark is this?" Jacob repeated.

"Urbanus made it"

"When?"

"Today"

The girl stood and handed the bowl of nuts to Gaius, giving a quick slightly tearful and embarrassed look at Jacob as she did so. Jacob now saw the plot unfolded before him and was trying to frame his next words.

"You want me to witness, on today's date, the Mark of Urbanus for the sale of the olive grove to Fortunatus?" Gaius tipped the nuts behind the bench again.

"Pick them up," he ordered the girl again. Jacob moved from uncertainty to anger at what was now for him a visual sexual assault at an innocent's expense. He knew now that his role of scribe for Gaius was unlikely to continue, and his next action may even render him homeless. Before the girl could take the bowl and repeat her humiliation Jacob snatched it from Gaius.

"Please let me do it for you, sister." He took command in a situation where he held the moral high ground. Jacob rapidly picked up the nuts while Gaius and the girl looked on. It only took a few seconds before Jacob was upright again with the bowl. He thrust it into Gaius' midriff intending him to take it. Gaius had a mixture of anger and a

102

little uncertainty on his face, especially now that Jacob was standing in his space. Gaius was used to having Jacob sitting. Now he was standing in his face and two or three inches taller. He was younger, fitter and looking a physical threat. Jacob's humble demeanour had all but disappeared.

"You want me to witness Urbanus' mark today?"

"Yes." Gaius for once had uncertainty in his voice.

"And you expect this deed to be legally binding?"

"Of course."

"Urbanus died two days ago and is buried in the grounds described in the deed. I don't think the family will want him and his ancestors dug up to have another Island, and I don't see them acknowledging a deed that Urbanus signed two days after he died and witnessed by the man who led the burial. Do you?" Jacob moved away from Gaius and began to collect his materials into his bag. Jacob felt that he had burnt his boats on his job with Gaius but he had done no wrong. He did not persevere with the conversation that had put Gaius so much on the back heel. The information was not public. Gaius and

103

Fortunatus might well repent of their action and Jacob could keep his job. He may even keep the new accommodation if the two deceivers wanted to keep the attempted conspiracy quiet. It then occurred to Jacob that he was now vulnerable to Fortunatus' thugs to ensure his silence. Here was a mess not of his making, and not for him to solve. Gaius was uncertain as to his next move. He was also conscious of his lost face in front of his slave.

"Urbanus died you say?"

"Yes."

"Why was he not buried outside the wall?" Gaius was scrambling to be in control.

"The family ancestors were buried in that plot before there was a wall."

"We will talk of this tomorrow, Scribe," was all Gaius could summon to control the situation.

Jacob conceded stability to a difficult situation. "Yes Sir." His bag ready to lift, he nodded towards Gaius. "Good day Sir. Thank you for your hospitality." Gaius returned the nod. Jacob left and felt relief as he stepped over the mosaic dog into the heat of the open street. His mind was still reeling from the events of the last few minutes. He then felt a deep concern for the trapped slave girl and what Gaius would do now to her to vent his frustration and anger and to regain face.

His anger bubbled within him as he headed for Marcus' home. He longed for the security it seemed to offer and the chance to vent his concerns in confidence. The frustration of his own weakness in the face of such injustice by powerfully corrupt men and the vulnerability of slaves meant he hardly noticed the details of his walk from the one house to the other. As he turned to Marcus' street he stopped and took some deep breaths. He had been walking vigorously in the heat but it was really an attempt to control his feelings before meeting Marcus and his household. He was not one to burst in with anger. He wanted to show a spiritual peace. He was also annoyed with himself that one of the besetting images of the confrontation with Gaius was the female slave's naked rump as she picked up the nuts. Gaius seemed to have found a weakness in his composure and he hated to admit it to himself. He turned into Marcus' porch.

Judith met him at the entrance as if she had been waiting for him. "Welcome Jacob," she said before he could speak. Jacob expected to kiss her on the cheeks but she was ahead of him in the exchange.

"Bless you and peace to this house." He looked beyond her for Marcus.

"The master will be some time," she offered. "He apologises and asked me to look after you until he comes. Please come this way." Jacob followed her through the courtyard for a few paces. "Please sit." Jacob sat on a bench in the shade with a view over the tiled square punctuated by potted herbs. Judith had prepared a bowl of water and a towel beside the bench and she suddenly busied herself talking off his sandals. She was aware of Jacob's uncertainty. "This is your traditional welcome? Yes?"

"Yes Judith but you really shouldn't." Jacob was moved more than a little by the humility, affection and attention. The cool water on his feet was extremely refreshing. He had no choice but to see down the front of Judith's front dress as he watched her service to him. Her cleavage was wide between her the roundness of her breasts. Today was becoming a challenging day to a man with a healthy libido and

106

nowhere to take it while keeping his moral stance. She towelled his feet. The memory of scripture was strongly upon him as he recalled the woman anointing Jesus' feet. "Was the Lord ever frustrated so?" he wondered to himself. Judith emptied the bowl into the herb pots and the water spilled through or over the pots and streamlets wet the tiles. She crouched to do so and her attractiveness in movement became striking even in her innocent actions. For the first time he admitted to himself that he was in love with Judith and it would take discipline refined in a forge to carry him through his emotions. She stood and turned while holding the empty bowl.

"Would you like to eat now? I have some goat's cheese ready with tomatoes and basil. We went for fresh bread this morning."

"Judith you are wonderful. I had a little bread earlier but I have space for more" He complimented her service but it was a slight release for his affection for her. His thoughts passed through the moments of her time as his catechumen and her attentiveness and willingness to learn the faith and its practise. He was ever looking forward to her being in his Sunday group in those days. She eventually brought Marcus and Jacob's closeness with this household was growing.

107

Jacob reached the table and sat. Judith brought the pre-prepared food, set it in front of him and made to leave. "Are you not eating with me?"

"It is not my place."

"In Christ there is neither slave nor free. Please eat with me." There was eye contact that made it clear to both of them that there was a bond forming between them. The eye contact lasted. It brought a renewed tension to Jacob about Judith's bondage to Marcus and he broke his gaze. Judith smiled, gave a slight bow, and went for her food. She knew now the pattern of what she had to say.

"Marcus is a wonderful master," said Judith when she returned. "He makes us all feel part of the household and makes us understand how important each of us is to the work, as if we are part of his family. Our work is valued. We want to work. It is the same for those on the farm, in the vineyard and in the bottle workshop. Everyone sees the need for their work and how they benefit from it. There is no need for a whip."

"I think I can see that."

108

"He makes us feel like brothers and sisters. He has always treated me like his sister." Jacob felt some reassurance that there was no physical relationship between Judith and Marcus. "He does not force us into partnerships like some masters. He gives us freedom to relate to those we wish to."

They ate in silence for some moments. Jacob was wondering where Judith's conversation was going. He had no response but to nod his attentiveness as he chewed.

"He always said I could have a relationship with anyone who I choose." It dawned on Jacob where this was really going, but he could not see the path to the conclusion. Marcus must have left this opportunity for Judith to talk alone with him. "I said I would like to choose you." Jacob found his food lodged in his oesophagus again and drank some water. Judith was a nervous about Jacob's lack of response to such a disclosure of her feelings and worried she had overstepped her position, or that she was not going to be accepted. Jacob still needed reassurance of Marcus' approval. His chest was uncomfortable with the lodged food and he hiccupped. Even if he could talk through the discomfort, he was uncertain what he should say. Judith, now starting to lack confidence began to talk quickly. "He said that if you

109

said yes to me he would give me freedom as long as I remained as his housekeeper. He said you would not want me as a slave or a kept woman but that you would want a wife." She stopped, and her eyes were moist. Please help me Jacob I am feeling foolish after saying all this."

Jacob's emotions were churning. He drank and thankfully the food moved to his stomach. He put his food down. He moved to where Judith sat and beckoned for her to stand with him. He was deeply moved and he could not prevent his tears. He put his arms round her waist and held her.

"I love you. I think I have always loved you."

Judith reciprocated the tears. "I know I have always loved you. All through the time to my baptism I loved you with a hope but never believing you could be my…" There was no right word to use for her hoped relationship. She stood on her toes and kissed his wet salty cheek. He felt her face against his and hugged her closely without a word for what seemed an age: neither wished to end the moment.

Eventually, Jacob broke the silence, "And I was expecting to start the conversation over our meal that I have had an awful morning."

110

Humour seemed to be the way forward. Judith stepped back with an open mouthed smile that wrinkled the corners of her twinkling eyes. She stepped forward again to hold him again. "You beautiful man!" and squeezed her arms round his ribcage, her face pressed to his chest. The moment lasted many more heartbeats, Jacob smelling her hair against his cheek.

"No, I really have had an awful morning. Now it is important to you as well. I may have lost my job as scribe to Gaius and I might have been made homeless. I might not be able to support anyone else, let alone a wife yet."

"I think Marcus has something in mind, but we need to wait for him." They broke the embrace and Jacob pecked a kiss on her forehead. "I have no dowry. I have nothing but my love and service to give."

"I have a bucket, a bowl, two tunics, sandals, a stretcher to sleep on, and a broom." With perfect timing, Judith spoke after a pause.

"Such riches!""

111

They both laughed. Then they hugged again. They finished eating. Jacob helped Judith tidy after eating. That was novel for her. He simply wanted to be in her company rather than be separated as she rinsed plates in an earthenware basin in another room. There was little conversation for some time. Not a lot could happen until Marcus came home. Both had found a relationship they wanted but did not know how to move forward with it. They moved around the courtyard as Judith talked about her cultivation of herbs. Jacob felt they needed to share more of their past.

What happened to you before you came to Marcus?

"I used to be in a household in Thyatira. I was with the family since I was a little girl. I don't really remember my mother. They were good to me and I wanted to stay with them. They were getting old and the master died not long after I went there. He was a trader. The son took over and everything went wrong. He made me take part in orgies for his friends. I think they were helping him with his debts. I became pregnant. He took too many risks with the business, his mother told me, buying too many things that never made a profit. After a few years they had to start selling property to meet their debts. They had to sell nearly all the slaves. His mother gave me an amulet as I left. It is the only thing I ever held as my own. He brought us here to sell us because he thought there was more to be made from the sale. He herded us like cattle. My son's feet were bleeding on the walk and he was crying. He was too big to carry by then. We had to sleep in the open air while the young master slept in an inn. It was cold that time of year. That was the only time I nearly ran away but there was nowhere for us to go."

"At the slave market I had to take my clothes off in the crowd and buyers were abusing me and other women. I don't think many had any intention of buying. Anyway, Marcus saw me and bought me. I wanted Agathon to come with me but he was sold to someone else. I just had time to give him my amulet. It was all I could give him." Tears were welling up and her last words were choked off. Jacob did not make the link with the youth outside Fortunatus' house until he woke up with the realisation a few nights later. Judith composed herself. "What about you? Where were you before you came here?"

"I got away from Jerusalem before the destruction. I found people of The Way in the wilderness and they cared for me. I began to believe in The Lord Jesus with them. When it was clear that Jerusalem was a ruin we moved to other cities and joined their churches. I eventually went to Antioch and worked as a scribe while learning the

113

faith. After some years they asked me to become a deacon. The church there was growing and there were several deacons. They asked me to come here after a visit from Onesimus so about four years ago I came back with him. Gaius had made it known he needed a scribe so I went to him so I had work of sorts. In the first year in the church here I met you among the catechumens. Until an hour ago I thought I would always be an unmarried disciple."

In the middle of the afternoon with heat still abundant, Marcus returned. Judith was instantly running to rooms to start serving again before Marcus called her name and she came to him. "Have you asked him?"

"Yes." Her averted eyes and the demure smile gave Marcus Jacob's answer.

"You have my blessing and your freedom."

"Bless you Master! Thank you." She was effusive, almost jumping off the ground. She looked to Jacob, who was approaching to greet Marcus.

114

"You are a man blessed by God if he has given you this woman." Marcus hugged Jacob with back slapping and a wide smile. "Will you marry her?"

"I want to but I need to tell you about the morning I had."

"I have a few important things to tell you too and an offer to make." They all moved into the room where Jacob and Judith had eaten. "Right! You first." They sat down. For all her new freedom, Judith continued her service as before and she brought Marcus the same prepared food as they had eaten earlier. Marcus listened in silence while eating as Jacob outlined the details of his morning's exchanges. He frowned and muttered appropriately punctuating Jacob's report. For the first time in her time in Marcus' service Judith moved to sit in his presence, closely beside Jacob.

"I think I need to go and meet with those two," Marcus responded when Jacob had finished. "I have an offer to make to you that I was going to make earlier. I am going to offer the same terms as before I heard today's news so as not to exploit your uncertainty. I need a secretary but more importantly I need a capable estate manager after I go away next week. You will have plenty of time to work as deacon, I

115

think, but there are a few journeys to take you away from town as well. I have a house on the farm to offer you with the work about a mile to the north. I still want Judith to be housekeeper here. Does that reassure you about your security as a married man? I am guessing you don't really want to work for Gaius any more? Do you want a job with me?"

Jacob was instantly much relieved. "Thank you again Marcus. It would be a privilege to work for you."

"Very good!" They stood and acknowledged their agreement with another manly hug. Marcus began outlining the responsibilities Jacob would be taking over in his employer's absence including the proposed guarded wine transport to Thyatira

"Are you in Rome for long? Is everything well?"

"Family matters," was all that Marcus would say. "Now what are your intentions regarding my erstwhile slave who is to be homeless and destitute with her freedom unless she continues as my housekeeper?"

"It would be my joy to me if she could be my wife."

"Since I am the closest she has to a father, I undertake to furnish the house as your dowry. I have arranged my passage to Rome so I hope you can marry before I leave next week. I will happily provide the feast here."

Jacob and Judith looked at each other, overwhelmed by the generosity Marcus was showing.

"Would you like me to break the news to Gaius? Would you like me to find Fortunatus for you? You can stay here tonight if you want to get your things."

"Thanks again Marcus. I don't have many things to carry."

"Given the muck you unearthed today I think I had better come with you. I'm worried for your safety. I have to see the new procurator later so I'll let him know about them."

Jacob gave his farewells and headed for Chloe's home and the clergy meeting to set some of the principles of the new gospel. A few minutes later Marcus set off to see Gaius.

117

Chapter 11

"Why are you so angry John?" Onesimus was wearing his fatherly face with a penetrating eye contact.

"This book has to contain much more of the Lord's condemnation and judgement. Sorry I don't mean to appear angry: I just feel strongly about it."

Jacob had a hard task concentrating after the day's momentous changes to his life. "We have very little of the Lord doing condemnation though," he offered.

"The Lord fulfilled the scriptures so we should have the judgement voiced in the scriptures." John's voice rose again.

118

"We have to be careful we are not writing what we think the Lord should have said. The Pharisees condemned Jesus because they didn't expect a Messiah to say what he did and do what he did. We could be just as guilty." Jacob was getting weary.

John threw his head back and breathed deeply. His voice rose again. "We are being guided by the Lord now. We are being given his guidance. We have corrupt powers ruling us and misguided sects perverting The Lord's words. We have half hearted people of The Way that are not working hard enough to proclaim His Word. Surely they need warning of the Judgement to come."

"These are harsh words from you John that have to be balanced with the service of a Lord who came to show the Love of the Father." Onesimus held the same tone as in his previous offering.

"Daniel's vision was of Judgement that happened. The Father will Judge again."

"If you have a vision like Daniel's then let us know of it, but it will be a different book." Onesimus was firm and indicated an end to a diversion. John drew breath to remonstrate but Onesimus turned to him and held the uncompromising face of a father to a pestering child.

119

Jacob broke the tension "Sorry if this is a diversion but I think Daniel was written centuries after it says it was and was writing up a history claiming it to be a vision recorded years before." The silence that followed was either confirmation that it was a diversion, or that it was a profound thought that needed consideration, or hostility to a perverted viewpoint. Jacob began to feel embarrassed.

Onesimus was keen to get back to the real agenda. "We need to finalise tonight a way forward for Jacob on the birth story of the Lord, and a way of putting together a structure that fits into the…let us call it a "Gospel" since Mark recorded his as such…all those sayings and parables for which we have no context. We have little or no knowledge of the Lord's infancy, but such that we have must be enhanced by what we believe are the fulfilled prophecies that must have taken place." The next few minutes were spent offering scriptural prophecies appropriate to the subject matter.

"Behold a virgin shall conceive." Pudens made his first contribution.

Jacob tried to make a representation amongst the chatter. "That is a mistranslation of the Hebrew. The prophet did not say that! He said 'behold a young woman shall conceive.'"

"We all believe that to be the true Word of God from the prophet." Pudens waved his arm vaguely in Jacob's direction as being dismissive as of a child telling a dream.

Jacob felt affronted. "So what did the prophet say in his native tongue then?" The room turned to concentrate on the new tension. Onesimus was conscious of yet another confrontation and more time to be wasted on a diversion so the point was not debated and he moved into a summary.

Onesimus began counting fingers. "Firstly, Bethlehem. Then we need to link The Lord to David as 'Son of David.' He came for Gentiles as well as Jews. There is a link somehow with Egypt when we look at 'I called my son out of Egypt.'" Jacob was stressed and tired and resisted re-opening the debate that that prophecy about Egypt was a reference to Israel's history, not a prediction of the Messiah's origins.

"Now as for the sayings, in the absence of context, we use the most general terms appropriate to the inferred audience. Since this was

121

the New Law from the Lord, wherever it was spoken by Him, it was as if it was from the new Sinai, and perhaps Jacob could place the Lord speaking to his disciples as the Father once spoke to Moses on a high place."

"We shall meet again, all being well, in four weeks time and we will see how Jacob is getting on." Onesimus rose and held his back and leaned back to stretch. He called those present to pray, and especially for the Lord's guidance on Jacob's work."

Chloe heard the group moving and entered. "Jacob is getting married." She announced. Jacob was not ready for this but he had not sworn her to confidence when he met her with the news as he entered her house as the earliest of her guests that evening. All present turned with smiles and congratulations at what was entirely unpredictable to them. They had no knowledge of Jacob having a relationship with a woman.

"It might take a while for the new gospel to be written now." Pudens caused a knowing laugh amongst the men."

"So? Who and when?" Onesimus smiled benignly.

It will be soon because Marcus needs to be present and he has to go to Rome urgently, but I have no day yet. My bride will be Judith."

Chapter 12.

The light was fading as Marcus reached Gaius' entrance. The heavy cedar doors were closed, rather early as Marcus thought. He thumped the door with the side of his fist. It made an inadequate sound so as to alert any resident, but he clearly heard large snarling and barking dogs hitting the door on the other side. The sound was dying down before he heard Gaius' voice on the other side asking who was calling. The tone seemed to be of someone expressing surprise at the lateness of the hour, even though it was barely sunset.

"It is Marcus. I have important information for you Gaius." They had only met on social occasions hosted by the procurator but Gaius recognised the voice of his caller.

"Please wait. I need to restrain the dogs." Sharp abusive terms were used to induce canine obedience. There was silence for some time before Gaius returned and bolts were moved. The door opened. Gaius looked uncertain at this unexpected arrival, his face like that of a child holding a forbidden sweetmeat.

123

"Please come in."

In the first openness of the atrium Gaius turned, still looking uncertain.

Marcus began firmly. "Gaius, your scribe Jacob is now in my employment and I am bringing his resignation." Gaius drew breath but Marcus continued, deliberately stepping into Gaius' personal space. The visitor was fully a head higher than his host. "I am also here to collect any fees due to him." Marcus had no authority from Jacob to ask this, but was taking an aggressive initiative to broach the earlier events of Jacob's day.

"He has no fees due. He did not complete his work today. I was going to dismiss him due to his lack of honesty."

"His lack of honesty is refusing to sign as witness to a dead man signing away his olive grove you mean?" Gaius' spluttering attempt to respond was talked over. "If I was employing on reputation for honesty I would take Jacob before you any time Gaius. Casca knows of your plot, so if there is any threat to Jacob, I will know where to look, and so will his soldiers."

124

Gaius stepped back so was not looking up so steeply. Marcus had lied about informing Casca but in anticipation of his later appraisal to the Roman authority of the day's events.

"I think you had better leave before I release the dogs again."

Marcus stepped forward into Gaius' personal space again. "If that is a threat, Gaius, the reason I am still here is that whenever anything has put me in any danger, man or beast, I have killed it." Marcus' voice was barely audible but clearly heard. Gaius looked up, saw the penetrating eyes and looked away. Marcus held the silence long enough to cause discomfort to the smaller man and then turned on his heel towards the door. "Goodnight Gaius. Thank-you for your time." Six brisk paces moved Marcus to the door and he left, closing it gently behind him. He did not want his back to Gaius for more than was necessary. Gaius with his shuffling heavy walk moved to the door and shot the bolt. He leaned on the door for more than a minute breathing heavily, not from the exertion of walking but as anger built. He turned back to the living quarters of his villa, looking for someone on whom to wreak his ire.

Marcus strode towards the Procurators' private reception. The following day was the public handover of authority in the barracks before the soldiers and local authority figures. It occurred to Marcus that he was likely to meet Gaius again. He would be alert as to how Gaius faced his Roman superiors in the brief time they would talk.

As he reached the torchlight of the barrack gate the sentry challenged him. It was the new guard relieving those who were to march to Rome the following day. Marcus found it hard not to salute.

"Marcus to see Gallus and Casca. I am expected."

The sentry did salute. "Sir, you were my first centurion." He stepped forward, stood to attention and Marcus saw his face in the torchlight.

"Hello soldier. Sextus is it? Stand easy. I'm retired now."

"Good to see you again Sir! Please enter."

"Thank-you soldier. I know the way."

Marcus strode across the paving to the Procurator's house. Sextus had signalled to the guard on the door of Marcus' permission. A

126

spear was moved to indicate access given and Marcus moved into a villa courtyard. The two procurators were each holding a drink and chatting in the open air. Others of Gallus' selected guests met in clusters around the atrium. A young Greek male slave in white linen moved to hold a tray of earthenware cups of wine in front of Marcus and he lifted one. He had a moment of satisfaction to realise it was one from his vineyard. Gallus could not take too many bottles back to Rome so the guests were treated to his new vintage. Marcus approached Gallus and Casca. The latter showed more maturity than when he had last met him, but the same youthful smile. Gallus and he were sharing amusing memories of mutual associates. Gallus saw Marcus approaching and hastened his story to its conclusion and turned to him at the final word, giving little or no time for the laugh that would otherwise have been expected from Casca.

"Marcus. Glad you could make it. Do you remember Casca? I think you met many years ago." The greetings were enthusiastic. Conversations ranged around news of families and filled in gaps in career paths. At an appropriate juncture Gallus brought the serious concerns to the fore.

"Casca is agreeable to non-uniformed soldiers going with you with your wine shipment."

"Yes just let me know when you have the shipment planned so I have some time to roster the men. I assume you are going?"

"Ah! That's the thing. Gallus knows I really must go to see my family in Rome and I thought this might be an opportunity. Two things, gentlemen, and I am so pleased you are together. Would there be space in a ship for my trip back to Rome? Secondly I have engaged a new steward who will be managing things while I am away. Would it be in order for him to lead the shipment? It will not be ready for a few weeks." Gallus spoke first after a brief nod from Casca.

"We have to put in at Athens with a delivery on the way so I trust you don't mind the delay, but I have no problem with giving you passage." He looked as Casca.

"My only concern is that soldiers only take orders from soldiers. Your man regardless of loyalty must be in their control in what is a military situation."

"I am sure he understands that."

128

"Is he ex military?" Casca asked. Marcus was skating to find an answer that did not betray Jacob's presence at the Jerusalem rising.

"I don't know all his background but I doubt it. He is a scribe that came from Antioch about four years ago. He became secretary to the magistrate. I do need to talk to you both a little on this." Marcus looked around to see if he was going to be overheard. "He had a run-in with Gaius and Fortunatus this morning. They were cooking up a deal to take the olive grove from Urbanus and asked him to witness Urbanus' signature." Marcus paused for the question.

"Why would he not witness a signature? That is his work is it not?"

"The main problem was that Urbanus was already dead and buried. Jacob had been present at the burial. Gallus will tell you the history I am sure, Casca, but these two belong under a rock. They have been plotting to take over the olive grove to build another Island for their slave whores. If your new soldiers do not know the Island yet they will do. Tell them not to use too much energy with their whores or they will bring the house down." There was manly knowing laughter from Gallus and Casca, and Gallus turned to other guests from the close

129

threesome that they had been since Marcus had arrived. Gallus beckoned to Casca to meet another guest in the adjacent group and the conversation moved on. Marcus looked round to see a conversation engaging four men, two of whom were acquaintances from The Way and he moved to join in.

After social niceties of greeting Marcus the conversation returned to the cult of the emperor and what it might mean. It became animated on whether any one god could demand total and undivided commitment from a devotee in the face of the presence of other gods. There were no minutes to record the debate but all seemed to accept that a sop of acknowledgment to the Emperor as a god was preferable to a charge of treason by holding in strength to a single loyalty. Those of the way were reticent to say otherwise in front of witnesses.

Casca would have the responsibility of enforcing the demands of the Emperor cult.

The conversation moved on to a circus planned for some days ahead and the gladiators expected to fight.

Chapter 13

Jacob returned to the darkness of the street after his meeting with a strange sensation of being totally rootless. He had no idea what would face him if he returned to his accommodation in the Island, and that could well be hazardous. He felt as homeless as when he was lost in the wilderness to the west of the Jordon when he was found in his first encounter with the followers of Jesus Christ. There was something momentous happening. It had not been stated overtly that he was staying with Marcus that night. There had been no eviction notice from

131

Fortunatus and his rent was up to date. He could dismiss his meagre possessions as lost and the sentiment attached to them was minimal. He had not lost his scribe's materials. They were where he put them down as Judith greeted him. His personal manuscripts were in Chloe's house. He was losing a bucket, a tunic, a simple oil lamp and the litter on which he slept. He would have preferred not to lose that because it was the final gift to him of a dying man. He still felt that his now totally dark room in the Island was somehow no longer his. He also suspected that Fortunatus and Gaius would prefer him silent so there was some risk to returning to his room.

He resolved, however, that he would spend his last night in his room and give Fortunatus notice in the morning. He decided he would consult Marcus after that to gain what had occurred between him and Gaius. He set his face towards the Island. Clouds were temporarily hiding the stars. His light source was an occasional glow from a window or door until he reached the streets giving such night life as there was. Torches lit up some of the street beside shops selling food, some of the few two storey houses in the town. He passed the end of the street of the brothel and could hear bursts of raucous male laughter. It must have been the last night in town for some of the soldiers, or the first of the relief squad. The streets were less illuminated as he

132

approached the Island. He jumped as Doria stepped out of a dark recess and took his arm.

"Jacob. There have been two men waiting in your room since mid afternoon. I think they mean you harm."

"Thank-you Doria. They must be hungry by now. I have no food there. If they throw my things out can you rescue them for me? I need to come back another day."

"I'll see you on the Lord's Day Jacob." Amid the anxiety in Jacob emerged joy. It was his first indication that Doria had joined the faith. He moved towards her vague figure in the darkness and hugged her briefly. He was fairly sure his affection would not be misunderstood but still felt unsure about hugging a prostitute in public. It suddenly crossed his mind that word getting back to Judith about him holding a prostitute in public might cause some tension. There was a brief uncertain silence.

"I need to go back to the square," Doria said.

"I'll walk with you. I have to pass that way now."

133

For some paces there was silence between them as they walked. Doria broke it. "Chloe is wonderful. I wish I could be her slave."

"She does not have slaves. Those in her household are free women."

Doria stumbled a little. "How wonderful!" In a few more paces he heard Doria sobbing. "Why does the Lord let me keep having to do these awful things to stay alive?"

"We cannot change all this at once but we will. The Lord give you strength."

The silence continued punctuated only briefly by Doria's sniffles after her weeping. They came out of their street and entered the square. Jacob turned to wish Doria a farewell but was interrupted by rousing male laughter to his right. Several soldiers were approaching, most of whom appeared to be off duty. A glint on armour showed that at least one soldier was not.

"There is someone who has had first choice at the fruit shop."
There was laughter. The soldiers were looking at him with Doria.
Before he could react he heard Marcus' voice from among the group.

"Jacob? Is all well?" He turned to his companions one of
whom had been the gate sentry earlier. "This is my secretary and
steward."

"It must be his payday." The soldiers laughed again seeing
Doria with him.

"This is Doria, my neighbour." Jacob ignored the banter,
speaking directly to Marcus. "She warned me I have intruders in my
room who mean me harm."

"I think we have a law and order issue before we relax, men."
Sextus had overheard Jacob's urgency.

Marcus spoke with quiet assurance but he had a slight slurring
that indicated he had been drinking wine. "These intruders are
preventing Jacob having his house farewell party. He gets married this
week. We need to celebrate his news don't you think? That third shop
on the right sells wine. Come with me Sextus to help carry bottles for

Jacob's party." Marcus walked away with Sextus and the other three gathered round Jacob with pats on the back. Jacob acted with smiles but cringed inside in case he had another fit..

Doria made to walk towards the corner where she normally solicited but Jacob called her back. "Please may I borrow cups Doria? I only have one." She returned to the group of men but stayed behind Jacob.

"I normally eat with friends; seldom at home." Jacob told his new companions. "Doria worships with our group" was the only introduction he could think of to explain Doria's presence. It was obvious why she was on the street this night. "She is my neighbour and warned me of the intruders."

"Are they armed?" One of the soldiers asked Doria. He spoke with a very thick accent placing his origins in the far north west of the empire.

"I think so, but not with swords."

"We can take them on. We always have at least two of us armed, even when off duty, in case of trouble with locals."

136

"It will be very restricted for space in The Island."

"Thanks Jacob. I am Anthony. This is Gordius. I understand we will be going on a journey with you." Gordius held Anthony's arm in concern.

"We don't know whose listening." Gordius was using hushed tones. His eyes indicated Doria, now slightly behind him.

Jacob was at a loss, not au fait with the details of the wine transport journey and assumed the journey was the imminent walk to the Island. He missed the secret warning between the two soldiers. Marcus returned with Sextus. They had acquired burning torches with the wine. They set off, Marcus with Jacob and Doria led the way at a brisk pace the flickering lights reflecting brightly from the white walls of the houses.

"I don't want them to know I warned you." Doria was earnest. "They will make my life terrible."

"Take Anthony by the arm. It is what they expect of you is it not? You two stay back" Marcus and the others walked on ahead.

137

At the Island entrance they met two men coming out. There was uncertainty until Jacob recognised his belongings in the torchlight. "Those are mine."

"We have thieves have we?" Sextus was an intimidating challenger.

The two dropped Jacobs things. His earthenware cup, unbroken, rolled on the beaten earth. Behind the torch it was difficult to see the identity of the accusers but they were well built and outnumbered the accused by several. They assumed they were soldiers but on whose authority they were present was uncertain.

"We are the landlord's men. We are evicting a tenant." Fortunatus' man spoke nervously. Jacob recognised him as one on the branders and one of those who held Doria as she was whipped.

"Is his rent not paid?" Marcus had his arms folded. The question was penetrating and all knew the answer. The silence was lengthy.

"Well in that case," Marcus continued, "You had better put this tenant's property back. Please inform Fortunatus that his tenant is

138

giving notice and will be leaving in the morning. We will wait here until you leave."

"Wait here." Sextus, ostensibly policing a moment in which bystanders could be put at risk addressed Anthony and Doria who had arrived just at that moment. All stood quietly until the two intruders exited. The torch followed the men as they circled the Romans with Jacob beside Doria, who was on Anthony's arm in the second rank.

Fortunatus' men were soon out of reach of the torchlight, and the group stood still in the noise of the cicadas.

"Now!" said Sextus abruptly, "something about this man having a farewell night in his accommodation and a celebration of a forthcoming wedding."

"I'll get the cups." Doria passed through the group and deftly mounted stairs. Jacob picked up his stretcher and bucket containing his cup with his spare tunic over his shoulder and followed. He was carrying all he owned bar his scribe's equipment. He was aware of the narrow passageway's looming shadows in the following torchlight.

Jacob placed his meagre possessions in their former places. The room still looked very bare. The Romans following him filled the room considerably more that it had ever been in Jacob's tenancy.

"You get some space to yourself." Sextus mused, "but not for much longer." There were chuckles from his companions. "At least you are lucky not to have to live in barracks and camps all your life."

Doria silently rejoined them with her cups and wine pouring began. She again took Anthony's arm even though the earlier charade was over. At least this time it seemed the cups were not to be used by men about to use and abuse her. In the absence of chairs, the men squatted, leaning on the walls. The one item left by Fortunatus' men was a single lamp on a recess shelf. It was a small earthenware bowl containing olive oil and in it a floating wick awaited a flame. When Jacob lit it with a sliver of wood and its flame borrowed from one of the torches, it hardly made a difference to the light in the room, but it would be the only light when the party goers left. The sound of wine pouring into cups began behind him.

"A health to Jacob!" One of Doria's cups was put into his hand.

140

"You should get to know these men Jacob. They will be your guards on the wine transport in a few weeks." Marcus spoke.

"How much of that wine will be ours by the way?" Sextus' riposte brought a laugh.

"Less than the bandits got last time I hope. If you capture the bandits you will get a reward, and if the wine gets through there will be another." Marcus' summary of the gravity of the operation caused silence for a few seconds.

"Will there be any wine left after Jacob's wedding?" Anthony caused more mirth.

"Not too much wine the first night or you will sleep." More laughter showed that Sextus' innuendo was not lost.

Gordius was quiet beside Jacob. The conversations developed between Sextus and Marcus. Anthony and Doria involved themselves with each other.

"You're the one on duty tonight?" Jacob broke the silence.

141

"We take turns to look after the others. This will be my only drink tonight."

"You are close friends?"

"We have been in this unit for about three years. We first met up in Vinovium. We were building a new fort there to guard the river bridge. It is good to be back in warm weather. It rains icicles horizontally. I don't know how Anthony reached adulthood. He was born near there. His father made bricks."

"Where are you from?"

"I am from Gaul. How about you?"

"I was born in Jerusalem and left before its destruction."

"Can you use a sword?"

"I am a scribe."

"You fight with a quill."

"Words can be a powerful way of changing things."

"Try me."

Jacob thought for some seconds before he spoke. "Everyone is loved by the true God or we would not be here: from the lowliest slave to the highest ranking king."

The silence lasted until Jacob began to feel embarrassed. Eventually Gordius spoke. "I just wish we knew who the true god was then. I have to make sure the Emperor is among them. I need a god that looks after me when swords are getting aimed at me. I don't rate the love of any of the gods of those I ran through with mine. " Another silence followed.

"The words were powerful though. They made me think. If we find we are taking armed bandits on I hope I can rely on you. I wouldn't rate your chances much between a bandit with a sword and you with a pen."

Jacob tried to move the conversation to those parts of the world he knew little of. Gordius became animated about the large island to the west of the empire. It was so green and tree filled and with so much rain. Yet how cold it could be in the winter time, and how dark the nights were for such a long time in the late season, yet so light for

143

so long in the summer. He had even seen snow to the depth of a man's waist.

In another lull, Jacob noted the quiet affection growing with Anthony and Doria. The torch light was flickering over them. It struck Jacob as to the colour of Anthony's hair. Was it a trick of the torch light? Jacob eventually framed his question to Gordius.

"No it is a sort of golden colour," was the reply. Many people in that area had golden hair, and not the coppery colour you find among some Romans, I have never been there, but some of the soldiers who have say that well to the north of Gaul you find people with almost white hair, and I don't mean the old people." There was another pause.

"I need to piss. While I am out I will check those rats have gone away and are not hanging around waiting until you are on your own again."

Sextus overheard. "Good idea. Marcus' wine has done its job." There was a general movement in the room. Sextus grabbed a torch and stooped to exit the door. Marcus followed. Jacob decided to join what was likely to be a men's moment beside a wall outside. He preceded Anthony through the door, but then realised as he descended the stairs, Anthony was moving upstairs with Doria.

"He had better leave her a good tip." Sextus was blunt in his expectations of Anthony's motives as they stood in the shadows by the back wall of the Island. He meant Anthony to hear it. Two floors above through the open window Anthony could hear him. The drink was talking amongst the men and they were slightly too loud for Jacob's anxiety about the neighbours, even on his last night in the building.

As they left the wall, Jacob voiced another thought to Gordius that made him curious. "Anthony is a very Roman name for someone from the land of the Celts."

"That is not the name his family called him but we needed too much spit to pronounce it so we called him Anthony. He always seemed to want more money for the bricks so we called him a name that means 'priceless.' He was always hanging around the fort wanting to be a soldier and had tremendous strength from carrying those bricks he delivered. He had the makings of a good soldier so we recruited him. Sextus and I took him under our wing in his training. We've been close friends ever since. Now. I see better in the dark without a torch so I'll

145

slip away. Now if you had to hide to watch this place where would you be?"

"They would see you coming with lights behind you if they were by that last corner of the street we came down. If they were waiting for all of you to leave but me then they would be behind us in the olive grove. They would have circled round after they left. They still have their orders I suppose."

"Rather than have this threat you should stay with me from now on." Marcus was decisive. Leaving Anthony in Doria's room the others each carried Jacob's possessions back to Marcus' villa through the dark streets. Sextus' torch was dying as they reached the door.

Marcus called Judith who in turn summoned domestic slaves to place Jacob in his allotted room.

"Tomorrow" Marcus stated, "I will take Jacob to the farm." Once Jacob had left for his guest room, Marcus continued to Judith. "And you will go to Chloe's house so they can start to make you a wedding dress."

Sextus declined Marcus' hospitality. He was concerned to find Anthony and return to barracks. Marcus could see through the ruse. The soldiers had yet to sample town night life and Marcus, using his long military experience had seen Anthony as an aggressive leading spirit amongst his contemporaries. Sextus as decurion did not want Anthony out of his sight for too long.

*****

Anthony kissed Doria passionately at her door having gifted her generously from his wage received that day. As a slave she would be obliged to part with her earnings he but suggested she used a portion of his gift on her own comfort. He was very attracted to the girl, but did not analyse if the attraction was simply due to his lack of contact with women for so long, or if there was a more enduring link that would lead to a relationship for the rest of his legion's billeting. He dare not think of any relationship beyond that. He hardly expected the women he remembered from his home community to be available for a relationship when, if ever, he returned to that extremity of the empire.

The door on which the foreman had cracked his skull swung shut leaving the dull light of Doria's oil lamp showing to Anthony

147

around the door's edge. Doria had told him the story of what seemed to her both Jacob's bravery and her thoughts that he was divinely blessed, given that night's conclusion.

He waited for at least a minute until his eyes adjusted to the darkness of the corridor and the stairs. There was little noise from the other apartments as it was now past an artisan bedtime. He felt his way down the narrow staircase, his large frame stooping as he felt the walls. He turned the corner to where Jacob's room door was to his left. At the bottom of the stairs he could see the ghostly night outside the external doorway. His hearing was the more acute due to the darkness. There was a sound. He froze.

It was coming from outside. Totally shadowed figures appeared in the frame of the door below him. They were inching their way up the stairs just as Anthony had crept down. Anthony had the advantage of his eyes now well adjusted, though his potential assailants coming out of darkness had lost the benefits of starlight. His suspicion was right. It was those confronted earlier returned to their original project. The shadowy outlines suggested at least one sharp weapon. Anthony was not armed. He was not the object of the potential attack but he was not going to be a collateral casualty of the dark either. He

148

was also allied to Jacob, his soon-to-be-married friend of the evening so those coming up the stairs were enemy. At least he had the advantages of surprise, coming out of pitch blackness and being higher up the stairs.

Jacob's door was set back a cubit under an arch, as all the doors in the Island were. The last movement Anthony had made before the figures appeared below was to feel the corner of that arch. He slowly and silently set himself for action. Given his size and strength he had a formidable reputation as a brawler amongst his unit. He also brought a Celtic originality to the unarmed altercations common amongst the ranks.

The first assailant felt his way up the stairs and reached the corner of Jacob's archway entrance. The unseen left-handed Anthony launched a straight left to where he adjudged the shadowed face to be. He was slightly closer than he thought. The punch landed at power but no recoil of the victim's head was possible against the corner of the arch. There was a soft thud with the hint of the sound of breaking bone and the scraping of skin and bone on brick. There was a sigh and the sound of a slumping body sliding down the wall. The second assailant had no concept of what had happened in front of him but assumed that

149

his companion had been struck from someone in Jacob's doorway. His feet felt his accomplice's legs on the floor as he tentatively stepped forwards. Anthony repeated the same blow with the same power on the second face. His second victim fell unconscious down the stairs making dull thumping sounds in the process but with a clattering of a falling dagger.

Anthony moved stealthily down the final flight with enough space at the bottom to pass the moaning conspirator. In the starlit open air he moved towards the town centre with the hope of finding his friends. Gently he felt his left knuckles, suspecting bruises would be visible next day.

Chapter 14.

By mid morning it was very hot. Marcus had not stopped from waking. He had taken Jacob with his few chattels to the farm and left him with his field slave Abraxas to tour the various crops and to settle the scribe in his new accommodation. On returning, Marcus had walked Judith to Chloe's house and left her with the women to organise her wedding dress. He had found Onesimus and agreed the wedding time for the following Lord's Day. The bishop understood the haste, given Marcus' intended departure for Rome, though Marcus would not be pressed as to his reasons for the journey.

Back in his atrium Marcus was alone, having dispatched the rest of his household on various errands preparing either for the wedding reception or for his long absence. It would not be a lengthy celebration lasting days, given the host's pressing departure for Rome, but it would still be worthy of a Roman citizen's home.

As Marcus left for his intended meeting with his bottle makers as part of the organisation of the wine shipment to Thyatira he was confronted at his door by five of Gaius' local armed enforcement unit intending to enter uninvited. Their weapons were not drawn.

"We are here to arrest the scribe Jacob." The leader was sweating under his leather helmet. Marcus stood his ground.

"Firstly, he is not here. Secondly what is he supposed to have done? Thirdly what makes you think he is here? The only offence I can see right now is your trespass in the house of a Roman citizen."

"I need to search for him."

151

Marcus' repetition was spoken slowly and deliberately "Firstly, he is not here. Secondly what is he supposed to have done? Thirdly what makes you think he is here? The only offence I can see right now is your trespass in the house of a Roman citizen." Marcus was quite used to addressing armed men with authority and stood squarely in front of the first policeman. The officer knew of Marcus' connections with the military.

"He assaulted two bailiffs at his former home last night causing serious injury."

"No he did not. With me and with several Roman soldiers he left the Island and spent the night here. He was violent to no-one, though the soldiers moved two intruders on without any physical contact. I have to pass the Magistrate's so will come with you now if Gaius is there. Move please!"

Though it was phrased as a suggestion it was clear Marcus was giving an order. He brushed past the turning leader and between the group behind and into the street. His pace was a double march that the squad behind failed to match in both speed and togetherness. At the magistrate's building, without breaking step he strode up the steps

152

through the portico and past the guard to the entrance. The squad behind gave the guard reason to believe Marcus was entering on business.

Within, Gaius was standing in front of and talking to one of the assaulted bailiffs of the previous night. Without waiting for Gaius' reaction as the legal authority in his appointed place, Marcus strode up to the unsuspecting magistrate.

"Jacob did not do this!" Marcus gestured to the injured bailiff. "He was with me and several independent witnesses last night." The squad behind shuffled in to stand behind Marcus.

Gaius began. "This man is the least injured of the two." Marcus looked more closely at the bailiff. His face was a mess. He had a broken nose, two very black eyes and still had caked blood on the back of his head and neck. "The other was thrown down stairs and cannot walk. They were bailiffs removing an offender from his lodgings when they were set upon at the door by a madman with a club. Since it was Jacob they were evicting we have to believe this is his doing."

"Believe something else Gaius. I came back with Jacob from his lodgings last night. There were three soldiers with me that can vouch for this. We carried his property away and there was no violence." Marcus thought for a moment. "In any case, there is no space to carry a club inside Jacob's old lodging, let alone use one. These pieces of low life said they saw Jacob there, did they?"

"They were at Jacob's door and they were assaulted. They are not low life. Please stop being so offensive."

"Scum, then. Have you ever been in that rat hole in the dark Gaius? Did they have torches to see who hit them?" There was a pause. "No, I thought not. Do I get the soldiers here to verify my account?" Another pause ensued. "So we will assume there will be no more harassment of my steward shall we?"

Gaius tried to maintain a quiet dignity in a situation he had clearly lost.

"Good! Thank-you Gaius. I am glad we have cleared up this misunderstanding. Farewell Sir." Marcus tried to be respectfully tactful knowing Gaius could well be vindictive and plotting if he could not have some of his face saved. For the second time Marcus passed

154

between Gaius' shuffling force and left the building. It was now imperative to see the Procurator both to clear Jacob and afford him some protection. Casca should be apprised of the witness afforded by the future guard of the wine shipment. It might well be that Casca would have to warn his soldiers to show restraint. Relations between the local community and Rome had been amicable for some time, but any difficulty would be met with overwhelming violence by the military. Marcus had a suspicion that the violent force in the dark was Anthony but did not want to betray him. The perpetrator could have been any soldier or soldiers leaving a prostitute and happening across hostile men in a dark passage.

Chapter 15

"We have no proof The Lord was born in Bethlehem. I have emphasised the prophecies. I would write what I know because there is a danger of making things up to suit a false ideology. That would make us no better than the heretics we are writing to counteract." Jacob was replying to the accusation by John that his first draft of an account of the birth of Jesus was a bit contrived. Jacob was again tired after a day walking on the farm, around the vineyards and spending what seemed an age going through lists of those with whom Marcus had dealings. It

155

left little time in Chloe's house catching the rest of daylight meeting his promise to produce enough advancement of his document to merit the meeting with his fellow clergy.

"You asked to list the descendancy of The Lord from David since the Messiah was to be the 'Son of David' yet there are gaps. We know very few of the Lord's ancestors past Joseph the carpenter and Mary his mother. I have to write from a position of faith, not fact, and that is risking heresy. However, our faith tells us that since He is revealed as the Messiah, then the prophecy must have been fulfilled. I am writing an account of possibilities.

"The Lord is the fulfilment of the 'time.' 'The time has come', we believe both He and the Baptist said this. As John has said, and as our Pharisees said in Jerusalem the time is based on Jubilee, when all debts are forgiven for ever and God's people are at one with God the Father. I represent this by having the descendancy listed in groups of seven, and the seventh seven is the birth of the Lord."

"Why you feel so strongly about the descendancy coming down to Joseph I fail to understand since you are insisting on a virgin birth using the mistranslated Greek version, because then The Lord is not descended from Joseph at all."

Jacob held his hand up to a clamour of counter argument. "Please let me speak to the whole of my writing to now and deal with it as a whole, otherwise we will never finish."

"If we are to have the birth of the Messiah then it should be more portentous than any of the births we find in scripture. Isaac was promised by the JHWH with the coming of angels, even with the scepticism of his mother Sarah. Thus we have the dream of Joseph. Speaking of Joseph, the importance of dreams for that son of Israel is reflected in the astronomic event of the star in the birth of The Lord in an actual stellar event rather than a dream. You have the Gentiles worship of The Lord with the magi, and therefore the convergence of all insights from all peoples into the one true God presaged in them.

"Remember we have a rich heritage of Gentiles worshipping the Lord, the best example perhaps being Ruth."

"Worship would include the offering of gifts and I have presumed to bring a visual aid from our brother Marcus with his good will. This is a gift he received from a beloved friend who had been in

157

Persia. It is a container made of beaten gold. Within is a very costly ointment made fragrant with incense.

"The deliverance of Israel from Moses by Pharaoh is the prophecy background of the slaying of the infants by Herod and the coming of the New Israel out of Egypt as The Lord returns to the land of His birth. Archelaus would be as good a reason as any for coming to Nazareth instead of Bethlehem. They say he was worse than his father. Even the Romans thought he was too cruel."

"My next project is to look at The Lord's meeting with the Baptist and his early ministry. I assume I am following the same pattern as Mark in his work. I am still very uncertain about what still feels like making up the story to fit the beliefs."

Onesimus, with his paternal voice spoke before several others made a sound having drawn breath. "We are writing truth, rather than history. We are showing God's revelation to us, not writing a report."

The statement held the room in silence for a few moments.

"We are using language as symbols representing a greater truth than the words can express," he went on.

158

Jacob asserted, "The heretics think that as well, like those that talked of the infant Jesus turning mud balls into sparrows for the Pharisees, but it does not stop their word-symbols being ridiculous."

"The scriptures are full of symbolic things:" Onesimus avoided the barb in Jacob's interruption. "Joseph's dreams to his family and the interpretations of Pharaoh's. There are the visions of Daniel and Ezekiel. Were they visions or were they simply trying to tell a truth in symbolic language? The Lord was always using symbols in his teaching to convey a truth. His talk of the coming of the Kingdom as a bridegroom to the wedding is one. Our Jacob here must be learning what that expectation is like." He smiled. Jacob returned it. There was another silence. John's eyes were glazing. He was in his own reverie. Onesimus noticed the lack of concentration.

"I think we have filled an evening successfully, thank the Lord. I trust we can meet again this time in a week. Jacob might find his new work and his wedding slow his progress but we continue our prayers for his endeavours. We look forward to his writing on the Baptist and the Lord's meeting with him." He continued by calling the meeting to prayers and he gave a blessing.

159

Chapter 16

Jacob and Judith were picking their feet over the dusk-lit path to their new home some thousand paces from the town gates. Judith held his arm at the elbow. She was still wearing her red wedding dress. Marcus had enabled her to look the part of a Roman lady, supplying the materials to Chloe and her seamstresses.

After almost two days of a wedding celebration they were tired but joyful and with a profound sense of closeness. There was no need for words. This was their first time alone since Judith risked her feelings in Marcus' atrium. Fresh in their minds were the images of embraces of farewell as the couple left Marcus' house and their guests. There were also the earlier fleeting but profound and tearful moments of standing before Onesimus and pledging faithfulness to each other before the Lord. There were so many images of smiling faces in animated conversation, all with goodwill. Even the outgoing Procurator had made an appearance as a guest at Marcus' invitation. They had said their farewell to Marcus with some regret. It would be many months before they saw him again. He and Gallus were sailing on the early morning tide. Given Gaius' animosity, Jacob felt less secure as a result.

Jacob was musing about how God given moments of such import like his wedding, or like this life itself, were so fleeting from an eternal being. Now there was no sound but evening birdsong and the rustle of vine leaves from a cooling sea breeze at their backs. Their new marital home was growing before them with each step. It retained a warm stillness from the heat of the day as they entered. All of Marcus' staff were still in the celebrations so the house was empty.

Judith immediately busied herself lighting lamps paying attention to several in their bedroom. A mattress was a new experience for Jacob. He had returned to sleeping on the floor several times in the week he had used the bed since moving into this farm house. It suddenly dawned on him that after all the emotional tension of his feelings for Judith before the shock of her overt expression of love for him, for all the anticipation of the wedding and for the social whirlwind that was the post ceremony celebration, the moment had arrived for a consummation for which Judith was matter-of-factly preparing a room.

161

"I need to wash". Jacob moved to the north room where buckets had been thoughtfully left full by the women house slaves that stayed here. They would not be back tonight as they would be both celebrating still at the wedding feast and clearing up afterwards.

"I do too." Judith was anticipating Jacob's anxiety and she moved beside him at the water. "Hold me." They embraced for some time.

"I will never forget you washing my feet. Let me wash yours now."

"We will wash each other." They embraced again, feeling each other warm through their clothing. When they moved apart again, Judith removed the shoulder clasp of her dress and lengths of rich material were being peeled from her. For the first time in his life, before him was a woman showing flesh while being willingly accessible to him. Inelegantly he removed his one garment. They embraced again, this time naked. Points of reflection shone from the one flame in the room on curved flesh.

They used the sponges Marcus his given to the household. Highlights then twinkled on water droplets on flesh. The cool water

162

was stimulating and refreshing after the heat of the day and the nervous but happy tension of the event. They dried on the course cloth available to them and without a word moved hand in hand to their bed.

Jacob had experiences of roundness, softness, warmth and closeness.

"What are those scars?"

"They were on my belly after I had my baby."

There were pecks of kisses and hands through hair. There was musk in Jacob's nostrils that was entirely and uniquely Judith. There was eye contact and each witnessed moisture in the others'. They held the moment. The breeze outside had stopped. Neither said, "I love you." Words were redundant.

In a few moments there was penetration.

"Sorry." Jacob knew this was not just about his pleasure.

"Do not worry. It will take longer for you next time in maybe a few minutes. Please stay close to me." Jacob's uncertainty was replaced with embracing reassurance. Judith could hear Jacob's

163

thudding heartbeat as she rested her head on his chest. His hand caressed the curve of her waist and hip. The caresses developed into kisses and a deepening passion. Judith was right: the second time was much longer lasting.

As his climax approached Jacob looked into his wife's eyes. Her irises had rolled up out of sight behind her eyelids and she was shuddering. Her irises returned to see his face as he began his orgasm. Then began an experience that he believed was literally a divine touch to their lives. It was not just the physical spending of his seed. He had a moment of what was at least déjà vu. It was as if he was recognising Judith's face again after seeing her multiples of times over generations from of old. He had a sense of wonder he had never felt. "It is you. It really is you." He gasped.

"Yes!" she breathed.

He rolled to her side and closed his eyes, holding the embrace. He could see her face even behind his closed lids, as if burnt on his retina from looking at the sun. For the first time he understood the meaning of "Abraham knew his wife Sarah."

Chapter 17

164

After Jacob had left the celebration, Onesimus left his small group of fellow guests and made an effort to reach Marcus before either or both were engaged with other guests.

"You leave tomorrow."

"Yes. It is not a journey I relish."

"You mean the travelling or the destination?"

"A large measure of both."

"If you want to unburden yourself I would be willing to listen."

"Thank-you Bishop. Your prayers for wisdom in dealing with my father would be appreciated."

"Just remember that you now have a greater Father from whom all the meaning of 'father' flows. He will strengthen and guide you when the time comes."

"Thank-you Bishop."

"I have a favour to ask you."

165

"If I can, I will."

"Please can you take some manuscripts to Rome with you and find Bishop Alexander at the church there. Greet him from me in The Lord's Name and deliver them. He needs to know of our project as being worked through by Jacob, but there are copies of Apostle Paul's letters he may not have seen yet. Jacob copied these some weeks ago and I was waiting for a messenger I could trust."

"I most certainly will do that. Thank you for letting me serve you. I must talk to you now though before I go. I am worried about developments about the new emperor cult. I wonder if the church everywhere should be making preparations for going into hiding. I have not forgotten the persecutions in Rome during my youth. When an emperor wants to be made a god then those who don't comply are labelled traitors. Other propaganda follows based on either ignorance or deliberate lies. I picked up the other day the gossip that is going about in common soldier's circles. Apparently the followers of Jesus are ritual cannibals eating someone's body. We are also conducting Thiestian feasts eating someone's son."

"This is terrible."

166

"It seems to be building up against the church. I dread to think what will be ahead of me in Rome because it all seems to flow from there. Domitian is pushing this divine emperor concept to the limit. We have yet to find out how it is to be enforced, but we should be thinking about how we will react when we have to make a choice about worshipping before an image of the emperor when to refuse will mean we are put in front of some judge on a charge of treason. Around here I wouldn't fancy our chances with Gaius judging us."

"You must start making contingencies especially to save the scriptures. You can't just wait for the tramp of marching men looking for you."

Onesimus replied in his paternal tone. "Still, many were inspired to join us when they saw that we have a God to die for, and who died for us. It may be that we are called to be the ultimate witness to the Lord. The final days may be with us when this comes."

Marcus paused for thought. "I wonder how solid our support will be when bodies on crosses line the road with birds pecking their eyes out, and the stench of rotting flesh and flies and maggoty wounds.

I have been part of Rome at work don't forget. There was no glory in martyrdom for those who opposed my troops when we had our orders."

Onesimus took the quiet voice of a parent telling an enthralling story to a child. "The glory of martyrdom is beyond the pain of the flesh Marcus. We all have death to face in this life. I just pray mine will not be pointless and I see the Lord coming."

"It is not just about you and me though is it?" Marcus was beginning to feel agitated. "Someone has to keep the message and the truth for those left behind if the Word of the Lord is not to die out. It will not serve the Lord for us all to perish this world and let the liars rule after we have gone." His raised voice caused some heads to turn though no-one could have heard his full sentence in the hubbub of wedding guests in full conversation.

"The Lord has always called others. Paul used to persecute those of The Way before he really saw the truth behind the message of those he was trying to kill. Even if the Lord does not come in our time, there will be others called to take our place. Seeing our witness will be their calling."

168

Chapter 18

Marcus breathed in the salt air and wiped a droplet of salt spray from his face. The bireme had left his home port and was having its first pitches into the swell of the Great Sea. It was his first experience of a military vessel since crossing the channel back to Gaul from Regulbium many years before. Being a supernumerary took nothing away from his sense of order and readiness to obey. He realized just how much he was conditioned by his old life.

Gallus returned from stowing his possessions and carefully moved across to join Marcus, pausing for balance as the random movements of a pitching and rolling deck moved under him. "That chest of yours with your name. It looks like it was carved by a child."

"It was carved in by a child. Me. It was one of the few things ever given to me by my father. It was maybe the only thing that I could say belonged to me at the time, so I felt I had to put my name on it. When he saw it he ranted for hours about the damage I had caused."

"He seems such a controlled and dignified man in public. I suppose we all have a public face and a private face."

"Maybe the people in the powerful man's private lives have to suffer for the image in his public one. My mother used to say that if you want to find out someone's faults you have to marry them." Gallus laughed, and there was a pause as they looked back at the receding town.

"We have to call in at Athens. I have a report to deliver, and diplomatic papers to collect there for Rome. Sorry I couldn't have told you earlier. There are a few matters back there about piracy that Casca and I don't want in the public domain. It should add only a day or so if the weather is kind.

Marcus felt happy to be seeing Athens again. It would give him an opportunity to visit the altar of the Unknown God that had given him the inspiration to begin the search that led him to a conviction about Jesus the Christ. He was not about to mention this spiritual journey to Gallus. Followers of Jesus were still suspect after the persecution of Nero almost two decades earlier. If Gallus, friend though he was had a choice between friendship and obedience to an order to arrest him, Marcus knew the choice that would be made.

"I look forward to seeing Athens again." Marcus had an ominous feeling about his visit to Rome and coming confrontations with his wife and his father. He had had such confrontations before, eventually leading to his retirement to his vineyard. The two regrets that troubled him were his guilt that he felt he had abandoned his son to the political plots and machinations of Rome and his tainted family, and his lack of a close personal relationship in the otherwise joyful life of the vineyard and his new community, especially amongst the followers of The Way.

"Have you worked out what you are going to say to your father?"

"Not really. That will be the usual disaster, whatever I hope to achieve with him and whatever reconciliation I try. He wanted to live his life on the back of whatever success he saw for me in Rome's power structures. I refuse to play his scheming games. I even married in his convenient alliance of families to try to please him. Rome is a magnificent city. It's just that it is inhabited by vipers. It reminds me of

171

the game children play when one is standing on a pile of hay and goading the rest to knock him off, and eventually they do, only for the next one to start goading those on the ground when he gets up there."

"What troubles me most is that I don't know what I am going to say to my son. I wish I could get him out of there and bring him back with me but that would cause conflict."

"Can you not order your wife to join you? You have that authority."

"I do not have a happy marriage Gallus. The present situation is the best we could work out. Octavia gets her social treadmill in the scheming gossiping circles she enjoys with her family and my father. I get a peaceful life making wine and walking with my God. That is not to say I don't have a sense of family obligation when it comes to young Marcus. What bothers me is how his mind is likely to have been poisoned by his mother and grandfather. I am pretty convinced that if Octavia is with child as the gossip you passed to me says, it will be my half-brother she is carrying. I will have to acknowledge the poor little bastard as mine to save the face and honour of the dynasty. For all his political astuteness my father's brains are in his balls. I could see his

172

lust for the girls in the family such as my cousins. Sex is only about power to him. We also have Diocletian's morality laws overshadowing us."

After a pause, Gallus said, "That at least gives you some capital in negotiations with your father and your wife does it not? I mean, you do not have to recognise the child as yours. Clearly the sums will not add up given the time you are away, and no-one in Rome could argue with you."

"Thank you Gallus. It takes a politician to see that. You could be right." There was another pause.

"Keep this to yourself. My report going to Athens is to the Provincial governor. I am recommending that Gaius is replaced. I have all sorts of suspicions of corruption. The hornets' nest in this is that these cities along here are used to being almost self governing. I think I could see you doing the job properly in his place. Think about it. It at least gives you a position in the community that Octavia might approve of to leave Rome with you and get your son home with you. See if the Governor approves first though."

"Would I have the time?"

173

"You have an able steward don't you? He is mightily respectful of you and he seems a capable sort. Surely, he can look after your businesses. My informants tell me he has an insight into Gaius as well since he was once his scribe. Your confrontation with Gaius is still reverberating around the town by the way. Casca is likely to have had a word of warning to him about his bad breath before you get back as well as asking penetrating questions about where tax money is going. The other thing to mention is that you have the detail for the wine transport. A routine patrol will start marching past your steward's house. They will check when it is ready."

Chapter 19

Jacob awoke with happiness in his heart. He attended to his prayers and for the first time he was joined by his wife. "God be merciful to us and bless us," he began and continued a psalm. When he closed his eyes he could still see the image of Judith from the night before. They offered the coming day. They remembered Marcus beginning his sea journey. They held all aspects of the work ahead of them. As they finished, the women that shared the house returned from Marcus' house where they had stayed. Judith took over her supervisory role, leaving instructions before her return to Marcus' house in the town.

They all ate a simple breakfast together and Jacob began his several tasks for the day. He had to visit the workers who made the leather bottles. He had to visit the site of the wine vats. He had to call on the farm workers. He had to call in to Marcus' house to look over the documents concerning the coming trade. After that, hopefully by mid-afternoon he was free to visit Chloe and continue his work on the new document of the Good News.

If his eyes felt tired, he reasoned, he would visit Pheobe before returning to his scribe's work.

The heat of the day was rising as he walked towards the town. He reached the ridge of high ground upon which the Roman road ran straight to the town, about half of a mile to the stone arch in the town wall. Coming down the ramped rough stone road from the gates he caught the sun's reflection on one of the helmets of a group of marching men. Marcus had warned him that patrols might begin and the planned transport of wine that disguised guards were to accompany. He resolved to wait under one of the few trees that afforded shelter

175

from the sun. It was a tortured gnarled thorn bush, not quite tall enough to give him standing room, but it gave him some shade and the benefit of a cool breeze on the hill top.

He was reminded of Jonah sitting under his gourd and took it as a sign that he was in the right place in his calling, uncomfortable though he was in the presence of Roman soldiers, a repeated experience now about to be visited on him. Carried on the wind he began to hear the voices of the soldiers in an unfamiliar marching chorus. In a mantra of prayer he was calming the moments of panic he had felt. He was ready to rise from his haunches when the body of men approached. Their marching chorus had ended. The order to "halt" was given when the squad leader saw Jacob. It was Sextus, and Jacob recognised Anthony and Gordius in the ranks.

"A cheer for a married man!" The squad raised a unanimous shout followed by laughter. The night of drinking enjoyed some days before had become known in the ranks before him. Sextus joined Jacob close enough for their conversation to be private. After smiling congratulations Sextus' voice dropped.

"Any news on when the shipment will be ready?"

"I am going to check now on the bottle making. The wine is certainly ready. All should be arranged in two or three days."

"The suspicion is that you will be watched leaving. We don't want to be seen attached to you. On the day we agree, four of us will detach from this unit as we march this route and join you. Our route is circular so takes us back to the barracks by a different way so hopefully no-one will see our scheme. Where will the train be leaving from?"

"The house down this road, then up this hill to where we are, and then the road to Thyatira."

"Tomorrow we will drop off our packs here for the journey. See you soon. Farewell." Sextus barked the order to march and the squad passed Jacob with each soldier smiling or smirking, with particular recognition from Gordius and Anthony. Anthony was by far the tallest amongst his comrades. Jacob watched the soldiers for a few moments until the birdsong and the breeze had displaced the sound of tramping feet. Jacob set his face to the town.

In the leather workshop there were only two of the four workers present, neither of whom held their tools. When Marcus had introduced Jacob to this place before, there was the atmosphere of

177

urgency and creativity. This time there was a sense of relaxation. Jacob assumed that with the master away there was an immediate loss of discipline.

After greeting them he asked, "Where are the other two?"

Aethon was the younger of the two present workers. "I think Acteon has gone for more leather. I don't know about Jason."

"We are sending the wine to Thyatira in two days. We should be filling the bottles tomorrow. They are needed by this evening at the vineyard."

When Jacob turned, the older worker, Ladon had put on his hand guard to begin pushing the needle into the leather of his next bottle. Jacob had the distinct feeling that no work had been done that morning, some two hours before the normal start. He moved to the end of the workshop where the completed bottles were stacked. He was counting them. It would be a few minutes of mental exercise.

He had reached the twenties when the door opened and Jason entered. "In honour of Jacob's wedding I thought I would stay and give my woman one as well."

178

The other two were staring blankly at Jason, but without comment. There was clearly mirth in their eyes. Jason was confused by their expressions. Why weren't they laughing?

"Greetings Jason!" Jason spun round. Jacob was aware that this would not have happened if Marcus had not been absent. "Thank you for honouring my marriage. I am also honouring my master even though he is away by earning my name as a faithful servant. I will be answerable to him when he returns, and while he is away, you are answerable to me. You have around two hours of work to make up."

Jacob returned to counting the bottles and the others began being industrious in silence. He was relieved to find there would be enough bottles for that week's shipment. He returned to the workbench.

"I have a story for you. There was a vineyard owner who went on a journey. While he was away, his slaves stopped working and the vineyard became overgrown. There was no wine produced that year. Now what do you suppose the vineyard owner did when he returned?"

"He would punish his slaves, I suppose." Jason said. He briefly held a canine tooth over the corner of his bottom lip.

"You understood the meaning of my story then?"

"Yes Jacob."

"The God of my faith is watching all of us all the time. One day he will return to His vineyard and we will all answer to Him." Only Aethon worshipped with the church, but the others were aware of Marcus' commitment to The Way and its influence on his concerns about the welfare of his workforce. Now they realised Jacob was of the same persuasion.

"Bring all the bottles to the farm as your last job tonight. Tomorrow we need your help with the bottling so come first thing, please. See you later." Jacob left as the others muttered their farewells.

Ten paces from the door Aethon called. There was no-one about as he ran to join Jacob.

"I keep getting teased about being a member of The Way. They are saying we eat babies. I don't know what happens after we leave for the teaching. What can I tell them?"

"Tell them we eat bread and drink wine as Jesus did with his disciples. Aethon, we have disciples who have suffered died as
180

witnesses for the faith and we will all live after death through Jesus' death on the cross, so we have nothing to fear from jokers telling lies. If they are joking that is their problem with your faith, not yours." The young man looked doubtful but looked at the floor and nodded. Resolution seemed to come to his face and he looked eye to eye with Jacob again. He was of a similar height.

"Thank-you Jacob." He turned back towards the doors of the workshop. Jacob paused for thought and called him back.

"I still need one more drover for the wine shipment. Do you want to join us? It might give us chance to talk more about our problems when we talk with others about the Way. It looks like we might get more difficult moments in the future." Aethon was impressed to be asked. He had never been more than a few thousand paces from the town of his birth so it was an exciting prospect. He beamed.

"Yes of course. Thank-you Jacob. Thank-you!" He turned with a jump and trotted back to the workshop.

Jacob turned and after blinking he closed his eyes again to be sure. He could still see the bright image of what must have been

Judith's face when he closed his eyes.. He had a pang of emotion. He was missing her already.

Chapter 20

Doria moved down her stairs and past the door to Jacob's former room. He mind was on her work and praying to her new God in the name of Jesus that she could be faithful to Him even in the loathsome acts she would no doubt have to perform this night. They were less loathsome than being beaten.

She could hear sobbing through the door. On an impulse she opened it and looked in. It was an opportunity for kindness such as that given her by her former neighbour, and a way of living this new faith by sharing the compassion if she could. The girl inside was crouched on the floor half clothed. Aware of the new entrant to her room she looked up hoping for any comfort that might be on offer, but she was dreading the return of those that had left her maybe an hour before.

"They raped me." What had been quiet sobs became a real howl of bereavement. Doria realised there were no words that could be of any use so she crouched silently beside the girl until sobs took over from the keening that preceded them.

182

"My father sold me." The girl shuddered and heaved another sob.

"We women have to stick together. I have found a new faith and it actually cares about us whatever mess we are in. They have raped me before as well. What is your name?"

"Rebecca. My father was in terrible debt. He sold me. He said I would be a house servant. They are making me a prostitute." The last word was only half spoken before the sobs choked it off."

"It is what they made me as well. Is your owner Fortunatus?"

"No it is Gaius. I thought he was going to put me into the house of his scribe as his servant but there was an argument. It was awful. Gaius kept making me show my bottom to the scribe but he refused to agree to whatever Gaius was up to. When the scribe left he caned me and pushed a stick up me." Her mouth set in a way that was refusing to let her burst into tears again at the memory of the violations. Her hand was vaguely indicating the area of her earlier pain. "Then he said something about getting back the money he paid for me by sending me here. Today three of his men then brought me here and.....used me. It went on for ages. I was a virgin." The sobs returned.

183

Doria by now had wet eyes and a tear running down her cheek. She put her arm around the girl. "Rebecca we'll be best friends right? I am Doria. I will take you to my friend's house tomorrow. I go and pray with them and we eat together early in the morning. Those rats that use us don't come near at that time."

"I think the scribe you meant was Jacob. He used to live in this room. He is a lovely man. He would never use us like those swine that work for Fortunatus or Gaius. Gaius sacked him but he has a new job now as a steward. He sometimes prays with us as well."

Chapter 21

Judith left her new marital home with a bundle of her freshly made bread en route to Marcus' house in the town. It would be her first sight of the house since her wedding celebration ended for her as she left with Jacob the evening before. She spent the walk planning her work and the allocated duties of her fellow slaves. Then she realised afresh that she was no longer a slave and was again moved emotionally at the thought.

Marcus had hosted events before but never the overwhelming celebration of the wedding. She had no illusions about the work ahead, returning the house to its normally ordered state. For once she had lacked control over the catering and despite the joy of her centrality in the wedding, her mental discipline as a housekeeper was never far from her mind. "And I always thought my calling by Jesus was to be as Martha in the home of her sister Mary," she thought as the party continued into its second day.

In her previous daily life she had only left Marcus' house to go to the market or the merchant houses while performing her duties, or to the worship at Chloe's home until the wedding. It was new for her to enter the town gates on a morning. This was one of the quieter gates. Most of the trade came from the port and the coastal roads, but it still had it's proportionate quota of beggars and tradesmen. One of the beggars was urinating against the town wall as she approached the ramp before he turned with his exaggerated limp back to his squatting place.

"Help a poor man lady?" he called on sighting her. "I haven't eaten for two days." His tone was redolent of a child that had spilt its milk. Judith had been accosted by beggars many times before, but had

185

responded in her slave state as being poorer than the beggar. The market square beggars, for the most part, knew her. She resolved to give him one of the loaves. For the first time in her life she had the stewardship of property, and she was steward of her master's property. She felt slightly dizzy with the realisation. She swung the bag of bread from her shoulder and reached for a loaf. She offered it to the man who seized it hungrily. Without even a hint of thanks he sank to the floor intent only on the food in his hands. Two women under the arch of the gate were watching. They suddenly tried to out-shout each other.

"Bread for the poor!" One shrieked. "I have children to feed." One of Gaius' men was supervising the gate and interposed himself between the women and Judith.

"And I have a household to feed," she said. The sense of power from moments was now utterly submerged in the opposite. The depression of that moment stayed with her as she continued her onward walk through the gate towards the house. She failed to look at others in the street.

"Mamma!"

"Agathon." The lad leading an ass was the baby she thought she would never see again. He was now taller than she was but she clung to him and wept uncontrollably. After a few seconds she controlled herself and looked into his face, only to choke back another sob. "What have they done to you?" She traced her finger over the scab on his forehead as if a mother's touch would heal it.

"They said I had run away, but I hadn't. I have your amulet, see. I serve Fortunatus. The man who did this died soon after. There must be a god who smiles on me."

"We have a God who smiles on both of us. Can you come back with me to my master's house? It is close by."

"I cannot. They might beat me again or torture me for running away. I will be close by. I have to watch out for my master for a train of asses carrying wine. And tell my master when I see it. Don't tell anyone I said that or they will beat me for that as well."

"Is you master buying wine? He could get it from my master. He owns the vineyard to the north. If you are by the north gate I will see you again later." Judith hugged him again. Agathon this time looked around over his mother's shoulder to see is they were being watched. They weren't.

"I have great news. My master gave me my freedom. I am married. I have much to tell you but I don't want you getting into trouble. Oh my boy it is so good to see you. Here is some bread for you." Judith picked up the bag she had dropped unthinkingly. Fortunately it had not been contaminated by anything on the ground. They parted, each looking over their shoulders to wave as they got further apart. Agathon, now Onesimus, looked at the bread and back to his mother. He moved back to his slave duties, a little happier for his encounter.

Judith reached Marcus' threshold moments later and tried to put out of her mind her recent experience. She had a house to manage for an absent master, and she was not about to fail in her duty.

Chapter 22

"Which mountain was it?" John asked.

"You know very well this is a figurative mountain. It is a metaphorical mountain. It is a symbolic mountain. If this is to remain readable there are only so many times I can say 'Jesus said to the crowds,' or 'Jesus said to the disciples,' or 'Jesus said to the Pharisees.' We don't have a context for the sayings so this is the best way of including them all. It is a mountain because it is the new law on a new Sinai."

"It strikes me," John continued, "that this would be an unrealistic long speech to be so full of little sayings."

"So your answer would be what?"

"I would interweave it in a thematic way so that it flowed like a speech."

"In other words you would make it up." Jacob continued as John opened his mouth to object. "I am trying to be faithful to what we believe were actually words used by The Lord, not put in The Lord's mouth what I want him to have said to suit my own political or doctrinal agenda. I know you want me to have Jesus hammering hell out of the Romans John, but the evidence we have talks of Him proclaiming a Kingdom that will outlast anything the Romans have or ever will have. In any case, if we want to avoid another bloodbath like that from Nero in Rome or Titus in Jerusalem we need to show the love

189

of the Lord, not the sort of polemic that threatens and provokes the Romans."

"I'm sure the Lord would have fired up his followers for this Kingdom. He must have had visions like those of the prophets. He must have been as confrontational, if not more so, than the Baptist."

"The parables are confrontational, but they all seem to be attacking false positions and hypocrisy when they are not kicking the rich in the backside. They are not whooping up a big judgement day, they are laying down a way of dealing with this life now, especially in attitudes to wealth and dealings with each other, especially the poor. Above all the door is always open to the opponents to repent and join the Way, not shove them into Hades."

John had his face set with thin lips. He was not getting his way, and the consensus around the room seemed to be with Jacob. Onesimus intervened in his usual calming tones.

"John, I believe there is credence in your expectation of a judgement. I believe that you can give an airing to your views, if not even visions, in your own book. What you are saying are the words that would be said by The Lord from His position of victory. I say again

190

that you should write this vision in your own document. It may well be edifying for us all."

"Now," he shifted in his seat, "is there any other matter we want to go over?"

Pudens cleared his throat. "I think we need to emphasise that The Lord is greater than the Baptist. Mark's description of the Lord being baptised is very matter of fact, almost that Jesus was just one of the crowd, all of whom were subjecting themselves to the Baptist's prophecy and greatness."

"What do you suggest, bearing in mind this means rewriting a scroll?" Jacob was being patient, but tiredness was creeping up on him. He was ready to go home.

"Why don't we have the Baptist objecting to baptising someone greater than him. After all, such a great prophet would surely recognise the Lord for who He was, given that the Baptist was a gifted prophet and was preparing for the Messiah who was standing before him at His baptism." Pudens waved his hands back and forth sideways, and gesture of his that went with what he considered a fait accompli. "And another thing, since we are on the same sequence, why don't we

191

expand the details of the thought patterns of the Lord while he was in the wilderness. We all believe that he was planning his ministry and setting aside the alternatives of raising an army or outdoing the Romans in administration. I wonder if it passed through his mind that he could have re-organised Rome in the same way that Joseph sorted out Pharaoh and Egypt."

A brief silence followed as the clergy thought through the implications. Onesimus broke into the meditation. "If it is delicately done to give an outline of the sorts of strategies Jesus would have set aside before beginning his Ministry. Now what would He have been tempted to do? Raise an army is one."

There was a discussion lasting a few minutes, and Jacob was given a verbal outline to fill out. "Is it not unrealistic to have a devil talking to him?"

"We have scriptures describing angels talking to our Israelite forefathers. I think we have the latitude to construct a fallen angel trying to mislead Him. We have plenty of evidence of Jewish leadership misdirecting the faithful." Pudens was solid in his conviction.

192

"Thank-you Brothers." Onesimus was bringing the evening's discussion to a close. "Jacob has a new wife to return to and he needs to be through the north gate before it is closed. He also has much to do in his new responsibility in Marcus' employ so we need to be trusting and patient. Now let us pray."

The brief prayers ranged around the people in the church's concerns, but some seconds of silence surrounded the prayer for Marcus, whose position somewhere distant and on the high seas brought a sense of concern.

When Jacob closed his eyes in prayer, he could see the image of his wife's face. For all the other surrounding issues, joyful anticipation of reaching home to Judith filled his mind once more.

Chapter 23

"You and Marcus have a different aim from us. You want to get your wine through to your merchant. We want to catch and crucify robbers." Sextus walked on his way to where the uniformed soldiers were still standing easy waiting to return to barracks having detached the convoy guard, now re-garbed to look like mule drovers. Their swords were hidden amongst the panniers on the beasts. He was out of

193

earshot as the leading soldier was being given instructions but occasional nods in his direction indicated the pattern of the conversation. The conversation over, the leading man called the remainder of the squad to order and they began their journey down the hill from the farm to take the valley road back to the town and eventually the barracks. The track was rough and narrow so marching was hardly the word to describe their single file progress.

The beasts of burden were led up the hill with their escort of three of Marcus' slaves, Jacob the steward and the four soldiers. At this stage there was very little conversation. Most were watching their footing on the uneven bare earth and stones. Sextus was wondering why the engineer Marcus had not made a decent Roman road on his land here yet. Anthony was minding his feet to avoid the mule standing on his foot. He was having a little nostalgia remembering leading oxen loaded with bricks. Two of the slaves had been on the previous trip that had ended in robbery and the death of Marcus' previous steward. They felt a little apprehensive but were assured to have professional swordsmen alongside.

The thorn bush at the crest of the hill came into view, and shortly afterwards the gate of the town in the distance. They left the

194

rows of vines with some final stumbling uphill steps and reached the road. They paused to order themselves for the long trek, but, Jacob thought, to enable anyone from the town planning a robbery to see them in the distance. This was the time for ease. The mule train would not be attacked on the open high ground. The time for concern was in the passes through the hills ahead. There were several that would afford opportunities for ambush.

The high streets the Romans built made much sense from a military point of view. They gave a wide view of the countryside and great opportunity to see attackers coming. They were not at all ideal for drovers and traders with beasts needing a regular supply of water and grazing. The path would soon take a downward slope to the road that followed the waterways. The animals set the pace. The soldiers would make a much gentler pace than that to which they were used when marching. They would also forego the break they anticipated every thousand double paces.

The breeze of the upper slopes would eventually give way to the sheltered heat of the valleys. The rest stops would be about cooling themselves and drinking as much as sitting. It would possibly be on one of the rest stops, if an attack were to come that the group would be least

195

prepared and vulnerable. The soldiers, with Sextus in the lead would surely have thought this through. If there were no excessive delays they would hopefully make the journey with only one night to sleep on the roadside. They would be extremely tired towards the end of the second day but at least they would be able to sleep securely with the task completed. Then they would have the journey back later the next day with a lighter load, albeit another temptation for robbers. Jacob had instructions to barter for indigo and woven cloth for either Marcus' household or for onward trading, and he was supplying Chloe's household with some of her raw materials.

Jacob took time walking with each of Marcus' men in turn. With Aethon he talked of how the first disciples had dealt with hostility, especially Paul, who once may have walked this road himself.

It was late morning as the mobile group moved down into the first valley, albeit higher above sea level than where they began as they climbed towards hill passes. Marcus' men watered the beasts from the valley stream. Two of the soldiers sat, but at the ready. Of the other two, one faced up the valley and the other down, alert to anyone approaching especially anyone potentially of hostile intent. There was little conversation. Most had a feeling of foreboding and they were

196

occupied either with servicing animals or eating. Such rest as they had was welcome.

The soldiers changed role from rest to lookout. The watered animals ambled out of line to graze on the waterside grass and the slaves themselves had brief respite with their food. All too soon, with an unspoken consensus the order of the train was restored. Before motion began, however, Sextus ordered a halt. Visible in the haze on the path ahead was a similar sized train of beasts coming towards them. In their present situation there was space. If the train advanced there would be a close quarter meeting of beasts and men as they passed each other, something best avoided. No-one expected this to be a hostile group on a trade route. A group intent on robbery would be unlikely to provide their own animals, but this could be a clever ruse to take a merchant band by surprise. Sextus was not taking any chances.

If peaceful, the oncoming group would probably take the place by the stream just vacated. Either way a conversation was likely to ensue about any news either travelling group might have to offer. Jacob's group wanted to conceal weapons both to avoid the other train being concerned about an attack, and to alert anyone on the road to whom they might later converse that the group they passed was armed and guarded.

Gordius was beside Jacob. "Can you really use a sword?" This was a reprise of their first conversation on Jacob's last night in the Island building. It dawned on Jacob with some fear that he might really be expected to use one. His mouth went dry and had a bitter taste. He dreaded coming to from another flashback and betray his former part, albeit minor, in the Jerusalem uprising, but he stayed in the present with Gordius.

"No."

"You can at least hold one as if you can when the time comes. Any scum attacking us will not know you can't and they will be less likely to attack if they think we are all capable of taking them on. Those who lose skirmishes are usually those that shit themselves first and run away. Robbers only rob because they think they have a weak group in front of them. There is a sword for everyone here." Gordius looked twice at Jacob who was watching the approaching group intently. "Did you not know that?"

"No."

The approaching train were much closer but still out of earshot when Sextus looked round to check his group's preparedness. There was immediately something in his face that showed he was anxious about Anthony's bearing. Anthony had his back to Jacob.

"Anthony don't you dare take action without an order. Relax. I don't think they are robbers but I'm not taking chances." Sextus returned his alertness to the approaching group.

Jacob's train were standing well clear of the stream and the path, far further than would have been usual for passing traders. The oncoming group moved to the water as expected. Their attending men waved. Sextus, now relaxed, walked back to Jacob.

"Go and ask if there is anything on the road we should know about. Tell them we have not passed anyone." Jacob strode off to the man that had led the first animal.

"Greetings. How is your journey? We have seen nothing to speak of today."

"Greetings to you. There are only a few shepherds this way since we left Thyatira." The man coughed heavily and spittle dribbled on to his unkempt beard. The coughing fit lasted some time, and returned each time he was about to speak again.

"May my Lord and God heal you in the Name of His Son." The man raised his hand acknowledging a prayer, though Jacob doubted he understood the reference he meant.

"A safe journey to you," the man eventually wheezed. "I get this from the scurf from the animals and always have." Jacob could see the drover was keen to attend to his animals and Jacob was anxious to be moving after this nervous delay. He reported his brief conversation to Sextus who received it with a nod. Without another word, they all began to move.

Sextus looked back frequently as they climbed the hill pass until the other mule train was tiny in the distance. The path became narrower and hugged a line beside the also narrowing stream. With further progress there was room only for single file walking, each man ahead of his beast. Fighting in this terrain would be difficult with no manoeuvrability to outflank the other force. The steep hillside either side of the path gave little footing for any force attacking from the side.

The soldiers could relax, just for the moment. Walking gave them enough exertion.

At the head of the valley there was a col as the path widened. The stream was just a few scrubby plants that thrived in damper ground. The next valley opened before them. They could see sheep grazing on the hillsides in the distance. There was a clear view. There was no ambush likely for some time. After the long slow climb the soldiers did, this time, want their thousand pace rest. The drovers welcomed another stop and dropped to sit on the ground. Again the beasts wandered in search of grazing amongst the stony soil.

All too soon the trek restarted. The routine of the journey became settled. At each site providing an open vista they stopped, and ideally that open vista allowed for water and grazing. Each man largely kept his thoughts private. Jacob looked at his beast and was reminded of Balaam, though his animal had been well behaved unlike the creature of the scriptures. His beast was obviously seeing no angel, and neither would it be saying anything soon. He wondered if this was a sign that they were all on the right track as guided by YHWH.

The evening sunlight was behind hills and they were looking for a place to settle for the night. They were in a valley by the bend of a deep stream, almost a river. There was a bend in the river, slow moving and shallow where they settled, but deeper downstream after the bend, and rapids could be heard hissing upstream, out of sight. Bushes punctuated the riverside. There was a wide flat piece of ground behind which there was a craggy cliff once carved by the water that had now retreated over hundreds of years to its present course. They had a clear view for some distance either way until the curves of the path took it out of vision.

Soldiers and drovers each had a watch. The supply beasts were unloaded to give what comfort could be afforded for those sleeping outside. No fire was made or welcomed. It would assist an attacker in identifying the victim before it would provide light to see the attacker's advance. It took some time to unload the animals. It would damage the merchandise if they lay on the bottles on their panniers. The beasts were tethered together. They may wander, but could not wander separately for any distance.

It made a relatively decent position to defend. The sentry need only watch two points. No attack was likely from across the river and

202

none from the cliff. Only the path ahead or the path behind allowed access. Most expected that any attack would be from a following force. Only the Thyatira merchant had any inkling of approaching goods. Any villains were likely to have been watching for Marcus' wine shipment leaving or been informed by one or more of his staff, innocently or otherwise.

They dined on cold lamb with bread. The lamb had been killed and cooked fresh and stowed well enough protect it from insects or in the heat of the day just passed or it would by the time of eating be starting to go off and be riddled with maggots. There was fruit to follow. The wine was off limits given their need for vigilance.

They settled in the last vestige of light to their sleeping arrangements near but not directly under the cliff. The animals were ambling near with Aethon taking the first watch with Gordius. The soldiers had reasoned that the most likely time of any attack would be in the hours close to or just after dawn but they had to be prepared for any eventuality. Sextus had given instructions as to the watches, and had educated his men as to the moving stars. When a given constellation had reached the land feature from their vantage point, they were to wake their relief.

203

Strangely, Jacob was not long awake. He had memories of sleeping in the open air going back to his terrified state in Judea after the destruction of Jerusalem. Sleeping on the ground was back to normal after his marriage bed. The soldiers slept as on a campaign. Sleep was a duty under orders if they were to be alert when they were needed. Their weapons were to hand in case of the call to fight.

There was a hollow in the cliff face for the sentry, who would be completely out of sight for an attacker rounding the path. Ears were the most acutely used sense, listening for any sound that was not the water. There were no cicadas. They did have an ear to the cliff above in case of a reconnoitring presence. There was none.

Only Aethon did not sleep at all that night. Once he had been relieved and Anthony had taken over from Gordius the ground afforded no position for him to relax and rest or give him comfort. He reconciled himself to being awake, but at least he was not walking beside an ass. He was still listening just as he had been listening when on watch. Now, at least, he was not worrying about where the beasts were going if they moved.

Jacob, in his dream was listening to the Jordan again and waiting for the Ark of the Covenant to cause a path to part the river in front of him. He was worrying that anyone else should touch the Ark, and several of the church members were in danger of doing so. Sextus woke him. It was as if nothing had changed since he lay down. The two that had been relieved were settling to their chosen bed hoping to snatch just a little more sleep before loading up the beasts and the trek beginning again.

Sextus walked to the sentry point swinging his sword as an exercise. There was just the hint of deep blue replacing the black in the eastern sky behind the cliff. The stars of his sleeping moment the evening before had moved. It was not often he saw Venus as a morning star but here it was. The looming shapes of the beasts were suddenly there in front of him. He kept his distance. He did not want to cause them to start. He stood by the water and reached with his cupped hands to pull a mouthful to his lips. He stroked his cold wet hands across his eyes. He turned his back to the water and urinated. He was looking again and again to the path round which they had come the night before. All remained still. He felt an urge to move his bowels and resolved to do it where the beasts were. He would be as innocent as they were. Having done the deed he walked back to the river, slipped

205

off his clothes and paddled knee deep in the water and washed himself. He had no intention of being sore from chaffing around his backside on the long walk that day.

While in the water he was taken by a strange glow behind the hills to the south, roughly from the direction they had walked. It was a strange light beyond his experience throwing the hills in front into shadow. It was definitely from the land and not the sky. It could not have been lanterns or torches. Needing to confirm what he was seeing he walked swiftly to Sextus.

"What is that light?"

"I don't know Jacob, but I won't let it be a distraction. That could be what the robbers are wanting."

Jacob returned to the river. Daylight was becoming more in evidence and progressively made the strange glowing disappear. He could now see the land delineated quite clearly. The sun would soon be with them though it would be some time before it appeared over the cliff. By then, he hoped, they would be long gone. It occurred to him that this would have been time for an attacking group to strike, when at their most vulnerable. They would all be tired from an interrupted sleep and they were likely to be physically stiff from the previous day's walk.

Time passed. Eventually Sextus, now clearly visible in daylight left his post and strode back to the sleeping group. The day's work was about to begin.

He continued to act as sentry as the others performed such ablutions and toilets as required at the waterside. The soldiers stayed alert and were one at a time off guard. The slaves reloaded the beasts. Anthony took his turn at the river side and took a liberty, moving into the deeper water for a swim as his wash. He had left his clothes by the waterside where the bushes afforded some shelter.

The beasts were loaded again and almost all was ready for the journey when the fears of all present were realised. From the direction expected five men with swords sprinted into sight. Sextus bawled "Guard ready!"

The beasts were lined up and still tethered to each other and the train was quite close to the cliff. The three ready soldiers formed a rank between the rear of the last animal and the cliff. It prevented a flank attack. The drovers remained between the animals and the cliff as

207

a second rank. Having reached twenty paces distant, the attackers paused, having little expectation of such armed resistance. The leader was working out options. There were five armed men against three but a frontal attack was the worst option. They began to sidle around the group hoping to breach a line either through the animal cordon or from behind it. The animals as one became restless and brayed. The drovers were holding on to the reins both to keep the animals between themselves and the attackers, and to avoid a stampede, such was the growing panic amongst the beasts. This was surely more than the result of robbers arriving on the scene.

Jacob was surprised how irrelevant details of the scenery were crowding him at such a fraught moment. The sunlight reached the water's edge behind the wary attackers in their sideward shift, keeping space to swing a sword, but remaining close enough to cover each other. The five then split into a two and a three, the three matching the three disguised soldiers, and the two moving gradually to the front of the train for a flanking attack, eyes still intent on the three armed defenders.

The group of three attackers were distracted briefly by a fast moving light across the cliff face but kept their attention forward. What

208

they had not seen to their left was the cause of the light: Anthony's had crept silently from behind and with a sideways full swing of his sword beheaded the first of the two sideways moving robbers. The sun had reflected from the sword. The head dropped like a vegetable and rolled as the body slumped. There was a massive spray of blood. His companion turned, startled and rapidly alert to the movement beside him, aware of another armed man. He was too late to avoid the sword that with Anthony's return sweep hit him across the bridge of his nose as he turned. It went through his face and stopped but an inch from severing the top of his head. His cry was momentary but enough to alert his conspirators of action to their left.

When they glanced the image was terrifying. Their two associates were dead on the ground and there was a fourth armed man. This man was naked and his body was as if it had been half painted with blood. The unpainted half gave the image of sun glistening on water droplets and an unreal golden or copper coloured hair on head and body. This was the biggest man, if man he was, they had seen. What was also ludicrous and jarring in this situation was that this naked swordsman had an erection.

209

The balance of opposing forces was now radically changed. The three soldiers, with Sextus in the middle, began a slow advance. The three bandits were now clearly the group being defensive. The beasts were still disturbed and as a group were dragging the four drovers away from the cliff. They were barely being controlled.

Into this exceptional set of circumstances there was a whole new dimension introduced. Rocks began to fall from the face of the cliff and the ground shook. The trees by the river waved in unison and everyone fought to keep their balance. It was an earthquake. It was as if a god had decided to act with displeasure. In difficult conditions for progress, the bandits began an ungainly run away from the scene in the direction from which they had come. Maybe, one of the escaped bandits was later to reason the bloodied figure by the river was a god or his agent. The soldiers did not pursue. They kept their rank and were disciplined. They did not know if the bandits may have had support around that corner. It was doubtful but possible.

For a time, all seemed out of control for any decision of certainty. After what seemed an age, the ground ceased its movement. The drovers had kept hold of the beasts and the braying and bucking and struggling ceased. The soldiers watched the corner from which the bandits had come, but they were certain there would be no return. Anthony was the first to move.

"I'll go and get washed again."

Jacob was in a space by himself on hands and knees. He was vomiting up his breakfast and crying. He was muttering something about a temple but the words did not make sense. All others looked anxiously back to the corner from which the bandits disappeared, but most felt there would be no return.

Sextus walked across to look at the bodies. "Any of you men recognise these?" he called to the drovers. In twos the drovers left their colleagues to mind the animals and looked at the cadavers. They did not know them, but mutilation would have made even acquaintances hard to know. They had not recognised any when they were running to the attack so this was mere confirmation of the fact. When Anthony, dressed and ready came to look at his victims, Sextus was holding the loose head by the hair, its gaping jaw drooling bloody spittle. "Do you know him."

"Not until today I didn't. We weren't really introduced."

"One of the others that ran away had two incredible black eyes. Did you see him?"

"I was a bit occupied over here for that."

"Yes! Well done soldier."

The stores being half used, the load was re-organised and the bodies were laid over the final beast. The authorities would take care of them in Thyatira. In due course they moved off leaving a trickled and sporadic trail of blood on the path.

Jacob, walking beside the fourth beast felt very unsettled. He knew he had had a mental return to his trauma in Jerusalem but had little idea what those around him had seen or heard. He had vomit on his front, but the soldiers had battle experience and had witnessed the reactions of newcomers to such violence. The last earthquake he remembered was at the time of the fall of Jerusalem. He wondered if this was another portent.

After a long time of silence Gordius shouted back to Sextus from one end of the procession to the other. "You know why they ran away?" all were waiting for a punch line. With perfect timing he

212

answered his own question. "They did not know what Anthony was going to stab them with!" The black humour brought long lasting laughter and they were able to relax. While retaining alertness they felt sure that the rest of the journey would be uneventful.

Chapter 24

The earthquake that struck as the attack took place hit the town with force. Most of the buildings had walls collapsing and pan tiles slipping and crashing to the earth. Judith's son, the young Onesimus was leading his ass to collect a slaughtered pig from one of the butchers' shops beyond the olive grove. He was in open ground beyond the Island and holding on to his panicking beast. The olive trees were waving in unison as if to each other. Women at the well ahead screamed in panic. He watched with awe as the Island that had been just behind him began its collapse. There were shrill screams of mothers and howling children in sheer panic from inside. The roof and walls fell as if in stages. By the time the shaking underfoot ceased in what seemed an age of violence there were but two craggy end gables standing upright and between them a dusty heap of broken bricks and dust. The shocked silence was punctuated by the sound of sliding bricks and debris. Then there were muffled sounds of moans mostly of

213

female voices, and a baby was crying somewhere from an air pocket in the mound. The men that lived in the building had already left for their places of labour.

Onesimus ran to the mound and was lost as to where he should start. Beams jutted out and he thought of crawling in spaces to see if he could find survivors but he was very frightened that he too would be trapped. He could hear the baby and the direction in the mound where it would be. He found what he thought would be the nearest point of access and began to throw bricks from in front to behind him. A small landslide of bricks came down on his knee when he made some headway. By now the word had gone around and others were beginning to scramble alongside him. At first it was the women that had been gathering water. One of them was howling about her "children being in there." Soon some of the men folk had left their work and were trying to reach their family members. It was an age before they unearthed their first body. It was a woman. Her body was as pale and dusty as a statue. Her head had been in rubble and dust. Her arms were trapped and she had suffocated. One of the men further along realised who it was and he ran and cradled her head in his arm. His tears were silent for a few moment before he screamed to the sky a long piercing, "Why?"

214

The baby was still crying an alarm call that kept beckoning them to greater effort. They scrabbled and dug the whole morning without rest. Onesimus used his animal to haul a beam out of the pile. His mind then turned to his errand. He did not want another beating and he began to move towards his original goal. On arrival the shops were empty of their proprietors. He reasoned that they must be dealing with the aftermath of the earthquake and began his walk back past the Island either to his master or to the gang leader to report.

Chloe's household with their visitors had finished prayers. Rebecca had taken much comfort from the support of the women and mentally agreed with Doria that they were a great support to her. They were moving to the table to eat when the whole house began to shake. She wondered if this must be a sign from God. Apart from a few broken pots and toppling tools and roof tiles and dust in the atrium there was little damage so a brief clear up made time for their breakfast being slightly late.

The gaggle of conversation sharing the experience as they began to eat was interrupted by Judith arriving. She had been going to the market when the earthquake hit them.

215

"The Island has collapsed. Anyone in there could have been killed. They are digging to find survivors."

Rebecca and Doria looked at each other with recognition of the import of the news. On impulse they were ready to run to join the excavation for survivors. Martha spoke for the first time that morning. "Don't leave here until we know more. The Lord may have just given you your freedom."

It was not that they had lost their home, but that they were not in it as it was lost. Had it not been for this community, they would not have been praying, and they would be under the rubble. It crossed Doria's mind what Martha was suggesting. For all Fortunatus and Gaius knew, they were indeed under the rubble and they had lost their investments in these slaves.

Chapter 25

The weary train arrived in Thyatira with the sun still above the horizon. It had been arranged for the drovers to take the goods to the house of Obadiah bar Nahum and Jacob had the directions to the merchant's property. The soldiers separated from the main group and headed for the barracks with one of the beasts bearing its gory load.

216

With some recognition of what had happened at the start of their day, they could see broken tiles in the road and some cracks in the walls. Generally, though, the community was quiet and the damage had been manageable.

Jacob arrived at a large complex surrounding his villa. Obadiah's men were quickly on the scene to relieve Jacob and his assistants with the animals and the load. Marcus had already arranged the price, and Obadiah had done much of the preparatory work in securing the train's goods for return. Jacob was greeted warmly at the door and there was immediate recognition by the rich man of his new arrival's cultural origins. The hospitality was generous for all of the drovers in servants' quarters but Jacob was singled out for Obadiah's company that evening. The soldiers were due to join the drovers after reporting to their superiors at the barracks.

Jacob was offered the customary courtesies of a fellow Jew to a new guest.

"You are the new steward serving Marcus? How did you come into his service?"

217

Jacob remained seated upright on his couch as his host reclined. The food was beginning to arrive.

"I was the scribe for the Magistrate and Marcus made a better offer for my services. Marcus would have been here but was called urgently to Rome for family reasons. I do not know the cause. Thank you but I have an eating disorder that prevents me from eating while reclining. Do excuse me keeping this posture as I eat."

"Of course! Of course!" The older man waved his hand dismissively. "We will discuss trade tomorrow. I see that you are tired from your journey. At least you were not robbed this time."

"There was an attempt on us. Four of our men have taken the bodies of two robbers to the Romans."

"You put up a fight?" Obadiah made noises of satisfaction clearly praising the success in combating the threat to one of his trade routes. "You must tell me about it."

Jacob was obliged to keep the identity of his swordsmen in confidence. "We have some trained swordsmen in our number now. They were ready for an attack and dealt with it well." Images of the bloody conflict passed through his mind again and Jacob shuddered. Obadiah could see Jacob's reluctance to go into detail.

"It is a shame we must deplete our profits to pay mercenaries." Obadiah slipped a morsel into his mouth. "Still it should give some deterrence to our thieves once the word gets about amongst them."

Jacob was aware of the movements of servants in the large room of which his companion's dining area was a vestibule. There was a heavily pregnant woman walking across making gentle supervisory orders to the servants. Jacob was concentrating on his host's conversation.

"Where did you originate? What is your family background?"

"I was born in Jerusalem." At that point Jacob was aware that the pregnant woman was in the dining area and was looking at him.

"My dear, are you well?" Obadiah asked her.

Jacob looked up. The woman's face was screwed up preparatory to bursting into tears, which she proceeded to do. Obadiah rose to his feet as quickly as his maturity and his plate of food allowed. She buried her face in his chest and wept. It was Ruth.

219

"This is Jacob." She said when after a minute she had composed herself. It was a fraction of a second before Obadiah recognised the Jacob she meant from the story of her past. It was some years since she had related it to him. As much as was seemly for a married woman she greeted Jacob with a kiss and looked into his face.

"I thought you were dead!" she sobbed briefly again. "What happened to you?" Jacob gave a brief history of his life since his escape, and that he was now a follower of The Way following his encounter with those that saved him in the wilderness.

"And what happened to you?"

Ruth sat with her husband and with animation outlined how she had been herded by Romans with other surviving women for sales at the slave auction in Syria and then at Antioch. Obadiah was trading in Antioch and happened on the auction and bought her.

He interposed. "I could not bear to see daughters of Rachel being bought and sold. I would have bought all of them if I could." The image had brought the memory back and he looked at the ground briefly. "I was trading on behalf of my late father at the time. I gave Ruth her freedom immediately and brought her into my home as a

220

servant. Now she is my third wife. She has given me five children, soon to give me a sixth."

"Do you know what happened to my family?"

"I saw your mother briefly as they herded us on the road but we were soon separated. I didn't think any men survived. Anyone in the temple would have perished. I heard they sent all its precious things to Rome. Have you married?"

"I married only last week. My wife is called Judith." He looked at Obadiah. "She is Marcus' housekeeper."

"I think I know her from one of my visits to the port. I stayed with Marcus then. I thought she was his slave."

"She was then. Marcus freed her and was generous with everything for our wedding."

"They are wrong in so many ways, but I see the followers of The Way are very generous. I see now that this Jesus must have been a great prophet, even to match the Baptist, but you cannot call a man a god. That is why we suffer so much from Rome and their mighty claims for their emperor."

221

"None of their Emperors has overcome death. There were many witnesses to seeing Jesus risen."

"Sadly all your witnesses are those who continued that perversion of our Jewish life and way. Why did Jesus not appear to his enemies and turn them round?"

"He did appear to the Pharisee Saul who was prosecuting the followers of Jesus. Jesus has left us all with a freedom, even to reject Him. That is why we are a threat to all authorities. They do not like slaves being told they are free and equal as brothers and sisters in Jesus Christ. In the same way the temple authorities did not like the poor and the lepers and the sinners being accepted and loved by The Lord, even though they were children of Abraham."

Obadiah seemed reluctant to continue the conversation and make any more concessions to his view of his faith. "You are not eating. Is the food not good?"

"Your food and hospitality are wonderful, sir. It is just that talking and eating are not an easy combination for me."

"Then we will maintain a prayerful silence before the Great One as we eat." He turned his attention to his plate again, and Ruth rose, held her hands into the small of her back and walked gently back to her wifely duties turning to give Jacob a smile as she left their presence. The smile was just as innocent as it had been in her youth in Jerusalem and he had a pang of nostalgia for days that could never return.

Chapter 26

Most of those digging in the rubble at the Island had lost everything. The few possessions that class of worker had lost was nothing compared to the precious possessions they, for the most part, had taken for granted: the close relationships they had with those who shared their hovels, be it partners, children or the elderly that enabled the young to be economically active while taking care of the children. A cross section of that demographic in the town was lost in the hours that followed the earthquake as the painfully slow excavation of the Island took place. Neither Gaius' police force, nor Fortunatus' employees were in evidence with even the primitive tools they had at their disposal. The imaginations of the frantic diggers brought up images of what the owners of this evident death trap might be doing.

223

"Everyone has said it was a death trap but they wanted to build another."

Occasionally bodies were discovered. After an hour or so, the crying of the baby ceased. Either the child had become tired of the wait for comfort or it had succumbed to its injuries. It would be another day before they found out. Miraculously the child survived but her mother did not. The mother was another of the prostitutes Fortunatus and Gaius housed there. As more bodies were dug out, mostly of young women, mothers or children, the despair built, and so did the anger.

"Why," someone asked, "are the soldiers not helping. It is them that kept using these women."

One of the tax collectors was standing in the distance watching, surrounded by several town residents that were unlikely to get their hands dirty. In their curiosity, they had no idea of the provocation their presence was giving the now utterly fatigued, unfed and desperate diggers whose whole life had collapsed with that building.

The bodies, with what ceremony was possible, were laid out in the open air inside the olive grove. There was no other shelter nearby

224

but the trees. Those digging the rubble would soon be digging graves and then with little idea where they would sleep the next night.

As the day wore on some of the market traders, completely without trade as householders conducted repairs, brought food produce for the rescue workers. It was eaten quickly from dusty bleeding hands.

One desperate man with his family still buried bellowed abuse at the curious bystanders. Someone in the by-standing crowd felt his dignity besmirched by such a peasant abusing him and replied. It was unwise and the trigger for a personal attack. This led to a riot. Most of those whose home was buried in the rubble paid what they thought was an extortionate rent, and for what? They did not even have safety. The men from Island were joined by discontented slaves. They had plenty of stones and other missiles available to them in every street. They were soon beating a path to Fortunatus' house.

The handful of Gaius force they encountered fled when they were stoned. They ran to inform their superior. In turn they were dispatched by him to bring out the Roman guard. Gaius hid himself in one of the temples. He had no idea where the mob was heading.

225

Hysteria was building. Someone had to be blamed and punished. All the pent up feeling was directed at Fortunatus and his house was eventually surrounded. Young Onesimus returning from disposing of broken tiles from his master's courtyard stood in awe from afar and watched. He had never seen a riot before.

Fortunatus and his household were totally unprepared. He was, of course depressed that he had lost one of his major assets. There were some armed men in his courtyard but they could not get past the missiles that were stoning them. The rampage was mindless and undirected, but the one consistency was destruction. When it was realised that Fortunatus had abandoned his house by some other exit there was looting of the status goods of the "wealthy" man. The crowd, some carrying goods was dispersing when the soldiers arrived.

Some were intent on looting from other wealthy houses as well.

There was no warning issued. In ranks of three, for such was the narrowness of the road in front of Fortunatus' house, each soldier at the front swung his sword. With the element of surprise none had thought to flee. The man that raised his arm to protect his face lost his

226

arm, severed just below his elbow. His scream alerted the rioters nearby. Beside him a man tried to duck the blow and the side of his face was sliced leaving a flap of bleeding flesh that included his ear hanging at his neck. He knelt whimpering in shock.

The attack was random and anyone in front of a soldier was going to be mutilated by a sword. The action lasted only a few seconds. The soldiers had done what was required and scattered the rioters. The crowd fled. The penalty for riot was crucifixion.

Young Onesimus did not know where he was to go, but he had to move from his present place for fear. Members of the crowd were running towards him and his animal was disturbed. There was no home to go to. He resolved to find the house of Marcus and his mother and go back to find Fortunatus when the streets were quiet. Surely he would not be accused of trying to run away in these circumstances.

He had heard of Marcus by reputation. He headed in the direction where he believed the house to be. The riot had not gone into this area. Residents here were still moving debris from their houses and clearing the street. He asked one man in the street for the house of Marcus and it was pointed out to him. Dusk was far gone when he

227

approached the entrance. Two of Marcus' women were sweeping the dust out of the door having cleaned the atrium of its debris and dust in preparation for builders when any could be found at this time of expected demand.

"Is this the house of Marcus?"

"Yes it is boy, but he is away."

"Is my mother here?"

"And who is your mother?"

"Judith?"

"You are Judith's son? Wait there. You can't bring that animal in here."

Judith was at the door in a few seconds, looking heated from the day's exertion trying to restore order.

"Agathon! Why are you here? I don't want them to hurt you for running away."

"There was a riot. My master's house has been under attack. There were soldiers with swords. It was awful. I don't know where to go."

"Stay with me tonight. You must go back tomorrow. I'll go with you. Tether your beast there. I am going back to my house very soon before it gets too dark. I don't know how damaged that is going to be yet." Judith briefly hugged her son.

When they left Marcus' house as the first stars showed in an indigo sky the streets were deserted. Towards the north gate there were several abandoned odd sandals and remaining debris whether from stone throwing or as it laid from the damaged buildings they did not know. It was just as Judith and young Onesimus with his hungry beast were going through the deserted north gate in the town wall that many miles away Jacob was being recognised by Ruth in Thyatira.

Apart from a few broken vessels the damage to Judith's new home was slight. Two of Marcus' slaves had been delegated to clean up debris so by morning the house was functional again and the morning of baking began again. The burden of carrying the bread to Marcus' house would be borne by young Onesimus', or Agathon's, as his

229

mother still called him, animal. Onesimus spent the morning with his mother but avoiding getting under her feet as the work continued. They updated most of the gaps in what had occurred in their lives since their separation at the slave market.

"They call them 'Christians' in Fortunatus' house." Onesimus was responding to his mother's disclosure of her faith. "They say they eat children. They eat flesh and drink blood."

"We do nothing of the sort. We believe we are all loved and God came to be one of us in Jesus, The Lord, to show the way of service and love for each other. The powerful people can't have slaves being loved by a God as much as they are, so they tell lies. We eat bread and drink wine."

By late morning mother and son and beast were climbing the road from Judith's home to the Roman road on the height of the slope that held the vines. Outside the distant gate to which they were headed they could see activity. The flashes of red cloth meant there were soldiers amongst the small, what appeared to be jostling, crowd. Several stakes seemed to be in the crowd's centre. The crowd was dispersing. As they approached, Judith and Onesimus realised with some trepidation that the stakes were in fact the crosses of crucifixion. There were four at this gate. They discovered later there were many more at other gates.

As they approached they were given barely a glance by the group of soldiers. Amongst the other bystanders Judith recognised the frail and bending figure of Phoebe who was weeping alone beneath one of the crosses. Onesimus did not know Phoebe but looked up to see that the figure on the cross was the man from whom he collected butchered animals for Fortunatus' household. It was one of Phoebe's sons, struggling to breath in his wracked posture.

The image of horror around filled several senses. One of the crosses held a body tied upside down, its late owner having bled to death from a severed arm. There was a smell of blood on the air, the groaning of tortured bodies and the wailing of several women. Judith simply said "Stay here" to her son and she approached Phoebe.

The comforting arm from Judith brought on a loud cry from Phoebe. "He did not riot. Gaius' men dragged him out of my house." She returned to sobs. Judith looked up to see the notice pinned at the top of the cross. She was able to read "RIOTER". Similar notices were over all the crosses.

Judith felt utterly powerless to give any comfort except from their shared faith. "The Lord will come to judge. His Love will give us strength. I'm sorry I must leave you now. Go to Chloe's house. They will support you." It must have taken a long and painful walk to get Phoebe to this cross, but Judith was very conscious of the delay in getting Onesimus back to his owner before the accusation of running away was undeniable, even if his master was amenable in believing him, or believing what to Fortunatus would be a strange woman open to being accused of sheltering a runaway.

Having delivered the bread and left instructions to Marcus' household, Judith set off with the young Onesimus. At the entrance to Fortunatus' house the remains of the Roman assault were visible. Dried blood and gore was spattered everywhere and one piece of maggoty flesh had yet to release its plague of flies. "Wait here!" Judith instructed her son.

Upon entry Judith found that there were several female slaves intent on cleaning the mess left doubly by the earthquake and the

232

riotous invasion. Although she knew some owners kept their slaves naked, and she herself had been abused at a slave market, it was still a shock to her to find the female workforce unclothed.

"Is your master at home?" she called to one working group.

"He is not."

"I have Onesimus with me. He could not get to the house last night because of the riot so I kept him safe."

"At long last. We need his mule and his help. We haven't got everyone back yet. They all ran away."

Judith returned to her son with much relief and said farewell once more. At least he would be safe for now. Maybe when Marcus returned, he would buy her precious son into the better conditions of her household.

Chapter 27

The drovers came home having taken the same time as their outward journey, but with the benefit of a journey that was less exertive. The soldiers remained attentive to their task. Jacob had

233

retained two of the containers of wine and offered them to the soldiers in thanks, and for the sake of the camaraderie they had enjoyed. Dusk was well advanced. Farewells said and Marcus' slaves dismissed with their animals, Jacob went indoors to see Judith.

They both had much to say of their experiences but tiredness foreshortened much of their narratives. For all the fear contained in his own story, it was the crucifixion of Phoebe's son that kept Jacob awake. For him it was clear that the Fortunatus and Gaius plot to secure the olive grove was still alive and the riot had presented them with an opportunity to remove or intimidate the family owners. For all the mistrust the Romans must have had for Gaius and Fortunatus, they were pragmatists when it came to keeping the peace, trade and collecting the taxes. They could seldom be trusted to win real justice.

The adrenalin kept him awake long into the night. When he was not thinking about the plot he suspected, his mind was back to his long train of thought on the journey home: the narrative he had to continue that was waiting for him in Chloe's house. That had excited him and built up an anticipation of making progress if only he could get to the writing materials.

234

His mind travelled over the following day's work. He had trades to conduct with the goods he had brought from Thyatira, and his diary for his report to Marcus, listing all the transactions and the money that had changed hands. It gave much input into the parable of the talents and so his mind was back on to the manuscript.

He disciplined himself in prayer and began reciting psalms in his mind, but it served to reactivate him rather than relax him. In the end he made himself picture walking the streets of Jerusalem, every corner and every house he knew, carefully avoiding those parts with such terrible images.

Judith's regular breathing beside him in the dark was a comfort and a joy, and, at last, long into the night he fell asleep.

When he was awoken by Judith rising to begin her day he felt, as expected, jaded from his shortened sleep. He was however, determined to be positive and prayerful about his day. He would be passing crucified men on his way to work but it steeled him to remember the central tenet of his faith: he had a God that raised His Son from the dead after precisely that death. Then he wavered in his

235

confidence. His past record of facing personal danger was not one to inspire hope of heroism.

Leaving Judith and her farm women to the bakery he strode up the hill to the town road. His legs were aching from four days on the road and he had a particularly painful burst blister on his heel. Sure enough, at the top of the hill as he turned to the north gate he could see the crosses. The area was deserted. As he approached he resolved to pass by without looking at the victims as emotional self protection. He held them in prayer. There were very few people in the streets beyond the gate. The town was still licking its wounds both from natural and man made assaults. He hoped the merchants he was about to approach were open for trade, especially for the indigo, since the rewards for a decent sale would reap Marcus a rich reward.

The market square was doing some trade but it was less that usual. He passed the doors of his old employer and the guards ignored him. He wondered that if he had been anywhere in the town that night that Gaius' men would have arraigned him before a judge for riot under false witness. The judge would probably have been Gaius so there would be little doubt as to the verdict. At least the procurator still had the final say on the death sentence but the Romans had little reputation for mercy or even of a stay of execution because there were doubts.

His mind jumped to the crucifixion story in Mark. Was it really the Romans responsible for the death of The Lord? Considering his narrative in anticipation, he did not want his document to provoke Roman revenge because it could appear to be anti Roman and inflammatory. The people of The Way were still under suspicion after the destruction in Rome those two decades or so before.

Then he saw the remains of the Island. He had averted his eyes from the crosses. The rubble before him of his former home was unmissable and he choked back a sob but could not avoid the flow of tears. The tears were not for the building, or of memories of a home that held few pleasurable times. He felt the grief of so many families for so many lost loved ones, most of whom he would have known; and what of Doria? Had she perished?

He had composed himself by the time he reached his first merchant. "Lack of sleep" was his reply when asked about his red eyes. Much of the conversation was the merchant's recollection of the earthquake and the riot. "At least I was not looted like some. Those that

237

got crucified deserve it. It is one good thing to come from the taxes I pay."

"There were some crucified that did not riot. I know at least one."

"They would have had a trial."

"If I had a choice as to whether to believe Gaius or the witness who told me I know who I would believe." Jacob then regretted his comment. He had no idea as to the loyalties of his client. He already had Gaius for an enemy without provoking public alienation.

"You were his scribe weren't you? Well you should know I suppose." Jacob was for once relieved that public corruption was so rife that the comment was seen as a throwaway.

Bartering took place and Jacob was pleased with his trade. "There is a ship due in for Rome today so your shipment should be down at the port today. My men will meet your carriers there this afternoon. Jacob suddenly had another task before he could get to his new manuscript.

As he walked back through the market he had the vantage point again of the port below and the ship mentioned must surely have been that rounding the headland. Jacob detoured to the bottle store to send one of the men to head for the farm where the indigo was stored and arrange its transport to the port. That done, Jacob went on the Chloe's house both to meet again, share the church's experiences of the recent disasters, and to discuss the trade of cloth that he had brought from Thyatira. Maybe then he could return to his priority in faith achievement and continue his manuscript to demonstrate progress to his clergy colleagues at their next meeting.

Once through Chloe's door he could sense anxiety. There was some joy at greeting each other again in that female community but as the conversation progressed there were references to vendettas being waged in the crucifixion of rioters, several of whom were presumed innocent. There was also the hearsay of the women in the market as the quest for scapegoats ranged around to blame for the earthquake itself and what had provoked the gods. The term "Christian" had been heard in a derogatory fashion. "It is an obscenity" someone said, "that they should only have one god."

"How many died at the Island?" Jacob asked.

239

"It looks as if the pile of bricks will remain so we don't know," said Chloe. Many of the men with the inclination to dig have been blamed for the riots and looting, though where they would put their looted goods is a mystery. Those that have not been killed in the streets or crucified are lying low."

"Do you know what happened to Doria?"

"Yes, but you have to keep the secret. Doria and Rebecca are here. No–one knows but that they are under the bricks. They were here when the destruction came. They were praying with us. Let Fortunatus think his prostitute slaves are still under the bricks and he has lost his obscene income. We will hide them here until we can find them a home in another town. We must be careful though or we will all be punished for either assisting slaves to run away or stealing them."

Jacob was trying to get a word in and eventually got his chance. "Who is Rebecca?"

"She is another of these unfortunates that gets abused by men to make money for Fortunatus, or in this case, Gaius. She was put in your old room in the Island. I thought you knew her. She was the one used by Gaius to try to bribe you."

240

Jacob suddenly had the unwanted image of the unfortunate Rebecca's bare backside in his mind, rubbed his eyes and tried to think of another question. Chloe moved him out of that mental room with a question of her own. "Your eyes are red. Have you been crying again?"

"I shed a tear when I thought of all the people I'd known in the Island, including Doria but I did not sleep much last night thinking about the death of at least one of Phoebe and Urbanus' sons. It looks like the plotters still want to build another death trap like the Island. You think they'd learn from what happened to this one."

"They would only think of the money invested in the slaves they lost. I hope they learn from getting hurt by losing a chunk of their god of mammon. They don't think of people except in how much they can make from them in money. They are Satan at work tempting us to be as they are: in comfort and wealth and other people are only there to serve them"

Jacob's mind was already moving to his manuscript in one of the church rooms Chloe had set aside in her house. Chloe's last comment inspired him in the narrative of the temptations to which he was turning his attention when he had his opportunity after their simple

241

midday meal. They were joined by all Chloe's women including Doria and Rebecca. They were now learning the dressmaking skills of the rest of the household until such time as an escape could be arranged to a secure home in another town, hopefully via a connection in the church there, or through a business connection that Marcus might have. Chloe's house was becoming crowded, and even visiting church members had to be kept from knowing about the runaways.

It was late afternoon when Jacob decided to walk down to the port to verify that his traded goods were satisfactorily received. It made a welcome break from writing after making pleasing progress. The tired feeling was catching up on him though after his lack of sleep the night before and he did not wish to make silly errors because of it.

Only a few paces from Chloe's door, however, there was the shrill call of a female voice from behind him. Judith had sent one of Marcus' very young slaves with a message. The breathless girl uttered broken phrases as she caught her breath. "Soldiers …. look for you." Jacob felt much alarmed. "Procurator wants ….. see you." There was some relief but still alarm. This was a new departure for such a senior Roman to see such a lowly non-Roman, but he assumed it was to do with the recent events on the road to Thyatira. Given the other preoccupations of the day, however, he was still worried. "Soldiers wait." The girl swallowed and resumed regular breathing as Jacob did an about turn to head for Marcus' house. It was a considerable walk. He would have to trust the transaction and transfer of goods had taken place that afternoon at the port without him. Such a summons could not be set aside.

He reached Marcus' house to find that it was Sextus and Anthony waiting for him. This time they were in full uniform to escort him. "Relax Joseph. I don't know the bulk of it but there is news of Marcus come with the ship today. The Procurator wishes to talk directly to you."

Jacob was cheered by the news that his friend was making contact, though a little surprising that it was through such senior channels. "I'm sorry to see your old home destroyed" said Anthony. Is there any news of Doria? She was a lovely girl. I was hoping to meet up with her again." Sextus looked over his shoulder and thought better of making an innuendo until he knew the girl was safe.

"She hasn't been found at the ruin yet. It doesn't look hopeful that she will be found now." Jacob kept his eyes ahead as they walked.

243

The conversation ceased for some considerable time. When Jacob glanced at Anthony's face further on, it was set with anger. A few moments later Sextus and Jacob jumped sideways in shock as Anthony roared like a wounded bull. "Why you fucking gods? Why?"

Sextus had seen this behaviour before and realised the immediate danger of irrational action by Anthony. "Attention soldier!" he bawled. "Stand!" Anthony, face still set obeyed his order and jumped to attention. "Right soldier" Sextus spoke as if on a parade, "you will control this. Is that clear?"

"Yes sir."

"This is another piece of shit in your life. We all get plenty of it and we dish plenty out. You will get over it son. Just don't do anything stupid that gets you or the unit into trouble." There was a pause. "Right?"

"Yes sir."

"Right, as you were. We'll move on."

"She was a lovely girl." Anthony swallowed.

244

"She was a slave and a prostitute. You would have to leave her when we go to our next post." Sextus spoke but was hardly tactful, as Jacob thought. The harsh reality was what soldiers seemed to deal in and though it was plumbing the depths of Anthony's feelings, the reality was all he had. The brief time of affection he had with Doria was all he was going to get. Anger was his outlet, but even that had to be controlled.

The rest of the walk to the barracks was entirely in silence. As they escorted Jacob to the Procurator's door, Jacob looked briefly at Anthony and said, "Sorry friend. A lot of good people died that day." Jacob had meant the people in the Island, but then realised that also dying that day were rioters, those that Anthony himself had killed, and the following day those that were executed and hoped that the two were not reading those deaths into his statement. "Thank-you both." Both the soldiers nodded their appreciation and farewell.

Jacob proceeded up the stairs to find two guards at the Procurator's door.

245

"Jacob to see the Procurator. He asked to see me." 'Asked' was a euphemistic word, Jacob thought but it was the least conflictual way of putting it that he could imagine.

"Follow me." One soldier walked to a door and rapped.

"Come!"

"Jacob to see you, Sir."

"Right." At the call, Jacob entered the sparsely furnished room. The procurator remained seated with a stone floor space before his chair. There was no indication that Jacob would be sitting with him.

"I have some tragic news both for you and for me. The ship that your master was on has been found broken up on the shore in Syracuse. No survivors were found. They recovered some of his possessions. I have lost several good friends but that is not your concern." Casca paused to consider his next communication. He did not expect those bidden by him to answer unless ordered to do so. This was no conversation.

246

Jacob was floundering with his feelings. This was the beginning of a traumatic onset of emotion. Marcus his employer, protector and friend had almost certainly drowned.

"There was a great storm that appeared to come out of nothing." Casca paused again. Jacob did not indicate it to Casca but he was praying that Marcus was safe, but still had a mental image of him floating in the ocean.

"Now I know that your master has a family that will inherit his estates. He has a young son and his father will probably look after the boy's interests. He also has a wife, so we will have to wait instructions as to how to proceed. Until we do, I will act as guardian to his property and expect you will be a good steward of his family's interests here. I will expect to report to me occasionally with an audit."

"I might be sensible if you did not tell his household if you want to maintain discipline," Casca went on. "If they think no master is coming back the slaves may think they can take the place over as their own."

247

"I will be honoured to serve his family as I have served my master. It is a terrible loss to me sir, and I am sorry about the loss of your friends."

"Thank-you steward. Jacob is it? While you are here, I received a report from my men on your trade journey to Thyatira. I feel that was success. If only we could identify the dead men we could perhaps chase down their associates. It is a shame we could not take any alive. We have a way of getting the names we need from such captures. You need to be aware that there could be reprisals against Marcus' estate. These criminals have a way of seeking revenge. We will be sending patrols your way on the north side. Hopefully that will deter them. If only they were as easy to hit as rioters. Have you anything to ask before you leave?"

"I have a concern about Gaius, Sir."

"So have I, and I have talked with Marcus on the subject. However he is a lawful authority for the town so I will not discuss him with you. That is all then?" Casca did not expect a reply. It was an effective dismissal.

248

Jacob felt at one remove from his emotions. It was an internal void of depression that could not be expressed in any real way. He passed the guards who gave him hardly a second glance. He walked back the way he had come. He reached the point of Anthony's outburst and felt very much like doing the same thing, but he withheld the anger and the grief. He kept the awful news to himself until his sobbing in bed that night alerted Judith to a problem. Swearing her to secrecy, he at last shared the burden of the news, and they both wept together, Judith's tears wetting his neck, and his wetting her hair. For all their hope of resurrection, the almost certain loss of their employer, friend and guardian left a gaping black hole of uncertainty in their lives.

Chapter 28

The bireme made good progress and its arrival in Athens was well ahead of expectations. There was a planned stay of hours while Gallus had his meeting and transferred documents and received reports for onward delivery to Rome. Marcus left the ship leaving a hive of activity as rowers and supplies were leaving or arriving.

249

"I have time to visit the Acropolis do I?" Marcus asked Gallus as the baking heat of the land warmed their feet a few paces after they stepped ashore.

"Yes. I should be a while and the rowers need a rest. Don't worry. I won't leave without you." Gallus stopped to let his companions join him along with the documents he had to present. Marcus walked on for the three miles or so from the port. It was his intention to visit the altar of the Unknown God, not just as a pretext to cover his commitment to The Way, but he had heard a story of Paul's visit whether apocryphal or not.

The last time Marcus had visited Athens he had been with Quintus so there was chance to reminisce. He walked briskly despite the heat. This, after all, was but a brief stay. At the start to the climb to the ancient temples on the mount, he was squinting from the brilliance of the white stones in the sunlight. He resolved to climb briskly and became somewhat aware that he was not a fit young soldier any more. He intended to see Athene's image before he left, because of its artistic brilliance. However he made his visit to the altar of the Unknown God a priority of this opportune pilgrimage.

250

In the courtyards at the top of the steps there were several groups in twos or threes about their business or worship. He felt as if he was the only solitary person in this area and felt the pang of loneliness for the friend with whom he shared this scenery on his previous visit.

He found the altar, and stood silently in the shade afforded, seeking to clear his mind of lesser preoccupations and give himself to the true God in this panoply of false ones including those that infected his own mind and inclinations. He was tired from a poor sleep on the ship. Its motion and his sense of nausea had just stopped short of sea sickness. He was also preoccupied with the family circumstances he might find in Rome. Together they made his task of praying very difficult.

The shuffling of a shoe on the stone paving behind him indicated he was not alone. His soldier's training made him feel uncomfortable when he could not see others about him in strange circumstances. He turned and walked back to be level with the new arrival and matched his posture facing the altar. The silence continued for some time and Marcus was gaining some purchase on his prayer life when the sound of the shuffling sandal restarted. His fellow worshipper either had a disability or he wanted attention. Marcus moved

251

sufficiently to look at the moving foot. There was a moment of recognition as he saw the foot describing the shape of a fish. The foot stopped moving. This was either a trap or this was a fellow worshipper committed to The Way. Since his fellow worshipper was alone, Marcus felt confident in declaring himself. "Jesus Christ Son of God and Saviour," he said, worshipping, and with a great measure of joy in his heart.

"Amen! Amen!" said his companion with equal enthusiasm.

The ice was broken. Marcus took the initiative and spoke. "I am Marcus. I love The Lord, but I am not yet baptised. I am here only for a few moments before sailing again. Are you from the church here?"

"Yes. I am Phineas. One of us comes here every day. Many of The Way heard that Paul came here and come to worship and seek this place out. We offer them fellowship and maybe help communication between the churches. Can we offer you hospitality?"

Marcus was immediately torn. He thought of the bireme waiting for him and this wonderful opportunity to experience another group of worshippers in another community. "I would love to but I

252

have a ship waiting for me. If I miss it I have no certainty as to finding another to take me to Rome. I am Marcus." They greeted with a kiss. "My Bishop is Onesimus."

"So sad you cannot stay. I would love to hear of Onesimus again. We wish you a safe journey."

Marcus was still going through the motions in his mind and prayer as to his next decision. He could at least delay the depressing conflicts he was expecting at the end of his journey, and fortify himself further for them. "I could stay but I need to get back to the ship and pick up my things. I have some of our writings to deliver by hand to the church in Rome. Our scribe has been very active, and we are recording more of the Lord's known sayings."

"How wonderful. I have a servant waiting at the base of the steps, or at least he should be there by the time we reach them after his errands. He will come with you, help you with your things and bring you to my house." They returned to the baking pavements and the glare of the sun on the white stonework and carvings.

Marcus was staggered anew by the magnificence of the buildings and statues around him and made appreciative noises.

253

Phineas heard the sound uttered. "God the Father is Creator and he made us in his image to be creative. This might all be to imagined gods, but it takes nothing from the creativity of The Lord in his children, even in their ignorance."

"So true! I still have a statue of Pan in my entrance porch at home to the disgust of my housekeeper. It is such a tribute to the skill of the carver." They began their descent.

"You can see my house from here."

"It is a wonderful view."

"Is it more impressive than Rome?"

"They are both uniquely impressive. It is not the architecture but the people that truly make the city it is. I think I would prefer Athens. All in all though, I prefer a community where it is possible to know everyone, including the slaves. I know then who I am meant to deal with to make the place as I would like it to be."

There was a pause as they negotiated more steps. "I pray that is also how The Lord wants the place to be."

254

"We are building the Kingdom of The Lord in big and small places. We are meeting some resistance though. It is why we are keeping our meetings secret now." Phineas the older man was getting breathless and stopped to catch his breath. Marcus paused with him. "We have heard rumours that some of the brethren along the coast from you have been tortured either to find out what we do together in worship and practise, or to make them confess to what they want everyone to believe we do."

Marcus set his mouth in an angry line. The growing hate of his life was abuse of power in any form, and torture ranked highly in that abuse. "It just shows how much of a threat our faith is to those in authority." The aggression that built up in him at this reported injustice caused him to descend the steps more vigorously. He had not realised and when he did, had to pause for some time for his new friend to catch up.

"I'm sorry. Your news upset me. I forgot myself." His apology actually meant he had forgotten Phineas, but the latter was unflustered.

"I understand perfectly. I cannot see my man yet. No. Wait. I see him coming over there." Phineas gave a wave, his arm high over his

255

head. At the base of the steps the young man jogged to their position. "This is," Phineas paused as he remembered the name of his new acquaintance, "Marcus. He has things to bring from the port. Go with him, carry his things and bring him home. I'll take these." Phineas took the small bag of market acquisitions. Thank-you Agapito. See you later brothers."

Agapito was a slender lad of around sixteen years old. He was looking at Marcus with an open smile. Marcus was reminded of a playful puppy wishing to please anyone and everyone. In his bleached cloth garment he was hard to look at for any length in the sunlight.

"Right Agapito," Marcus said a few paces into the walk, I assume with that name you are a member of the Church here.

"I chose that name when I was baptised. I loved the feast. To have the care and generosity of everyone made me know I was loved and I never forgot. It was the first time I ever remember not being hungry. The Lord comes to us in the kindness of His servants. That is when I really believed: when I knew what it was to have a full belly." Agapito talked non-stop with utter conviction. Marcus knew he would have little problem filling silences on this walk. He was setting a forced march pace, still working off his anger at the thought the abuse of power and of the innocent faithful being tortured. The lad was almost trotting beside him, becoming breathless as he chattered. He was telling his life story, but for such a young life there were a lot of words in rapid succession. He was a slave. He was harshly treated and abused. No, he didn't know who his mother was. He was eventually bought by Phineas and taken to the worship the same day where he was fed. The worship meant very little to him. The food did. That was two or three years ago.

The rapid fire words suddenly ceased. Marcus caught up mentally and realised the lad had asked him equally rapid fire questions. "I am on my way to Rome to see my family after several years. I became a follower of Christ because a slave of mine was such a wonderful example of living I became curious. I was also utterly cynical about the gods of wood and stone. No I am not baptised yet but I hope to be when the Passover comes. I might actually miss it if I do not get back home in time. I have a vineyard there. I have a very good steward who is running things for me." "Yes, he is a follower of the Way as well. He is a Deacon."

257

The miles were getting eaten up, even walking into the welcome breeze; half of which they created themselves. They were soon at the port.

Gallus had not yet returned but Marcus explained himself to the senior soldier supervising a deck squad. His collected one or two items from his possessions were and left a message left for Gallus. Marcus hoped to meet up with him in Rome and he relayed his gratitude. Please would he see that his wooden chest was delivered to his father's house?

Marcus had kept his old soldier's pole and the cloak and bags that attached. In addition he had the light wooden box containing the documents for the church in Rome. That fitted on Agapito's shoulder and after a drink of water they had a more leisurely walk back in what was now a more humid and hazy sunshine. Marcus had mixed feelings. He now had the uncertainty of finding another ship bound for Rome but was looking forward to new company and sharing the news from his church. Since it had a new document emerging of great significance to the church everywhere, Marcus was full of enthusiasm in anticipation of the evening's conversation.

"What name are you choosing to take at your baptism?" As his thoughts played out, he had lost track of Agapito's word bombardment. "Agapito repeated himself. "I chose Agapito at my baptism. What name are you choosing?"

Marcus was struck by the fact that he had not really put much thought to it. Jesus had changed several of his disciples' names when they followed him. "I think maybe Matthew. I was once a soldier entrusted with guarding the revenues bound for Rome. Now I am guarding some things more precious on the way to Rome: Jesus' Word in these manuscripts. I only wish my friend Jacob had finished his work. Maybe I will undertake to take that to Rome one day."

Marcus was met at the door by Phineas, who must have been looking out for him. "Come in my brother. I'm sure you are ready to sit down. It is all very well for these young men and their energy." His final comment was with a smile for Agapito. "Marcus, I have taken the liberty of inviting some of the church to meet you this evening. Do you wish to rest before then?"

"You are very kind to a stranger sir. Thank-you. I would love to meet members of the church. It is why I stayed in Athens." Marcus was shown to a room where he could sleep in a shaded if slightly airless room. After the broken sleep of the night, he was soon able to doze.

He was awoken by the smell of cooking food. This was welcome after having only the memory of salt spray and ozone in his nostrils and he realised just how hungry he was after the soldier cold rations he was afforded that morning. He moved from his room into the living area of the house where Phineas was standing holding a cup of wine.

"Wine my friend?"

"Thank-you"

"You can tell me your views on it. Agapito tells me you grow wine yourself." Phineas poured a cup of golden coloured white wine and Marcus put the cup under his nose. It was not as he expected and smelt resin. He tasted it.

"It this wine right for you?"

"It is a local wine. Maybe you don't know it. It has a distinct flavour from the resin we use here to seal the bottles. Maybe it is an acquired taste. Most of us drink it here. Tell us about your grapes."

"I grow reds that bring about a robust wine, much stronger than the local wines I remember in Rome. This is very distinctively different. I smell garlic in the air for our meal. Is the wine to take the flavour of the garlic away or the garlic to take the taste of the wine away?" Marcus had a mischievous twinkle in his eye and Phineas laughed heartily.

"What do you do Phineas?"

"I am a teacher of children. I teach them reading and writing skills. I used to be an athlete as well when I was young enough to compete. Some of the older generation remember my successes. I still coach young men in throwing the discus and the spear. I think young Agapito will do well at our games this year. I hear my guests arriving."

There was a tramping of several people approaching from the street and their chatter as they drew close. Marcus was introduced to some dozen men and each was offered wine by their host.

261

"I think there will be a storm," said one. The weather was then a topic of conversation for some time as speculation ranged as to the weather to come. Several farmers in the group wanted rain. Phineas noted that whatever the weather, farmers wanted something else, and a good-willed discussion to place on that opinion. The conversation was becoming oiled by the wine.

A lull in the conversation led one of the group to ask Marcus to introduce himself and to tell them about the church he came from. Marcus was only too pleased to talk about Onesimus, "who had been heard of by many churches," they said.

"He has a collection of Paul's letters he is building up." The reaction to Marcus' news was greeted with enthusiasm.

"We must have them copied."

"Phineas remembers Paul staying in Athens," said another. Marcus appreciated the confirmation that Paul's visit was not just apocryphal. Most churches would want to lay claim to influence or contact with one of the Apostles, he thought. It seems that in the doctrinal arguments that ensued, a reference to one of the earlier

262

generation of disciples seemed to lend weight to the views expressed, regardless of the reasoning of the saying.

Marcus was asked about his past and he outlined his military career, his retirement and his eventual move to his vineyard. He also spent some time rehearsing the interest and eventual commitment to The Way before describing his present church and its clergy.

Marcus was much impressed with the food. This was a sort of lamb dish with aubergines and cheese, heavily flavoured with garlic.

There was much interest in Jacob and the new document he was working on. He also described some of the documents he was carrying, including three of Paul's letters as copied by Jacob. There was an acclamation that they should be read to them, and the rest of the evening was devoted to their reading. Given that Paul had been worrying about the failures in the churches to which he was writing there was a discussion lasting long into the night about the failures of the church then and in the present. At last tiredness prevailed despite the enthusiasm and farewells were expressed.

As they were praying together as the group began its farewells they heard rain gushing outside. There was a clap of thunder and they

263

were conscious of a wind. "You may be seeing me tomorrow as well if I cannot find a passage home," he said.

The rain filled wind was in the faces of the departing guests as they made their way down the street, and Marcus was quietly pleased that he was not trying to sleep on the bireme that night. He quietly held his former shipmates in his prayers. They would be having a rough experience.

It was clear by the following day that no ships would be leaving the harbour in the morning, but Agapito, having been sent to enquire identified one ship that would be sailing for Rome when fair conditions allowed. With dampness in the air but reasonable confidence that the worst of the weather was past, Marcus himself walked to the harbour in the late afternoon to try to obtain passage. His carrier had come from Joppa and had put into the port ahead of the storm. There would be little comfort for him amongst the cargo of cedar wood. "The wind will not be favourable and the sea is too high," he was told by the ship's master. "We might make a start by first light. Be here then because we are already delayed by two days."

Marcus glowed at the success of the previous evening, but he was now resolved to face the family conflicts in Rome. For the first time he was impatient to do so. Much as he loved his life around his vineyard, estates and the church he was now increasingly aware as to its superficiality without the resolution of his long term division with his father and the growing rift with his wife. At the heart of the two was his son whom he last saw as a three-year old. With whatever he left Rome at the end of this trip, as after the storm just past, the air would be clear.

He returned to the altar of the Unknown God in the hope of a clearer strategy in his mind. The word strategy occurred to him and began military campaign imagery in his mind. In a military campaign there would be some intelligence of the enemy's disposition and motivation, their position, equipment, training and numbers. He would have lost one of the few advantages: that of surprise in that Gallus would no doubt have broken the news of his imminent visit.

The goodwill of his previous night served to build up optimism. He had very little hope of reconciling himself to his father, but at least he may find an accommodation or even an alliance by ceding paternity to this coming child and regain at least equanimity from his wife.

How would his faith help in this maze of mismatched relationships? His mind ranged back through some of the arguments with Octavia, several ending with her attacking him physically. They were not threats in any real sense. They were the wild flapping hands of a woman striking at his face or chest. Their only pain was the confirmation they gave of his desolation in what should be his closest social and family comfort: a loving wife.

Was it her fault? The lesson of the faith was to seek the best of the other, to forgive and identify ones own sin. Was her alienation really her frustration that she would never be an Emperor's wife because he was not a plotter or politically motivated like his father? Or was it that she could not find the closeness that he also lacked in a partner? He had dreamed of a close relationship with her, but the idealistic goodwill somehow ran into the sand.

Marcus remembered Livius his son. He was a toddler playfully climbing over his chest and trying to hide inside his toga. There were infant giggles. It was his son, he thought, because his

266

almost bald infant head had the shape of his bald ageing uncle, his mother's brother. The child's lips, pursed for a kiss had the same shape as his late mother's.

Oh yes! He thought of his late mother. Marcus came back from the frontier of the empire to find she had died months earlier. He had never removed the doubts in his mind that there had been foul play. His father would, whatever the cause of death, have wanted a new relationship, but was his mother's death really to make way for a new dynastic alliance. He returned from his next military posing to find his father widowed again. There had been no new step-mother since then. Maybe Roman families were not prepared to put their daughters at risk with such an unlucky future husband. Still, the old man always had his slave girls to molest. He had heard the squeals from remote parts of the villa.

He remembered Gallus' suggestion that he might be made Magistrate in Gaius' place. Would that give Octavia sufficient standing in a community to satisfy her ego even if it took her away from her social circles in Rome? Much as he wanted to influence his son's life, he could not take Livius away from his mother. He had enough issues

267

with his own father without developing the same dysfunction in another generation, if the dysfunction was not there already.

And what of this other child? Would Octavia want to get out of Rome to avoid the gossip? Would she be utterly hostile to seeing him or would she want forgiveness for the sake of security in her future. After all, the old man would not live for ever to keep her protected.

After losing track of the time he had been standing before the altar Marcus realised there were just too many unknowns for any strategy. He resolved to see the circumstances that met him in Rome and prayed that The Lord would guide his words and actions.

As he sighed and relaxed (he had not realised how tense he had become) he heard a familiar shuffle behind him. On turning he laughed with recognition when he saw Phineas again. "The man who walks on fish," he said, and they both laughed.

Chapter 29

As Marcus, relieved at last to be stepping ashore in the port of Ostia, looked around him and realised just how severe the storm must have been given the pieces of wood and jettisoned cargo in the water both inside and outside the harbour. He was thankful that he did not have his chest to worry about as he put his soldier's pole over his shoulder with his bags. "At least, he thought to himself," as he recalled the years of performing this action, "I am not carrying a shield, helmet and sword." The box of documents was light in comparison. His clothes smelt of resin and sawdust from his journey and he was tired again from lack of sleep from a choppy voyage. He had been largely ignored by the crew so he felt ready to talk to anyone going his way. There were no walkers, only slaves carrying goods or leading beasts of burden. He chose again to walk after the enforced passivity on his voyage.

After an hour of walking, meeting the traffic on the way from Rome to the port, he eventually caught up with a cart carrying corn. After hailing the drover he negotiated a ride. "That must have been a bad storm you had?" he asked, once sitting alongside. Pools of water by the side of the road testified to the downpour.

"Aye!" The drover had a speech impediment that made understanding him difficult. Marcus wondered if he had had his tongue cut out at some stage in his life. He did catch words about wrecks, but

269

no details. Laborious progress even on the well made road meant that it was late afternoon before they were on the outskirts of the city. There was a parting of the ways. Marcus jumped down and found his coins. The drover nodded his appreciation. He had gained spending power for no extra effort on his part.

Marcus had to walk through the centre of the city to find his home, adjacent to his father's villa. There were enormous building projects in progress. Slaves were active on the half built wall and supplies were en route or empty supply vehicles were leaving them. The early evening activity was increasing after the traditional quiet afternoon. There was still a coolness to the air and dampness to the masonry. The building work was not exuding the dust that would normally accompany it. Marcus continued his walk, moving into the less elaborate imperial buildings until he came towards his own street. There were few people around but on the open sweep of the climb he could see the end of his road from some distance.

There was a boy sitting on a wall that would have given him a great perspective down the road Marcus was climbing. The child had his knees to his face and his arms wrapped around his shins and he was immobile for the whole time Marcus was approaching. As he walked

270

up, the lad raised his face to see who was approaching. From the red eyes and the runny nose he had clearly been weeping. He rubbed his nose on his sleeve.

"Are you alright young man?" Marcus had a kindly but chirpy tone.

"I come here every day to look out for my father."

"Well he should be home soon. The work in the city is nearly over."

"No he doesn't work in the city. He is over the sea. He will never come back." The boys face creased into tears and he struggled to get his next sentence out. "They found his chest on the shore. They say he drowned."

Marcus had a lump in his throat. "Livius." The lad's face moved to look at the speaker who knew his name. Recognition dawned. He swung his knees round from the wall and squealed "Daddy!" and clasped his arms around Marcus' waist, burying his head in his father's stomach. Marcus could not return the affection with his arms committed to his possessions.

271

"You remember me?"

"I remember you leaving. I remember you turning and waving to me when I was in Mama's arms, and when we went back into the house someone said, 'I wonder if we will see him again?' It is the only memory. When I'm unhappy I come here to look out for you coming back."

"You are unhappy?"

"I was because you were dead, but now you are here. I must tell Mama."

"I think I should tell Mama, son. Where is granddad?" The lad turned from his trot. He had joy to share.

"I think he is in the city." The eight year old was jumping like a puppy eager to show the stick he had fetched.

"Daddy, are you home for ever and ever?"

"I wish I could be with you for ever but I have a vineyard that makes you your wealth for the future." Marcus would have liked to say he wanted Livius to come and see it but that might raise the thorny problem of taking him away from his mother. He choked back the words. They passed his father's villa, his childhood home: it brought back a feeling of a compost heap where things once vibrant now rotted. A few more paces brought them to their home's entrance, but Marcus was skating around the title of "home" for it. Little had changed. It was always a temporary place to live. When he was not on campaigns or stationed in far off places he was awaiting his next posting. Only for an all too brief period of intense domestic conflict was he there for any time before decisively heading for his life's dream of working a vineyard. How did he come by his vineyard? It all seemed so long ago now. Oh yes! It was there for sale after one of his soldier friend's uncles died. He remembered passing through there once and loved the landscape and the peace between the sea and the distant hills. He now had an established home and an estate, not just a dream to which to take a family if they wished to join him. The atmosphere of their last parting five years ago did not give him any optimism.

He walked through the portals and towards a smell of cooking food. There were chattering women. Octavia had retained old Fulvia in the house. Marcus thought of her as old since she had been in his parent's household since he was a child. She must have been his father's age. He walked into the room, sunlight behind him.

273

"Hello Max! You are early." Octavia spoke on instinct as the shape blocked the light.

"Mama it's not Granddad." Livius giggled.

Octavia turned. There was recognition. Then she took a sharp intake of breath that stifled a scream. She shrank back and had a distinct expression of fear.

"Daddy didn't die."

"Hello wife. You must have been eating too much of that bread by the look of you."

Octavia appeared to be gasping. Her arms lifted from the elbows two or three times giving the appearance of a dying bee utterly confounded by the glass in front of it. Marcus had to be decisive in the face of such surrender. He walked the four paces to his wife and held his arms around her shoulders, Octavia's head rested on his chest. There was so resistance to the affection. Livius joined his parents at their side, his arms reaching as far round their waists as he could reach.

274

"I'll finish this." Fulvia's voice gave permission for the re-united family to withdraw from the activity of the food preparation area.

They held their positions for some seconds, Marcus becoming aware of his wife's distended belly against the base of his.

"How long do you think you have before the birth?"

"Maybe another six weeks." Octavia jumped back as if she had been stung. "What happened to you?"

"I don't know what you think happened but I just landed on a ship from Athens."

"Your box was washed up. The ship you were on was wrecked on Goat Island. There were no survivors."

"Oh! No! Gallus."

"I hear they found a box of his papers when they found your stuff."

"I need to talk to you about this." Without even shifting his eyes downwards it was clear to Octavia what he meant. Marcus turned to leave. He lifted Livius and sat him on his arm. He was a big boy but his weight was no problem. "Livius my dear son, please can you help Fulvia. Mama and I have to talk." He kissed his cheek. Livius' pout showed he was disappointed but obeyed when Marcus put him down. A slight burnished glint from the shoulder of Fulvia's dress caught Marcus' eye. There was a bronze clasp in the shape of a fish.

"Right Master Livius. We have to take the stones out of these olives." Fulvia was well aware of the likely issues to be addressed by Marcus.

Marcus moved to the atrium and into the sunshine. "I need a drink. Have we any wine?"

"It is a new vintage your father got. I'll bring some." Octavia almost trotted. Within a minute she returned. Marcus had been noting how little had changed in his house.

"Thank-you. And you didn't use lead cups."

"I don't. And neither does your father now. He agrees that it leaves a metal taste."

"My father agrees with me for once?" Marcus sat down on a stone bench. Octavia sat with him at an arms length.

"You misjudge your father. He sobbed his heart out when he heard you drowned. He sobbed again and again. Today is the first day he has been out of his house."

"Did you sob?"

"I have been trying to be strong for everyone. Yes I did sob. Don't bring the bad times back."

"Is this a bad time? Is he the father of this?" Marcus nodded at her belly.

"He is saving my face and yours. No he is not, but he is pleased with the rumour."

"How is this 'saving face'? You are carrying a child that cannot possibly be mine. I could boast but I don't have manhood that reaches here from the other side of Greece." Marcus' voice was gaining in volume.

"I am at your mercy Marcus. I am so sorry." For the first time Marcus looked her in the eye. She really did appear contrite. There was a tear welling and she wiped it away. Marcus was expecting manipulation and histrionics, but this seemed sincere. All of his recent worship and prayer seemed in conflict with his gut feelings of betrayal.

"I have been faithful to you. I cannot prove it. It is women that get caught out." There was a pause. Marcus sipped. "So who is the father?"

"It is my fault." Octavia was computing words in her mind to confess. There did not seem any that reduced her sense of wrongdoing.

Before she could find the words Marcus said, "Not on your own you weren't."

"I am really. I abused a slave. There was a boy your father bought. He was innocent. You had been away for so long. I missed being with a man. I used to taunt this boy and flirt with him. It was like I could not help myself. He came to my bed and I used him. His seed came before I was pleasured. I feel so humiliated now. When I found out I was with child, I told your father. He went quiet for days but then told me he was selling this boy. He said we could not have the slaves fathering our family and laughing. The boy does not know it was him. He does not even know I am with child. He is somewhere in the north now."

"Your father spends all his time with Fulvia now. It started not long after you left. She is still a slave but she may as well be his wife. She may as well be Livi's grandma as well. She is wonderful with him."

"You've all changed. You were after big social occasions and nagging and trying to promote me. Fulvia was a sullen dark cloud in any room despite the care she gave me. Father was an ill tempered ruptured ox who blew up at the least frustration. Now you tell me he actually wept. Even for my death that's unbelievable. I might have thought this was a manipulating scheme of yours except you thought I was dead." As Marcus talked, Octavia was drawing breath to reply at the earliest chance.

She had tears in her eyes. She spoke quickly. "I thought that was my role to get you promoted. When our fathers arranged all this I came to do my duty and I thought that was what you all wanted. I always felt a failure and tried harder. Now I see we were going in opposite directions." The sobs started. "I thought I was doing the right things for you. I always tried to look my best. I tried my hardest to impress your father's friends for you." Octavia sighed her tears with the occasional quivering breath. Marcus looked at the floor. Had he misjudged her by such a margin all this time?

When Octavia spoke again her voice was slightly more self assured. "I felt so gifted and honoured by the gods when I was given you in marriage. Where did I go wrong?" The question was real: not rhetorical like a personal admonition. Marcus realised this after a silence and he looked up to see her penetrating eyes under a furrowed brow.

"I'm not sure you were. I think we were both misunderstanding where the other was. You are a daughter of Rome and its expectations. I came back from army life and hadn't found my new life path yet. I have found a happy place now, but I miss you and Livius."

280

"I thought it was because you loved Quintus and rejected me because I could not do what he did."

"I shouldn't have told you."

"I felt like I couldn't compete. He used to fight alongside you and he was made up in your mind as perfect: and he was dead so there was no way for me to reach his place with the gods. And there was that other thing."

"You don't have to bring it up again. I know what you are going to say."

"How was I supposed to compete with a dead man?" The conversation went no further because Livius chimed from behind them,

"Can I show Daddy my writing?"

Marcus resisted the temptation to dismiss his son again. He had too many memories of his own impatient father sending him away when he wanted to impress and be accepted. "I would love to see your writing Livius. Go and bring it." Then to his wife, "Why is Fulvia looking happy then? The last time she smiled was when Caligula died."

281

"You have to keep a secret. Your father forbids us to talk about it. She has become a follower of Jesus, one of the Jewish sects. They can be accused of treason if they do not swear oaths to the Emperor. Domitian now signs himself 'Lord and God.' The Jews can only call their God a god, and the Christians will only call Jesus their Lord. Most people say they are atheists."

"Christians? Is that what they are calling his followers?"

"Yes. But Fulvia had been very changed since she started worshipping with them. She has become quite lovely. It's like there is a peace with her and she brings it to the house. Your father is almost peaceful when he is with her instead of his old grumpy self. Nothing is too much trouble. She loves her work. I am thinking of going with her one day."

"I'm glad you think like that. I have a slave like that. She is called Judith." Marcus thought for a moment. "She is not my slave any more though because I gave her freedom and she is married to my steward now. I left the wedding feast to come here."

"Your steward is not a slave?"

282

"No. He was the scribe for the magistrate but I made him a better offer. Where do the Christians worship?"

"I don't know now. They keep it to themselves for obvious reasons. Some of them have been tortured and crucified. Judging by the dust on Fulvia's dress one Sunday I think she had been underground."

The sound of a child's sandals running on the stone heralded Livius coming with his exhibition of writing.

"Papa look I have been learning Greek."

"That is wonderful Livius. You are a clever boy. I have a steward who knows Greek, Latin, Aramaic and Hebrew."

"What is Hebrew?"

"It is the old language the Jews used to speak hundreds of years ago. Their religious books are written in it."

"Can you write Greek Daddy?"

283

"Greek is what I have to speak and write all the time where I live. It is strange talking in Latin again really after all this time. Now let me see what you've written. It is the story about a king. That is a big word. What is he called?"

"Agamemnon.

"Brilliant!"

"Can I leave you together?" Octavia was concerned to see the food was ready.

"Yes of course. I haven't really eaten since I was in Athens what with the rough seas and the maggots in the food. I really need to wash as well. I stink of wood dust and resin. I hope I have some clothes left here."

"Of course you have. I never gave up hope you would wear them again." There was reproof in Octavia's tone, but Livius did not pick it up. He was sitting beside his father, head on his elbow and arm as far round his waist as he could reach, waiting for more affirmation.

"You smell funny Daddy."

"I was on a ship full of wood and dust. I had to sleep with the rats. I think one has just come out of my clothes." Marcus tickled his son. The boy giggled. "If I smell funny I should get a wash and wash all the rats in my clothes as well. Mama and Grandpa won't want a smelly man at their meal either." Livius saw the necessity of being separated from his father again albeit briefly but still looked disappointed. Marcus kissed him on the head and stood up.

Feeling much more relaxed and clean Marcus wandered the rooms of his house feeling strangely remote from his possessions, as if they were from another life. He was still full of foreboding about another meeting with his father, despite news of his tears. Would he have been told that his son had turned up or would he get the shock that Octavia had?

Marcus walked into the atrium just as his father entered from the street. Livius had been watching out, eager to be the first to break the news. He was doing the excited puppy act again. It reminded Marcus of just how different his own childhood had been relating to his father. He could never have been so happy around his father's feet. He looked into his face. The old man had grown more lines into his skin and he had put on a little weight, but there was a more benign and

285

softer expression from any he had remembered. For once there appeared to be uncertainty where Marcus remembered tyranny. They looked at each other across the room, both a little uncertain. Marcus moved first.

"Give me a hug you miserable old so-and-so."

"What happened to you?" Maximus had a crack in his voice as he spoke but an inch from his son's ear as he held him, just a little woodenly as Marcus thought.

"I was on a different ship. I stayed over in Athens on the way."

"I just paid off your vineyard debts. I was arranging a passage to go over to see to your estate. You did well in getting so much of it paid for."

"Thanks Father." Marcus held back on saying that this was possibly the first praise he could remember hearing from him. As they withdrew from the hug Marcus picked up the half drunk wine cup from earlier. "You found a good vintage here: nearly as good as mine." Maximus smiled. There was a slightly embarrassing silence.

286

"Are you going to use that passage? I would love you to come and see how I've done, especially as you are now the part-owner."

"I'm getting too old for this sort of travel really. I just had to settle things for Livius when I thought you were not able to. I was worried for his future if anything happened to me. I feel these days I am too old for anything. I'm utterly weary of the senate bickering. It is like a yard full of geese. In any case, how do we manage to reason with a god? You can't say that to anyone though or you'd be on a treason charge."

"I hope you can stay with us for a while." Maximus' affection was wrong footing for Marcus. He was expecting abrasiveness and criticism.

"A few days I hope. We need to sort some things out don't we? You are going to be a grandfather again and I need to talk through things with my new business partner. I don't want to leave it too long before getting back. There are threats from a couple of schemers back home. I would trust my steward but I don't trust the law enforcers including his former boss. Besides, there are robbers around that attacked my last wine shipment. I want to get home and see how the latest one went."

"And I've just thought that if the word has got back that I have drowned it leaves my steward a bit vulnerable. I was at least able to influence the Roman cohort a bit in the face of the rats in the shadows. At the same time I should be here for the birth. I found out about that from Gallus, but he must have got it from gossip. The gossip was either complimentary about you or scandalous: depends which way you look at it."

"Octavia has told me all about it. I get whispers behind my back but rather that than knives. They have plenty of gossip but little else. They know nothing but wish they didn't. Octavia hasn't been out for months so the subject is a bit forgotten."

"I wondered about taking her back with me if she will go. That means Livi goes as well. How will you cope?"

Maximus looked pained for a moment. Marcus read his thoughts. "We will visit regularly."

"I have long ago stopped thinking I can influence your decisions." There was a barb in the tone. "I would have hoped Livius would get a good education here."

"If he comes back with me I have a steward who is a scribe with four languages. He will be speaking Greek fluently to the natives in months. There is no better way to learn than in childhood."

"What does Octavia think?"

"I haven't asked her yet."

"Asked? Is the Roman citizen using his authority then?"

"Who is going to claim paternity for this child? It would remove the scandal from your doorstep and a bad smell from you. I think you could endure a few months at a time without us. You have your friends and your politics. I could be here in a week if you send a message. In any case, you were always so busy you wouldn't see much of us anyway."

"It was always wonderful to come home to you."

"How can you say that? I lived in fear of you coming home"

"I always wanted the best for you."

"You wanted to live your life through me. You wanted to create me in your own image." Marcus inadvertently used Jewish scripture. Maximus was not familiar with it.

"You two are just like each other." Octavia came in on the conversation and sensed the building tension. Marcus resented the inference. Octavia was ahead of his reply. "Yes you are. Both bull headed: aggressive first and thoughtful later, usually with regrets. And yes I will come with you if you want that. I overheard you. Not because of my baby. You are different now. I don't know what it is, but I used to be frightened of being with you once but I am not now. I feared you being utterly outraged but there is something new about you."

"Maybe there is something new. I might be able to think what it is if my brain and belly get fed."

"Yes the meal is ready." They trooped through to the dining area. Fulvia was already serving plates.

"I want Fulvia to eat with us." Octavia and Maximus spun to look at Marcus as if they had misheard.

"What are you thinking of?" Maximus raised his voice.

"This is still my house. I want Fulvia to be my guest. She is your slave if you want to dismiss her." Livius sitting in a corner was aware of a new departure. Fulvia was silent but anxious, looking from one to the other of the adults in the room. "Let me help you serve, Fulvia."

Maximus was raging internally at the breach of protocol and remained standing. "Please sit there Father."

"This is outrageous."

"No it is not. Fulvia has been in our family for as long as I remember. She was the only affection I knew when I was a boy." Fulvia had tears welling in her wrinkle lined eyes.

"I know my place master Marcus. Please don't do this."

"We should all know our place. In my view those who serve best should take the highest place."

"What has come over you?" Octavia's tone was pleading. She was embarrassed.

291

"Now sit there you old volcano." Marcus pushed a plate into his father's hands. "Fulvia you sit with him." A second plate was handed to her. "Livi, come and get you plate please." He came forward and obeyed without a word. Octavia was standing slightly open mouthed and received her plate without comment. She sat.

Marcus took up his own plate and, still standing spoke in prayer. "Knowing our place before the one true Lord and God we give thanks for his gifts and His calling to serve each other. Amen." He looked round the room at the awestruck and confused company. "I am now what you are beginning to call Christian. Now let us eat."

Maximus was showing all the signs of deciding whether or not to leave. He had not touched his food when Marcus was two mouthfuls into his.

"We know when cats are friends or family when they can eat together without snarling."

"Marcus you are being tactless. Stop trying to humiliate us." Octavia's tone was pleading again.

Marcus chewed and eventually swallowed. "I am sorry if you think I am trying to humiliate you. I am not. I want us to be at one with one another without anyone pulling rank or standing on their pride. I love everyone in here, and God' loves us all."

Maximus at last took a mouthful. Fulvia watched and then took her first. Livius was eating with gusto and innocence. There was a lull for a while as everyone ate. It was still uneasy.

"They say that Christians are cannibals."

"That is rubbish and they probably know that when they say it. They are frightened of accepting that we are all born naked and have death rationed one each as well. They are only protecting their self interest. Most of the sayings of Jesus are about wealth and its misuse, not about eating flesh. And anyway, they don't eat flesh: they eat bread as they remember Jesus and His last supper with the disciples."

"The problem is not what is really happening, but what people want to believe is happening. I don't want you accused of treason." Silence ensued again. "I am already under a cloud. The Emperor is making adultery a crime and the tongues are wagging."

293

"Why do you think I came here right now? I had intended to come back later this year but the word got back to me from the military about your grandchild. I think the news was carried by Casca, but Gallus was the one that told me about it. Yes I will name the child as mine before either of you are forced into the embarrassing question."

"I'm finished Mama."

"Well done Livi. Please stay with us like a big boy."

"When is this ship going my way?"

"I have a friend that owns an empty grain ship turning round in about a week. It is going round the coast to Egypt. It has to call various ports on the way I'm told. I'm glad I'm not going now. It was bad enough having to deal with your death but I get seasick in the street standing in dog piss."

Marcus turned to Octavia. "How quickly can you be ready to follow me? You don't want to be giving birth on a ship."

"I don't know. This is all new to me. Can you sort it for me?"

"I'll find a passage for you." Maximus intervened.

"Am I coming?"

"Yes of course." Marcus and Octavia answered the excited Livius together.

"I'll miss you." Fulvia had grown used to looking after a child again. Marcus wondered why his father had not allowed her to have children of her own. It confirmed a long formed conviction of his that really the old man was heartless if not just insensitive to those around him.

As they were finishing their food, Marcus studied his father while the latter was concentrating on his food. He was a little bowed now, but he had a similar physicality with the broad shoulders and deep chest. "Why were you never a soldier Father?"

"I did as I was told by my father. You never met him. We dared not disobey him even when we were grown up. Your generation does not know it was born."

"I wonder if all fathers say that." Marcus was smiling.

"I have some urgent things to do for you tomorrow and you had better come with me. Some of those papers from Gallus survived.
295

One was making recommendations about you when you get back: something about a corrupt magistrate and you taking his place. I could see you as a policeman. I hear there are a lot of retired soldiers and other Roman settlers where you are."

"It gets us away from the plotting of the senate and whichever emperor is at the top of the muck heap. Is Caligula's horse still in charge of the senate or did Nero's horse take over?"

"Yes very funny. Gaius Caesar never did try to get his horse into the senate. That was propaganda. The losers always get the worst of the history. Right, my son, is Fulvia going to go back to her chores or do you want me to clean up after the meal?" Maximus' sarcasm was fulsome.

"Why not ask Fulvia?"

"Cheeky dog."

"We could clean up together. I will show you how water runs into a bucket. It is like magic."

Octavia moved to head off an open argument. "Come and help Mama, Livi, please."

296

"No seriously Father: we were all born equal but in this sick society some get dehumanised into beasts of burden while others play gods with their pathetic lives. In the reckoning of who owes what to whom, I suggest you owe a lot more to Fulvia than the other way round. I bet I get loads more work out of my slaves than another hundred masters around me that beat their bare arses with sticks or worse. I treat them like they share the ownership, and they work like they do. They know when they are well off and put their all into it."

"You'd better keep that to yourself all you'll be accused of starting a slave revolt."

Fulvia sat with her head down. She then looked up with dignity. "Master Marcus my life is not pathetic. I choose to serve. You say you are of Christ then so must you." Maximus and Marcus both looked quickly at Fulvia. It was the first riposte he had ever heard from her to any of the family.

"I did not mean you Fulvia. I mean some of the slaves I have seen in their dreadful conditions. Please can I talk with you about the church here? With your permission Father?" Maximus nodded, satisfied with Marcus' hastily added request to him.

297

Maximus rose to leave. "I can see you are tired, my son. We need to talk business in the morning. Please be careful. Christians are no more welcome than they were when Nero used them for torches." Then to Fulvia. "I'll see you when you have finished here."

Marcus and Fulvia waited until Maximus had left the house. Fulvia waited for Marcus to speak. "I have some things to pass on the Bishop Alexander. Can you tell me where I can find him?"

"I will see him when we worship."

"This really cannot wait."

"I can take you to my deacon."

"Thank-you, sister. It is a start. Bless you for all you have done for me over the years. When can you take me?"

"I will go when your father has a sleep after the mid-day meal."

"Thank-you again."

Chapter 30

298

"Quite clearly the fig tree was a parable, not a miracle." Jacob was trying to hold the line in being faithful to Mark's narrative. The small room circled with clergy was wrapt.

"We are trying to emphasise the consequences of not being fruitful with the work entrusted to us." John was equally emphatic as to the message to be portrayed.

"If ever anyone has access to both of these documents they will see the difference and they could be forgiven for thinking one of these is not accurate. My account already has I don't know how many extra miracles. If this has twice as many miracles as Mark, how many would the document before Mark have, if we ever found one? Ten less? Keep going back and we could infer there never were any miracles."

"Calm down, Jacob. You are getting close to heresy." Onesimus was stern.

"I am not saying there were no miracles. I am saying that if we keep doubling them then our readers will start being as sceptical about this as we are about the rubbish invented by the Gnostics. I am also worried that if we keep banging on about the judgement of an angry God we will lose the message of the Love of God the Lord shows us."

299

"I still think the judgement has to be emphasised."

"John, how much wailing and gnashing of teeth do you think we need in this book?"

"Jacob I think you are getting tired." Onesimus was gentle. "Maybe we should ease off in our expectations until Marcus returns. We know you have a lot to do."

The comment skewered Jacob's emotions but he held firm. "Thank-you Onesimus."

"I think we should give this a couple of weeks for our next meeting to take the pressure off Jacob a little bit. But, we do need to talk about the resurrection before Jacob starts that momentous last section. We really have to show our appreciation of all that Jacob is doing here and be a little less judgemental ourselves. I think Jacob expressed the trials very well without making this an anti Roman polemic."

"If the people in Jerusalem when Our Lord was confronting them were anything like those when I was there in the five years before its destruction then the Romans could have done nothing about it. Even when they had a day off from the Romans they were fighting each other."

"You have told us that before."

"Several times."

There were smiles around the room.

"So, what about the resurrection narrative?" Onesimus was soliciting items for the final item on the agenda.

"Mark does not even finish his story, but that does not mean we have nothing to go on." Jacob spent the silent hours of his walk back from Thyatira thinking about his very thing. "We have those appearances that Paul mentioned, but they are very sketchy."

"Not so fast! What about the moment of resurrection?" John was controlling but Jacob felt he had the authority of those in the room.

"We have little or nothing on that, and it is such a mystery it would best be kept that way. In so doing we keep the mystery in the same we do not tell everyone about the Father. How can we? He is beyond description. So is the resurrection." A silence gripped the room

301

for several seconds after Jacob spoke. It was not just an absence of noise.

"By the same token we could leave everyone a blank piece of paper and save ourselves a few meetings." The barbs in John's voice broke a profound moment.

"All we have is an empty tomb. We have confused and distressed women and we have a steady turning of the disciples from frightened hideaways to courageous preachers. The Way gets established in many cities across the world, but we have no record as to how. Paul goes to Damascus but we have no idea how the Church got to Damascus. Then we have Paul's writing about the appearances. At best I could weave the traditions around Paul's sketchy sightings."

"The sceptics could be equally destructive of our message if we they could say that we cannot even say what happened at the resurrection." John was not giving up.

"If they ask you, ask them what happened on the day of creation. Were they there? And neither were we, for both events. Our best evidence for the resurrection is that we are here now talking about it. Readers will see that."

302

"Maybe we ought to make an effort at a description of the resurrection event." Onesimus was looking for a compromise and progress.

John was emboldened by this. "I think there would have to be a shaking of the earth, there would have to be an opening of heaven, there would have to be angels and there would be precursors of judgement day like graves opened."

"So why did no one think to mention this so that we heard about it? We would hardly have forgotten about the earthquake last week would we? I think someone might have remembered seeing their old saintly granddad again."

"There have been many earthquakes. It is why the Jews thought God was behind the rebellion against the Romans."

"Then both the earthquakes and the Jews of any faction were wrong. I was there when the temple was destroyed. God did not do much, I'm afraid. I don't remember an earthquake: just a whole lot of screaming and death."

"You two are becoming very wearing." Pudens spoke for the first time for an hour. His intervention was the more effective for it. "We are on the same team aren't we? The old men need some sleep and it's not like Jacob to get so angry. I think you are tired my brother. Go back to your wife or she will have forgotten what you look like. John. Write your own book. I look forward to reading it."

"Let us pray." Onesimus' call was booming and irresistible.

As he exited and said farewell to Chloe, Jacob was beset on each arm by the enthusiastic Doria and Rebecca. "Is Marcus back yet?"

"Not yet, Doria. I will let you know when I know more." Jacob sensed a rising crisis in his life. Without Marcus to return, there was now the issue of the escape of the two slaves beside him. Sitting on the floor beside him was Martha, the escaped slave who had remained within these walls for decades.

Jacob looked down to be met eye to eye with Martha's gaze. Jacob could see she was aware of his thoughts. "Marcus is well. It's not what you think."

Jacob had goose bumps at what had to be a prophetic insight. For no rational reason he believed her, whatever she was meaning. Had she meant Marcus was really alive? Or was Martha seeing a Marcus in a heavenly place. All that was known, but not, in this community beyond the procurator and Jacob and Judith, was that there had been a shipwreck from which there had been no known survivors. Maybe Marcus had survived. Jacob was not going to pursue the conversation with Martha for fear of letting the intelligence slip and the insecurity that would ensue if it became general knowledge.

"Bless you Martha."

"And may the Lord bless you too Jacob. Beware those in the shadows tonight. They are of the night."

A full moon gave sufficient light to see the footpaths clearly. By the time he reached the chariot route the moon gave enough light to cast a straight shadow beside the kerb. There was no curfew, but there was an uneasy quiet on the streets since the riots. Martha's warning gave Jacob a nervous disposition. Who was going to be 'of the night?' What had she seen? If she had been given an image of a future event, could it be avoided?

305

Jacob's mind began to range around his tensions. He had yet to work out a way to approach Fortunatus about the young Onesimus and a slave purchase. His last contact with Fortunatus as Gaius' scribe did not have a happy result. Fortunatus was an unknown quantity given the loss he must have suffered with the destruction of the Island, his loss in rent income and the profits from slave prostitution. Jacob again remembered meeting the facial expression of his beloved Judith each time she asked if he had found a way of recovering her son yet.

His musings had blended with prayers for guidance when he turned the last corner towards the north gate. There were torches there under the stone arch. Soldiers were watching the gate. It was fairly normal to have men of Gaius' civil force watching the comings and goings, and supervising the tax collection in daylight but this looked like a departure. There were several torches compared to the normal single light. Jacob took a further interpretation of Martha's words. These were men in the light, not in the shadows. Jacob resolved to be a man in the light and strode directly and openly, conscious, for once, of his sandals beating the stones beneath them.

The soldiers were relaxed and engaged in friendly but loud debate amongst themselves, with occasional bouts of laughter. They heard Jacob's footsteps and turned quickly to see who approached. Seeing a single figure coming out of the shadowy street they relaxed again. As Jacob approached he could see the outstandingly tall figure of Anthony and soon recognised his former companions from the trek to Thyatira amongst the eight soldiers.

The soldiers' presence was official and the first conversation reflected that. Sextus asked Jacob what his business was.

"Going home after a long day of work, Sextus. I hope all is well with you all."

"This is official, Jacob. We are watching all comings and goings. We believe we have at least one and possibly two or three of the robbers we encountered loose in the town. We are not entirely sure that they did not get through the gate here first though. Anthony remembered the black eyes of one of those that attacked us and realised they could have met before. We tracked him down but he was ahead of us. Mind how you go. Oh! And sorry to hear of your news about Marcus; he was a great soldier and a good man to know."

"Thanks Sextus. I didn't know anyone else knew about it, though. I thought Casca was keeping the news secret until orders come

307

from Rome. I think I would prefer it kept quiet for a few reasons, if you don't mind."

"We got the news about Gallus so we put two and two together. Anyway, sorry. I know you were close friends. We had a great respect for him as well." The men behind Sextus were murmuring their agreement. Then a small piece of mortar landed beside them from the wall above. The atmosphere was instantly electric and swords were drawn.

"On the wall," one of them shouted.

"You four stay here. You three with me." Sextus move quickly along the wall at ground level with his three subordinates. Clouds had covered the moon. Jacob looked up to the top of the wall. It was too dark to see any figures out of range of the flickering torches. Jacob remembered Martha's words.

The remaining soldiers were distracted by their alertness to the presence of a criminal, possibly armed. Without further conversation Jacob moved through the gate and down to the path along the hill top. The crosses still loomed, silhouetted before the moon as it returned from its cloud. There were no bodies hanging there any more. The

308

soldiers on guard behind him at the gate were silent. It was eerily quiet. It would have been like this on Golgotha hours after The Lord and the two criminals beside him had been taken down. Jacob was moved to prayer again.

There was a reality about the cross compared to the idealistic emotional rush of a faith declaration. Maybe it was like the swell of pride of a soldier marching to cheering crowds compared to the real horrors of sword piercing the flesh of a men that had loved wives and children and mothers only hours before. Here was a real cross. How massively removed it was from the social warmth after a baptism or during the shared supper of The Lord. How much it must have contrasted for any disciples that had been there on Golgotha compared to the previous night in the upper room.

Jacob turned away and set his face to the north again. How different the church bickering of meetings, even about the scriptures, compared to the awesomeness of the reality of the cross. How wonderful the Lord's words and actions, yet how trivial the issues that beset and divided the worshippers. 'Who was greatest?" the disciples had argued. It had been like that for those churches to which Paul had written: argument and division.

309

There was a new foreboding that had not been present before the gate. What was it? Jacob stopped beside the thorn bush to reach the source of this foreboding in his mind. Then he located the anxiety. Had the villain or villains on the wall overheard Sextus in his commiserations over the death of Marcus? Did they know Marcus and now identify the vulnerability of his estate and those that worked for him? Were they known to the personal enemies? Jacob resolved to put the anxieties aside. He was powerless to change anything. He was looking forward to seeing Judith after such a long day, and only time would tell the outcome of the night's events. With hope, the fugitives would be captured by Sextus and his men and the worries could be put aside.

Judith was waiting for him by the door. She clung to him with the warmth of affection after a day's separation. "I believe I have news for you."

Jacob held her close. He thought about the peculiarity of the statement: there was news or there was no news. How can you 'believe' you have news? He continued to hold her closely in the moonlight before they entered the house. He waited for the rest of the news. He had no way of knowing whether this was an addition to the anxieties or a relief for one or more of them. He looked into her face, pale in the light. It seemed an age before she spoke again.

"My way of women: I always start before the full moon." Jacob looked back over his shoulder to the moon. It was most definitely full. "I have not started. I may be having a baby." Jacob returned to the close embrace that existed before his sighting of the moon. The moment was profound. There seemed to be nothing to say. Jacob's mind ranged around the news of births in scripture: of Isaac to Sarah, of Samuel to Hannah. Would this child be special? They remained in their embrace until his stomach made an un-aesthetic noise. They laughed. "You are hungry." She turned her back and with tripping steps moved back into the glow of lamp-light.

Chapter 31

The moon was in its last quarter as Jacob walked early to the north gate. Sun and moon were in the sky together. He had resolved that day to go to Fortunatus' house to purchase the slave he had named Onesimus. He had debts to pay off to merchants for supplies for the farm and the bottle workshop. There were tools to order for some of the vineyard workers. He hoped to visit some of the sick of the church,

311

including giving some comfort to Pheobe Then his project for the manuscript could be completed that evening. At least his accounts for the estate were available for anyone arriving from Rome to administer Marcus' will.

What had been a steady working through his work agenda was to be disturbed when he reached Fortunatus' house. There were two soldiers guarding the door. Jacob did not recognise them.

"May I speak with Fortunatus?"

"No. He is not here. We need to know where he is. What's your business?"

"I want to buy one of his slaves."

"That could be a problem. We are looking for him. We need to ask a few questions. When we do he might be unavailable for a while."

The other soldier laughed and repeated, "Unavailable for a while!" under his breath.

"We need to know who Fortunatus is dealing with. Who are you?" the first soldier asked.

312

"I am Jacob, steward for Marcus."

"Ah!" Recognition dawned. "Sorry to hear your news Jacob. Sextus told us about you. Marcus was a good soldier. We think one of the robbers you scared off was employed by Fortunatus. We have him at the barracks. He is in a little discomfort just now." The second soldier sniggered. "Now it looks as if his boss has done a runner. It doesn't look good for him. His property will be seized if he's guilty as well. That doesn't seem to amount to much now. This house, and the Island heap of rubble and the dead prostitutes under it. If you're buying his slaves you'd best see the Procurator."

"Shouldn't Gaius be dealing with this?"

"Well!" the soldier hesitated as if he was worried about saying too much. "He would normally but the Procurator is taking over this time since his soldiers were dealing with the robbers." Jacob was shrewd enough to read between the lines. Fortunatus and Gaius were closely tied in business. Maybe Gaius was at last being investigated by Roman authorities. Jacob turned for Marcus' house after farewells to the soldiers. He had at least some news for Judith about regaining access to her son. He resolved to go to the barracks in the morning to ask for an audience with Casca.

Once in Marcus' house, he eventually located Judith who looked distinctly pale. "I have been sick. It comes with babies. I'd forgotten how awful it was. Next will be indigestion for months. What women have to go through!" He held her in an embrace.

"I will need to see the procurator to buy your Agathon. Fortunatus is implicated with the robbers. His property is likely to be seized. I have to answer to Casca anyway until someone comes from Rome so I'll give him a report on the trades since we got back from Thyatira. It should give me chance. I think we need another worker, especially one that handles a donkey. I might put that to Casca without the personal story we have here."

"Thank-you Jacob." Her words were cut short. She ran off to the rear of the house. She was about to vomit again.

Jacob walked to visit Phoebe. There was again a distinct peace in her house as they overlooked the olive trees. She was remarkably composed and confident for a woman who had lost both her husband

and one of her sons in quick succession, especially given the trauma of witnessing her son's pain on the cross.

"I know how The Lord's mother felt." She said. "I will see my son again. He died as innocent as The Lord."

Jacob left Phoebe full of confidence to continue his writing. The old woman was inspiring with her quiet faith. On the way he intended to call on the bottle workshop just to check on progress. Ladon was working alone.

"Where are Acteon, Aethon and Jason?"

"Acteon is out on an errand. Jason is taking the finished bottles to the press. I don't know about Aethon. I heard he was wanted by Gaius' men."

"What for?" Jacob had a massive pang of anxiety remembering the terror Gaius' men had caused by the targeted arrests after the riot.

"I can't be sure but there is a rumour they are looking for Christians. He had been boasting about his faith to people he met in the market place. Mind how you go Jacob."

315

Jacob's mind was full of anxiety as he walked to Chloe's house. He was passed by a group of gladiators some of them swaggering and intimidating those they met. An event was arranged in the arena later that week. Jacob was praying for guidance in what was an increasingly uncertain time.

He arrived in Chloe's house to find a hive of activity. The women were tasked with what appeared to be a house removal such was the packing. Chloe was not among them. Jacob felt ignored. Onesimus appeared from the room they used for worship. He beckoned him to the worship room. His face was grave.

"John has been arrested. It has been hard to get facts but Gaius' men seem to be on a rampage targeting us. John started arguing with what seem to be Gnostic preachers in the square. Gaius' men decided to break it up but I think they are trying to cause a distraction for the Romans to get their minds off the robbers, especially Fortunatus. He has gone to ground, but that is where rats belong. It won't be long to find out where we meet so we are hiding the things we hold dearest. The scriptures especially must be kept safe. Do you think Marcus' house would be safe from them?"

"It could be." Jacob was thinking of the consequences of Marcus' death being discovered. Gaius would take great delight in salvaging his pride at the expense of the late Marcus.

"If they come here they will also discover Doria and Rebecca. They might have a problem proving any crime by people of The Way but harbouring runaway slaves is a different matter."

"How are we going to hide them?"

At that point Chloe entered and heard Jacob's question. "I think we could get them across town by them laying over a donkey like a body and us covering them with material or dresses as if we were moving our stock away for sale. Come on Jacob. You have to save the scriptures. You can't lose your present work. There is no copy yet."

"You weren't at Marcus' house to ask you but we asked Judith. She is expecting us." Onesimus nodded as if to ask Jacob's confirmation of the plan.

"When did you ask? I only left her an hour ago."

"Your Aethon came to me with the story. He was with John and saw him arrested. The lad then avoided Gaius' clowns by hiding

317

under the market stalls. I went looking for you at Marcus' and then came here."

"And my girls at the market saw what was happening and came straight here."

"Where is Aethon now?"

"He caught up with Jason taking the bottles to the vineyard. I think he'll be hiding among the vines until he gets help from you."

"What about John?"

"He is with Gaius for now. No doubt there will be Gaius' usual mockery of a trial and then he'll be up before the Procurator on a death sentence for treason. Knowing John he won't be quiet about his faith in The Lord. I don't see him offering any acknowledgment of Caesar as his lord, do you?" Onesimus' face was sterner than Jacob could remember. Even his twinkle seemed to have gone. He had always exuded the air that he had a secret and you had to guess it.

Jacob asked, "Why do you think we are under threat?"

318

"I have a gut feeling. That may be an insight from The Lord. It just makes sense. Everyone knows the story about your fight with the robbers. It is no secret about the arrest of one of them by the Romans. Most seem to think that was one of Fortunatus' goons. Fortunatus has gone to ground so we assume he is receiving the robber's goods. Gaius and Fortunatus are too close for comfort. To avoid being implicated Gaius is causing a distraction for the Romans in the name of loyalty to the divine lord, the emperor. Maybe that would take the heat off Fortunatus as well. He is looking for Church members to be scapegoats. I just pray Casca sees through it. Gallus would have done."

Soon the hasty preparation was ready for action. The beasts were loaded and the runaway girls were under the materials. Jacob realised that one of the beast's leaders was the young Onesimus. "How did you get here?"

"There was no-one at Fortunatus' house and I was hungry. I went to see mother. She put bread in my hand and sent me here."

"I really have to clear this with Casca. We can't be found with runaways on our hands." Jacob looked round to see Chloe.

319

"Chloe, can you trade these things in Thyatira? I have an idea. I would need to write you a letter of introduction."

"I could trade them if I had transport, but I need to stay here with my sisters to work."

Onesimus and Jacob found their way to Marcus' house trying to avoid main streets and crowds, carrying the precious documents. The short train of asses loaded with the produce from Chloe's companions followed a route through the town that was a frequently used by trader transport. Rebecca and Doria struggled to breathe easily as their bellies were crushed against the asses' backs and the weight of material pressed down on them. Arrival to be unloaded could not come quickly enough for them.

Upon arrival, Jacob took up his writing materials. He was addressing Obadiah in Thyatira. Chloe was sending two of her workers along with Rebecca and Doria in the train led by Aethon and two other slaves from the farm. There would be garments from Chloe to trade, but with the offer of a joint venture to set up a garment manufacture in Thyatira if Obadiah could find accommodation for work and domicile.

The hope was that the road would be free from robbers after the Roman sting operation.

Rebecca and Doria resumed their discomfort en route to the farm, Jacob himself leading the first ass with the two women companions. The beasts turned off the high road so were out of sight of the distant town gates. Jacob moved them all down to the farm to find Aethon and the men that had been on the earlier wine transport. They were instructed to leave and take the first part of the journey when it was dark, the girls hidden as before. When far enough removed they would move from their cover, and if challenged on the road would be passed off as slaves en route to a new owner.

Jacob hastened back to town to take his account of stewardship to beg an audience with Casca intending to ask for authority to maintain oversight of the young Onesimus to legitimise his position. At Marcus' door, Judith was waiting for him and as soon as she could she clung to him. "Please be careful."

"We all need to be careful. Let us trust ourselves to Jesus' safe keeping. We have been gifted with several pieces of fortune. We have been given each other. Fortunatus' foreman was struck down when he

321

was going to attack me. The earthquake saved us when we were being attacked. The soldiers might not be of Christ but they have done the work of angels in saving us from harm."

"Not Pheobe's son."

"He is not the only one to die on a cross, remember."

"I want my child to know his or her father, whatever our earthly fate." Judith's eyes were welling with tears."

"I know. So do I. God means great things for us. I must go now though or it will be too late to ask for an audience." Jacob went to fetch his accounts and gave another hug to his wife before leaving.

"Please be careful. I'll be praying all the time for you."

"Thank you my beautiful wife."

Jacob arrived at the barracks as the guard was changing. Anthony was one of the sentries being relieved with Sextus calling the marching orders. The latter pointed a finger to indicate where Jacob should stand and wait. The relieved watch stood down, Sextus returned to the gate. "Yes Jacob?"

322

"I need to see the Procurator. I have accounts to present to him but I need to clear what could be seen as a crime unless it is explained. I have a slave on Marcus' property but the owner has abandoned him."

"You mean one belonging to Fortunatus?"

"Yes. Fortunatus calls him Onesimus. He came to me when he went back and found the place deserted."

"We have a few other lost slaves because of this. Normally the magistrate would be administering this be he seems to be a bit short handed just now. Casca wants to nail him with Fortunatus but he can't prove they were in the robbery trade together. For once Gaius was not warned in advance of the patrol we were on with you and it is the first time a sting has worked in years. I'll see if I can get you to Casca."

At the door to the Procurator's house the sentry saluted Sextus and was sent to ask Casca for permission for Jacob to enter. A few minutes passed and Jacob was summoned. It gave chance for Jacob to ask Sextus what was happening in the search for those of The Way, and hoping for news of John.

"There is a hearing before Casca tomorrow. The charge is about causing an affray and risking a riot. After the business before Gaius' force are edgy. He does not have much respect after having a riot on his watch. I think he would arrest anyone for farting to regain Casca's confidence."

"What about him causing a distraction to take everyone's mind off Fortunatus?"

"That as well probably, but we are all being watched by a frightened emperor so any thought of treason and we have to prove where our loyalties are damned quickly. Casca is no fool though."

Jacob stood before Casca as on his last visit when he heard of the death of Marcus. "Yes steward."

"Sir, I am here to give account of my stewardship and to arrange the purchase of a slave who is under my control in irregular circumstances. Also, I did hope you might have news about my master's family." Jacob was doing his best to be confident but felt nervous. He comforted himself that Casca would normally have nervous, if not frightened people in front of him. Casca held his hand out for Jacob to bring the documentation he had with him.

324

Casca perused for some time. This was not merely a formality. "I see you have traded well with the goods from Thyatira."

"Yes, Sir."

"Does the estate need any more slaves."

"We have no spare capacity for transport when moving bottles or farm goods. I have to take workers away from production. This lad was from Fortunatus' estate and he is good with animals. He actually has one of Fortunatus' beasts. The lad is not trying to run away or steal the beast. He did not where to go when he found his normal home abandoned."

"Why did he come to you?"

"Marcus' housekeeper is his mother."

"And your wife."

"Yes sir."

"I take note of where he is. It's a bit of a mess at the moment. We need to sort out what has happened to Fortunatus. We also have to wait for instructions from Rome when Marcus' family representatives arrive."

"Yes Sir. Thank-you. Have you any further instruction?"

"No Steward. You appear to have things in hand. Dismissed." Casca talked as if he was ordering a soldier. Jacob made no further reply and moved through the open door, slightly relieved to have made the young Onesimus safe for now, and without threat to him or anyone harbouring him.

Twilight was creeping on as he moved again into the open air. Sextus had gone and the sentries ignored him as he left the barracks. Judith waited at Marcus' door for him.

"Thank the Lord!"

"What is making you so nervous?"

"It might be the anxieties of having a baby inside me now, but I don't feel all is well. What did Casca say?"

"Agathon can stay here for now. I think he should stay here tonight. They don't know where Fortunatus is and we have to wait for

326

news from Marcus' family. John has a hearing tomorrow before Casca. I get the impression Gaius is looking for the death penalty for anyone causing a disturbance. Let's go back to the farm before it is too dark. We might see them all before they set off for Thyatira. Everything is sorted here is it?"

"I have our food ready."

"Can we carry it?"

"If we must!" Judith had taken pride in the presentation of the meal and she sounded disappointed. Within minutes Judith had bags to carry. Jacob had his scribe's materials and the accounts he had brought from his presentation to Casca.

Some of Gaius' force was guarding the gate as they left on the road to the farm. Jacob and Judith were being watched in silence. It was as if Gaius' men knew something they did not. There was no relaxed banter or the ease of a group passing the time of their watch. Jacob kept looking over his shoulder. Judith and he would be vulnerable once they were on the open road.

327

Against the darkening sky Jacob could see bearded vultures moving over the expanse of the vines.

"They are a long way from home! They don't come out of the mountains very often." Jacob watched the birds landed out of sight.

"There must be something dead among the vines." Judith was stumbling on the gloomy stones of the road.

"I'll check in the daylight tomorrow; probably the remains of a fox. Bearded vultures usually go for bones and marrow."

On arrival at the farm the beasts were forming up the train and all appeared to be loaded ready for the gruelling journey ahead. The men had all done the trip before so Jacob was confident. He was confident Obadiah would see the benefit of the arrangement, and his doubts would be assuaged by Ruth, he was sure.

Jacob walked to the hillcrest road with the train as they stumbled and staggered in the dark. They risked all the women walking rather than hiding the two runaways. Being dark, it was unlikely they would be seen from the distant town gate as they left. Torches would have been visible from the town and could have aroused suspicion. He bade his friends and workers farewell with a prayer and a blessing.

Jacob waited until he could no longer hear the sound of animal hooves. There was no chatter by the men and women as they left. Jacob returned to the Judith, the only person left at the house. It was moonless but he was now familiar with the path, even in the starlight. She was again waiting at the door, anxious but more positive now that escaped slaves were no longer present to incriminate them.

"There is very little here to eat after the food we brought. We sent the last of the bread with Aethon and the walkers. I had no time to plan for this. I have enough stores to make bread for the household tomorrow but you will have to give me money for the market when you get back to Marcus' house. Did Casca have any news from Rome?"

"No my love, but it cannot be long now surely. I wish I could set store by Martha's prophecies. She gave the impression Marcus was still alive despite the news of the wreck."

"We have to get through one day at a time. I only hope they don't start hunting us down as people that follow Jesus. It has happened in other places."

329

"Onesimus thinks that Gaius would do that to take everyone's mind off the hunt for Fortunatus and the robbers. His hands are dirty with that. I was never happy working amongst him and his force. We have hidden all the scriptures. I don't think we will be worshipping on the Lord's Day this week unless we do it in our own homes."

"It wouldn't be the first time."

"No."

Chapter 32

For the first time in his life, Jacob kneaded bread the following morning, together with Judith, leaving her with the proving dough. He moved to his new scripture and with a great sense of fulfilment continued the narrative. There were parables he had heard told in Antioch. He felt the Lord with him in spirit, and was moved to write his final verse as the Lord telling him that. "I am with you to the end of time." It gave him courage to go back to the town with much more confidence than in the uncertain spirit in which he had left it looking over his shoulder.. He turned to look at the mounting pile of papyrus. It would soon be finished.

He kissed Judith and left the house full of the smell of cooking bread. He crested the rise on to the top Roman road and set his face to the town gates, and as he did so remembered the circling bearded vultures from the previous evening. He tried to remember the area of their activity but was immediately prompted by the sight of one rising, clutching a bone in its   claws. He headed through the vines to search for the source of its interest.

As he approached the smell was distinct. Through foliage he eventually discerned some paces away at ground level the movement of flapping material in the slight breeze. It was human remains dressed in Roman male gentry clothing. Standing over the body it was hard to recognise a face. Animals, maybe foxes had torn what they could of exposed flesh, and torn through what they could of the clothes to savage soft flesh. Eyes had been pecked out by carrion birds. The marrow bones of the shins had disappeared. Maggots were much in evidence. The only clue to identity of this former life was the colour of the matted hair, the buckle on the shoulder, and a ring. Jacob intuitively sensed it was Fortunatus.

Fortunatus had the means to be able to travel if he was fleeing. There would have been no likelihood of him being so desperate as to hide in the vines. The cause of death was unlikely to be of natural causes. Looking around there were signs of broken twigs and scuffed earth. The body had been dragged. Jacob had walked down the adjacent row of vines so had not seen the line of the drag. Now it was obvious.

He pondered what to do next. Jacob had no doubt it was to the barracks that he would report the body's discovery. Was the placing of the body on Marcus' property pertinent? Could it be an attempt to put Jacob himself under suspicion? That is if this was, indeed, the missing Fortunatus, enemy of so many, but implicated as a possible gang master for the robberies. There was no shortage of suspects who would have seen Fortunatus dead, but it would have severed a link that would have led to Gaius if he was also the beneficiary of crime.

As he retraced his steps towards the top road he remembered the previous night and the body language of the Gaius' guards at the gate. Given the previous record of corruption, was Jacob himself going to be blamed for Fortunatus' death? Jacob resolved to reach the barracks avoiding contact with Gaius' force. He may be, he thought, imagining the threat, but he was going to be behind Roman lines, metaphorically speaking if he was provoking Gaius.

As he reached the top road he broke a branch and twisted it back on another the indicate the row of vines. Then he glanced up the road to the north gate before dashing over the road.

It added a long time to his journey through vines and then the uncultivated foliage and scrub beyond Marcus' property. He skirted the town walls at distance thus reaching the east gate close to the barracks.

Jacob did not know the guard. He had a broken nose and looked long overdue for retirement. He was dismissive when Jacob asked for an audience with the Procurator.

"Who do your think you are, Jew?"

"I am Jacob, steward for Marcus. I have urgent information for Casca."

The sentry waved back to someone out of sight of Jacob in the courtyard. "Wait here."

The wound up feeling of panic began to rise in his gullet. For a moment he felt that this might have been a soldier in the line he attacked in Jerusalem. Had he been recognised? He calmed himself as the soldier studied him. No, this troop was in Britannia when the Jerusalem action took place. "Behold I am with you always." He regained his confidence with quiet prayer. The broken nosed soldier, standing at attention observed Jacob from the corner of his eye.

Through the gate appeared the man that broken-nose had beckoned. Equally curtly Jacob was beckoned to follow. He waited at Casca's house door while permission was sought for an audience. There was a guard at the door who seemed oblivious to Jacob's presence while his erstwhile escort disappeared into the house. He was a considerable time. Jacob felt that the wait was to remind Jacob of his station. The sun was hot and they were exposed to it. The soldier eventually returned.

"The Procurator needs a shit before he sees you." Jacob was left alone as his escort returned to his previous post at another door. He watched as the daily life of the barracks continued. Soldiers marched in small squads from one space to another and as labourers appeared and disappeared carrying stores from door to door.

334

Casca's voice boomed from an arched window above. "Come up steward."

Jacob found the room as before. His audience followed the same order and he was standing before the seated Casca. "Yes?"

"I have found a body amongst my master's vines. It has been in the open for enough time for animals to have made it unrecognisable. It looks from its clothing like that of a Roman gentleman."

"Do you think it is Fortunatus?"

"That is possible sir."

"So, I wonder who of about five hundred suspects killed him? You will need to lead one of my patrols to the body. I am not leaving this to Gaius. Wait downstairs at the door. Send my attendant in as you leave. He is in the room opposite."

"Yes sir."

Jacob waited outside as before until quite some time later his escort had formed There were four soldiers, one carrying a stretcher and another a blanket. Jacob's day was being eaten away with few of his duties performed. Judith's provisions had yet to be sourced and he

335

needed to see both the bottle works and see how the church in Chloe's house was faring. He also prayed for the group en route to Thyatira for their safe arrival and success of their mission. He was going to be frustrated for some time.

Chapter 33

Gaius's men had intimidated the market stallholders for some time after the disturbance in the market and the arrest of John. There was little co-operation from them, but he did at last get the identity of what appeared to be John's associate. He was one of Marcus' slaves and put to the work of bottle making. If he could undermine Marcus he would have been satisfied. Was the rumour that Marcus was dead true? He would find out in due course.

What had happened to that Christian John? Gaius was slightly heartened that Casca had taken the treason of the Christians seriously and witnessed John in chains on the way to a ship. Given Casca's comment the previous day, John was probably on his way to slavery in the mines somewhere in the empire. Shame the sentence had not been crucifixion. The momentum for the campaign would have been all the more supported.

336

The arrest of Fortunatus' man was more than a setback, but that man could not identify Gaius as an associate. The Romans had ways of finding out who Fortunatus' associates were if they could question Fortunatus. That body would be found soon enough with implications for the owner of the land or its steward. Fortunatus had enough enemies so who would point fingers at the officer delegated responsibility for law and order?

Now, prosecuting one Christian like John was like swatting a wasp. It was satisfying, but wasps may return. He had to find the nest and occupy the Romans with a surfeit of high treason charges. Now, where in this street was the bottle making building?

Gaius was making as to march ahead of his six men. If only he had the fitness of years before. He was out of breath too soon and his crotch-rot sore was playing up yet again. He arrived at what appeared to be the right door. He could smell the leather. He beckoned to his men they should enter. He followed them through the door. There were two workers occupied but sitting in dismay at the intrusion.

"We are looking for an associate of the one they called John. He is one of the Christians. What are your names?"

337

"I am Jason. This is Acteon. We are both slaves of Marcus. Who is John?"

"I ask the questions leather worker. You won't be able to sew leather any more if you lost a few fingers would you?"

"No Sir."

"So which of you is the Christian we saw with John?"

"Neither of us, sir. I think you might mean Aethon. He has not been at work for two days now. We don't know where he is."

"Where might he be? Where does he live?"

"He lives in our rooms but he has not been home either. I could ask the steward. I have not seen him since yesterday."

"I will ask the steward in good time. Where would he be?"

"He is out and about a lot, sir. I know he is busy about his master's business."

338

"If you were avoiding pain, where would you scream that he might be found?" Gaius leaned over Ladon with menace. His breath was foul.

"He might be at his master's house, sir. He is a freeman over me. He does not confide his business."

"Where does this Aethon meet his fellow Christians? We need to find a few traitors who deny the emperor his title." Gaius stood straight again.

Jason and Acteon looked at each other. There was silence until the man behind Ladon swung his sword down across the leather bottle that was being made. Both the slaves jumped. The moment was threatening but took on a comical aspect when the wielder of the sword found that it had gone through the leather and into the wood of the table and was stuck. The split bottle came up with the sword when at last he worked it out of the table. The bottle was difficult to get free. He then cut his thumb on the sword as he took the bottle off its end.

"We do not go with them sir." Jason was gabbling. "I think they meet with someone called Chloe."

339

"Who else is a Christian?"

"We don't know, sir. They are very secret."

"We have all we can get from these slaves. I think I know where Chloe's house is." Gaius beckoned to his men to leave. "They are the seamstresses from the market," he said as he was leaving.

Ladon and Acteon again looked at each other. They rose together and thought as one. "I'll go to Marcus' house. You go to the farm." Ladon chose the shorter distance, was first to the door and peered round it to see that the force had gone. Then they hastened to their respective destinations, fairly clear that Gaius's men were not going to be at the north gate to restrict movement.

Gaius arrived at Chloe's door. Without ceremony he entered and his men followed. Only Chloe and Martha were in the house. The other two were at the market stall and, of course the others were unaccounted for on the road to Thyatira. No-one was immediately visible to the intruders. Chloe heard the footfall and appeared from a room behind them.

"Welcome to my home gentlemen. Can I help you?" The voice was quiet and with authority. They spun round.

"I have reason to believe this house is used by Christian traitors."

"Whoever and whatever this house is used for, who are you?" Chloe knew exactly who it was but maintained her dignity as the householder before uninvited guests.

"I am the Magistrate. These are my men. We have reason to believe this house is used for practises that are treasonable."

"What reason?"

"I ask the questions."

"You are intruding into my home. We are law abiding and pray for the emperor. There is no-one here that has committed treason."

"Search the house."

"Stay where you are." Chloe moved into the midst of Gaius men. I've known you since you were children running naked down the street." She proceeded to name them one by one as she faced each of them. They looked away. "I know all of your mothers and fathers. Now go and ask them if you can call on me like this."

341

"And I suppose you know my name as well." Gaius was seething that his orders were countermanded and his men were in thrall to a woman.

"What is it?"

"I am Gaius the magistrate. We will search this house." His emphasis was on 'will.'

None of the group had seen Martha as she sat by the door from which Chloe had exited to the atrium. She was continuing to sew the hem of a linen garment partially obscured by a pitcher. "You are not Gaius. You are Amyntas. I have known you since you were a child." Gaius seemed to have his authority waning and was beginning to feel hysterical.

"I am Gaius. This house will be searched, now." His voice was shrill and feminine. His face was red and his lips set in a narrow line. He expected the men to move to order but they were still uncertain.

"You are Amyntas. I was there when you were born a slave. I was there when they gelded you, poor mite. You screamed and bled for

342

hours. I tried to comfort your mother as she nursed you but I was too young to help. They cuffed her when she tried to hold on to you and they wanted her to get on with work."

"Who are you, crone?" Gaius walked towards the voice that had so humiliated him

"I am Martha. You will not remember me. I threw the name they gave me to the evil one. I nursed you when I had use of my legs. The same people that made you a eunuch made me a begging cripple. I heard you married a wife. That would have been an interesting consummation. What did you do with her?"

Gaius was not a tall man but he now towered over the seated Martha and he saw her crossed and cruelly shaped legs. He would have struck her dead, but to do so would have brought him even lower in the estimation of his men, if that were possible. He aimed a kick at her. Limited though her movement was, Martha reacted on instinct to defend her body from the blow. It was with the hand that held the needle. It penetrated deep into Gaius' shin, just below the hem of his toga. Martha was send backwards with the impetus of the blow of shin to her hand and wrist, but she recovered quickly. Gaius staggered to

343

regain his balance and then reach the source of the pain in his leg. One of his men laughed nervously. Gaius could not tell which one had laughed but even bawling out one of his men for laughing would have been a losing strategy as well. He was torn between saving face after his humiliation by the women, or in trying to make his men frightened of him again.

"Would you like me to show you round my house?" Chloe was the hostess and in control. She addressed Gaius and all his men. Gaius took what seemed to be a way forward from his discomfort. He had extracted the needle from his shin and threw it down. He followed his men on Chloe's room by room tour, limping. There was absolutely nothing physical in Chloe's house to incriminate her.

"What meetings have you held in this house?"

"My friends and family meet here, and as you know we make clothing to sell on the market."

"Do Christians meet here?"

"Does it look like it? What do Christians do?"

"They practise cannibalism. They eat children. They refuse to accept the emperor as their lord." It struck Gaius that his direct question had not been answered.

"I know no cannibals or anyone that hurts children. What a foul thought! If I find out about anyone that does I will come immediately to you. Have any children gone missing? My women on the market have not heard of any. I don't know of anyone that has gone missing to make me suspect cannibalism. Do you know people that have gone missing?" Chloe, despite her diminutive size was controlled and the authority in the house. Gaius realised he was being walked to the door, his men shuffling behind. The thought of the missing Fortunatus crossed his mind, and those of his overhearing men. It broke his train of thought. Chloe wished him well at the door and suddenly he was on the street with lost face. His usual recourse would be to humiliate slaves in his house to compensate. This was not open to him yet and he had to re-establish authority with his accompanying force. His anger was clouding his judgement but he had no direction for his revenge. His thoughts again turned to Jacob and Marcus and his frustrated business with the Island project, his lost slaves and the near exposure after the attempt to hijack the wine shipment. At least his own men seemed to be loyal in doing his bidding. He resolved to arrest Jacob. Something had to be found to discredit him.

In his silence as he progressed back to his office he tried to piece together the confrontation with Chloe. How had he ended up so humiliated? How could one small woman and a crippled slave turn round a group that could so easily have committed an atrocity against them? His mind turned to sorcery, and he began to attribute that as another crime of Christians. Had he been overcome by a sorcerer as in the person of Chloe? Had he been cursed by Jacob? What was the evidence?

He said he was a Jew but not practicing. It was hard to tell the difference between Jews and Christians. Fortunatus had given that incredible account of the attack on the wine shipment via his robber band. The guards were either mercenaries or soldiers. Knowing Marcus' contacts they could have been soldiers. But what was the creature that came out of the water? They said he was a naked angel with golden hair and there was a flash of light and the earthquake, that same earthquake that wrecked the Island, symbol of Jacob's opposition. "He destroyed a major source of income for Fortunatus and me," Gaius reasoned to himself. Jacob avoided attempts at ambush. Did he have

346

some charmed way of foreseeing attacks on his person? Those sent to

end his influence at the Island were attacked by a mysterious force

from the dark.

The Romans seemed to be supporting him. Has he got them in

thrall as well? These were dangerous times. Could he trust his own men

to stay with him and avoid confession under strain. They weren't the

brightest individuals.

His mind full of such thoughts, Gaius returned to his office to

think about the way forward. He intended also to nurse and bathe his

sore shin after its penetration by Martha's needle. Who on earth was

that woman that had so unmasked his former station in life. He was

breathless and desperate to sit down when he did return.

Maybe it was time to force the discovery of Fortunatus'

remains and seek the arrest of Jacob as a suspect for interrogation since

the body would be found on a route normally used by him. It might

give a lawful reason to search Marcus' house as well. If it was true that

the soldiers had been talking about the death of Marcus that fateful

night of the arrest of the black-eyed robber there were prizes to be

picked there and who would know whether the false steward had made

347

is own profits by the missing property that would be noticed under audit.

Gaius looked at the mess of documentation in his room and cursed the missing scribe. At least Jacob had kept on top of the job.

Chapter 34

Jacob led the soldiers to the grotesque remains of what could have been Fortunatus. He was unfamiliar with most of the troop but he was pleased to have Sextus leading them.

"You say this is the row?"

"Yes Sextus."

Sextus ordered the man with the stretcher and one other down the row Jacob had indicated. The rest he ordered to walk separately down adjacent vines. "You never know what else we might find," he said.

Several paces down the hill and out of sight of the road, the soldier at the furthest row on the left called that he had found something. Sextus ordered everyone to stand still as he pushed between vines to find the soldier. Jacob followed. Face down in the earth was

348

another body. The stench of rotting flesh was apparent as they approached. The flies were around the cadaver in droves.

"Turn it over." The soldier obeyed, but had a look of distaste at the order. He used his foot. There was a mass of maggots on the underside that scrambled as one to hide from the light. There was no face to recognise and there was a massive stain of dried body fluids left where the stomach had been pressed to the earth.

"Recognise him?"

Jacob thought Sextus was using his black humour developed over years of witnessing the inhumane treatment of man for man. He was not.

"This is one of our robbers. I recognise the belt." The girdle around the waist, now serving most of its purpose in keeping the bowels inside the body's trunk was plaited strands of leather. There were two pieces of what could have been silver at its ends. "This one died of having his throat cut. Most of the blood ran away from the head. There was quite a struggle by the look of these broken branches. Someone is keen to get rid of our robbers. They must know someone important. Let's have a look at the other body."

349

As they picked their way back to the row of vines that sheltered the Roman gentleman's remains, Sextus commented, "Now we are a stretcher short."

"You can have my old bed. You might remember that." Jacob was pleased to get away from the grizzly sights and smells of the recoveries. One of the soldiers was dispatched to go with Jacob to the farmhouse." They retraced their steps up the hill to the top road and turned towards the farm. As they looked back towards the town gate there appeared to be a small band of armed men leaving to march towards them. They were not Romans so Jacob assumed they must be some of Gaius' force. He would rather have Gaius' men on the other side of a Roman line of soldiers than be confronted by them on his own. He walked quickly. His single soldier escort was well used to forced marching and was unperturbed by the heat. They walked in silence apart from the buzzing and whining insects busy in the noonday sun.

When Jacob arrived at his house the door was open and he could hear movement .inside. He was not expecting anyone home. Surely Judith would be at her housekeeping work for Marcus. He caught a glimpse of her rushing from one room to another. Acteon was standing alone in the middle of the room.

"Judith. Please bring some water for our guest. We are thirsty in the heat."

She spun on her heel to see Jacob and the soldier. Her face was full of anxiety and she was flushed. Without comment she rushed to the back of the house and brought earthenware cups of water. Jacob handed one of them and, duly transferred, to the soldier and he asked him to wait while he went for the stretcher. Jacob quickly quaffed the other and put the cup down. He beckoned Judith to follow him. He sensed her urgency to impart news.

In a whisper out of earshot of the soldier at the door, "Gaius is hunting down our people. He raided the bottle workshop. He was going to Chloe next. I am trying to hide your writings."

Jacob matched the whisper. "I have found bodies among the vines. I went to the barracks. This is why the soldier is here. I should be alright while I have them with me. Where is Onesimus?"

"He came to Marcus' house this morning. He was setting off with his household for Ephesus by the coast road. He was carrying the rest of our scriptures. He should be well away by now. When he heard that John is being sent to forced labour he knew they would come looking for us. Any one of us could be martyred, but the Word must be saved."

Jacob was by now on the way back to the soldier at the door, carrying the stretcher. "Let's hope it doesn't come to martyrdom. It's easy to celebrate it after the death of heroes we never knew. There is no glory in pain and death. I've seen too much of it. I'm going back with the soldiers I hope. I don't want Gaius catching me to ask why bodies have been found amongst our vines. I know who he'd like to blame."

"Can't we run away?"

"And then I will look guilty. Besides, I have to answer to Casca for Marcus' estate and then I would be the feckless steward as well. Acteon, can you help Judith for the rest of the day? Thank-you, brother."

Jacob returned to soldier and the hastened up the hill again to the top road.

352

It was indeed Gaius' men moving down the top road from the town's north gate. They had seen the distant figures of Jacob and the soldier walking away from them but had not for sure identified them or seen them coming out of the vines. Their task was to search for the "missing" Fortunatus amongst the vines and report back.

They turned into the vines and picked their way down the row, being surprised as they discovered the Roman force ahead of them. They continued warily, and with not a little confusion. The Romans were spread over several rows, clearly searching. Suddenly Sextus' voice boomed across the side of the valley, "Guard, to me. Ready arms!" He had seen Gaius' force. He was not going to be surprised. There was not going to be a negotiation over the possession of their gory find.

It took a few seconds for his soldiers to form up beside him. The bodies were now covered. Gaius' men approached uncertainly.

"We are searching for missing persons," said their leader.

"And just what made you think you had to search here?" Sextus had his face set and the tone was very sarcastic. There was enough room to draw weapons if necessary. Shields were up. There

353

was no doubt about their military readiness. The soldiers had their helmets on and were ready to defend or attack as needed. It would have been awkward swordsmanship among the closeness of the vines. There was no political reason for the military stand-off. The local force and the Roman military usually worked in tandem, but intuitively the Romans were ahead on this turf war in pursuit of corruption. After putting their own force in danger while combating robbers on the road, they were not about to cede the initiative to a force that was suspected of collusion. It was still a closely guarded secret that it was Romans guarding the wine shipment. The readiness of the Romans to take a military formation was still not a surprise to Gaius' men. They were increasingly aware of the gossip that they were in collusion. Their presence in that very location looking for a body could have been a massive co-incidence, but it was very unlikely. Gaius' standing with the rest of his contemporaries in the self governing town was already at a low ebb after the riots, and the riots, it was well known, were sparked by the collapse of the Island in which he held a major financial interest.

Gaius' men knew they were no match for the Roman force in front of them, even hampered as they were by the vines.

"I will have to report this to the Magistrate."

"You do that." Sextus was disdainful of this travesty of a military force confronting him. He watched as they shambled their way up the hill for a minute before giving the order to stand down.

By the time Jacob and his military companion reached the height of the road, they could see Gaius' men mooching away from them back to the town gate.

With the stretcher delivered Sextus ordered two of his men to load the stretcher with the decomposing remains of the two bodies. One glint caught Jacob's eye as they lifted the stretcher.

"This is Fortunatus." Jacob stated plainly.

"How do you know?" asked Sextus.

"This is his ring. He used it to seal documents." A maggot crawled over it to escape the light and disappeared under the stained toga. The whiff of the stench caught Jacob's nose and he narrowly avoided retching. His sadness came from the thought that he would never want to sleep on this stretcher again, even though these were not the first dead bodies to have lain on it. The first, at least, Jacob thought, remembering an old friend, had died in a state of grace.

355

"You don't have to come back with us Jacob. I can report all this to the procurator. He can liaise with the town authorities." Sextus was looking forward to getting away from the stench. The four stretcher bearers looked resigned to a brief uncomfortable time.

"I think I'd better come. I answer to the Procurator now until we hear from Rome."

Chapter 35

Gaius sat alone in his town official chamber staring unseeing at the wall. Who on earth was that woman on the floor who knew so much about him? His mind returned to his years of service alongside the two sons of the household during his childhood. He remembered them. They were bigger than him in early years. They took it in turns to beat him and bugger him. He would never forget. He remembered resolving that he would never forget. He always remained patient and faithful to their father and mother. He learned his service well alongside other abused slaves. He resolved he would wait his chance no matter how many years it took.   The first was on the road. He must have been about twenty years old then. Yes, he was convincing about

356

the robbers. He even cut himself several times to show how hard he had fought, but the poor son had no chance as three robbers set about him and stabbed him in the back. Gaius looked at his forearm to admire the scar. He remembered the satisfaction of the knife penetrating that son and the cry of pain that turned into a gurgle. No, Gaius was always a dutiful and peaceful man, eager to please. Who would have suspected this honourable manservant?

Then there was the party and the drinking a year or so later. They were all so very well drunk. "What was it," he thought, "that I put in his drink?" Most of the guests had gone and the son was vomiting. In the middle of the night he held the pillow over the comatose drunk until the silence lasted until the first birdcall. Of course he had choked on his own vomit. They all said that. And what a great comfort I was to their father. What a shame I could not have children as his adopted heir. Gaius smiled again. "I will always win. I will never suffer humiliation without revenge again."

But who was that woman? How did she know? She knew about my castration. I do not remember it but she did. And then his distant dream returned. There was that haunting shadow again of the girl that sang to him. She was the only person that gave me any

357

kindness: then there were those screams and she had gone. Gaius had

gone down the long passage of past memories he dare not enter, and he

had found the pain: not the pain of the knife or the beating or the

violating penetration: it was a pain deep in his chest, or was it his gut. It

was the shadowy and only comfort in his past, the only embrace that

meant something. It was that person that sang. She was not a mother.

Whoever it was she evoked the only positive emotion that existed in his

life apart from creature comfort and the joy of winning and they now

seemed so shallow. That must have been her, the voice, she that once

held him.

For the first time he could remember since childhood a tear

ran down his face. He chided himself for the weakness. His anger built

at this aberration. He rose and paced the floor. He felt he had nowhere

to go with his feelings. He sat again as the soreness in his groin built

again. He walked to the street entrance. At the top of the steps he could

see his task force returning to report. They arrived and stood at the

bottom of the steps looking up to him as their foreman spoke. "The

Romans found the bodies. They were there when we arrived."

Gaius thought a curse without expressing it to his men. He

stood silently for a moment then spoke. "The woman on the floor at the

358

garment maker's house is an escaped slave. She belongs to me. Go and bring her here. You'll have to carry her. If Phoebe is there arrest her and don't get into that argument you did before. You behaved like brats and she was your mother. Then I want you to pick up Jacob. There were bodies on his land. He is the primary suspect in murder."

The men looked at each other. They knew where the guilt lay and smirked to each other. "What are you waiting for? I want this sorted by nightfall." Gaius made a shambling turn and waddled through the door.

The men walked into Chloe's house. They upturned a table to commandeer as a litter for Martha. They lifted her under her arms and placed her in the upturned table as if she was being carried in majesty. They left the house. Nothing was said, even by Martha.

Gaius lost track of the time it took for the return of his men. The door was barged open unceremoniously and the four stepped through. The burden was heavy for them and they were hot from the exertion.

"Put her down. Now where is the woman that harboured this slave."

359

"The woman that harboured me is long dead." Martha had imposed her presence. She was hard to ignore but Gaius' men had to answer for themselves.

"The other woman was not there." The men were trying not to overbalance or injure their backs as they let the table to the floor upside down by its corners.

"That is a task for later. Now find Jacob."

"We have not eaten yet Magistrate."

"Neither have I. Go to it." Gaius moved to his table to complete his plans for the next entertainment in the arena.

The conversation amongst the men as they moved towards Jacob's farmhouse was about how Gaius could probably do without a few meals anyway but they were thirsty and could do with sustenance. As it was they stopped at the north gate where two of their colleagues were assisting with the tax collection and they asked to be fed from their bread and a sour wine. "We will repay you."

As a result of their conversation, they ascertained that Jacob had gone with the soldiers with their gruesome litter. They had passed
360

through the gate some time ago. There would be no point going to the farm. They resolved to wait at the gate while one of them went to the market for food.

Gaius sat and regarded the crippled woman sitting in the well of the table. His attempt to be overbearing and threatening did not work. Martha met his stare.

"It takes more than balls to be a man." Her voice was quiet and kindly, which made it all the more provocative. Gaius did his best to maintain composure as the model citizen of authority. Inside he was boiling.

"You are an escaped slave. I inherited his estate from your owner. You are now mine. I think I will put you out to beg as my master intended. I can't think what else you can do."

"I can think of several things you can do. You can accept where you came from and show that you can right the wrongs that happened to you and me. You can show that by treating people as you wish you had been. I am a skilled seamstress. I could also have been a loving mother. I dreamed of being a mother as I held you. You would not have lived if I had not fed you. They sold your mother before you

361

were old enough. Yes they gelded you. I could not be a mother after what they did to me. Yes you had it hard but at least they left you your legs. All you are doing now is making sure another generation goes through the hell we did." Her tone was even. The voice was of an old woman but he remembered it. The dark tunnel of infant memory briefly let light in for Gaius. There was silence for a long time.

"There is no other way. It would all break down if there was no control of idleness"

"Who is idle? I was making clothes for the people out there 'til your idiots turned up with not a clew as to how to move me. Have you missed me? No! You didn't even remember me. So why the demand I beg for you now? You don't need a beggar slave. It would cost more in slaves' time to have me moved around than I could make begging. To save face? You can't. Your men already despise you and laugh behind your back. The only reason I am here is because you made a fool of yourself trying to kick me when you can't lift your leg high enough."

"I think I'll have your tongue cut out."

362

"No. You can't bear the truth can you? You can change, or you can die an angry bitter loser. Giving me more torture won't change that: it will reinforce it. You will despise yourself even more."

Gaius' attempt to sit in overbearing judgement on his new slave, he had to admit to himself, had failed miserably. He could not reach the reason why. He still kept a silence to decide the way forward. Martha again broke the silence.

"Yes you are wounded by this awful world and so am I. I have found a way of living with joy in my heart and self respect despite having to have other people wipe my arse. You could have this joy as well."

Gaius came out of his reverie and was intrigued by Martha's last comment.

"Go on."

"I have a God who loves me as I am, equally with you and everyone else. He is the only God. All the other bits of stone and wood in the temples are just that. I believe in the only real God. He knows all things and has power of life and death over all of us. He will sit in judgement over everyone, especially those that presume to judge others, like you."

"Who is this god?"

"Only God knows God's name." Martha had cut through the sham nature of the temple religions of the town, and Gaius recognised that. "The true God has power of life and death. He overcame death."

Gaius realised that Martha was talking about the Christian God. In his mind he was in a fork in the road. He was intrigued by finding out more since he was desperate to build his self-esteem. A God like that made him feel better. His lower nature came to the fore, however: he suddenly had a potential informant in front of him about the Christians in the town. When his force returned they would take Martha back, and then keep a watch on visitors to Chloe's house.

Chapter 36

"And they knew exactly where these bodies were?" Casca was interrogating Sextus over the gruesome litter, now set down in the courtyard. A piece of putrid flesh fell away from the neck of the robber's body and exposed maggots scurried for cover.

364

"Yes sir!"

"I think we need to bring that force in for questioning, and maybe Gaius. We can't immediately assume he is implicated but he normally gives these men orders. Take the clothes off them and arrange to bury the bodies. The town force under Gaius can't investigate this. They smell more than the bodies here." Casca turned to Jacob. "You should get back to your stewardship. Do you want this stretcher back? I'll see you get it. I have not heard from Rome yet as to Marcus' will and his family's instruction."

As he strode through the barracks gate, Jacob remembered a parable told by one of the preachers in Antioch about stewardship, and resolved to add it to his gospel. It may have been told by The Lord but even if not, it was worthy of Him. "Back to stewardship." he mused. "This day is totally destroyed for work." He decided to head for Marcus' house and meet up with Judith again. He was beginning to feel hungry. He needed papyrus. There was more in Chloe's house. He would go there first, then check he bottle workshop, and then find Judith.

The heat of the day was just past its most intense when Jacob entered Chloe's house. It was deserted. He was most puzzled by the fact that Martha was not present. It was the first time in decades that Martha was not in that house. It was most ominous. Had Chloe been arrested with Martha? Jacob grabbed his papyrus and left for the workshop. In his hurry he did not see the distant group carrying a table, but they saw him leaving Chloe's house.

The workshop was also deserted and it began to feel that his world had disintegrated. All that was familiar and reliable was a void. His prayers for death in the desert on the way to the Jordan began to come to him. He needed a sign of hope. He began to panic that Marcus' house would be deserted as well. Thankfully it was not. All seemed to be functioning normally and tracked the source of a noise and found Judith with other women pounding something in a large pestle. Something in his mind was recalling more words he had written recently. "Women grinding at the mill – some would be taken and others left."

"Is this the end coming?" he imagined. He was filled with anxiety and yet there was a sense of reinforcements coming to a beleaguered force. He was not to know that another man who felt

366

cornered was at that moment responding to his minion's report that Jacob had been seen attending the house where Christians met. Gaius was marking in the clay in a message box a missive to Casca that a nest of Christian traitors had been discovered, and one of them was Jacob. Arrests were imminent. He sent the same minion with the missive.

Chloe left her companions to the rest of the afternoon's trading. The days were quiet since the riots and the earthquake. They would then close down the market stall and return home. Chloe had to leave early to see to Martha's personal needs, as well as then beginning to prepare the communal meal. As she reached her home, two of Gaius' men were obviously loitering in a space in her street where there was nothing to occupy them. One was urinating into a bush and the other sitting on the ground and one was idly doodling in some pavement dust.

"Why are you watching my house, Linos? Antipater?" Their names were spoken sharply. The doodler came out of his reverie and his companion felt foolish and his bladder was uncomfortable having his stream interrupted. They had been in the earlier search of her house.

Chloe spoke over the floundering attempts at a lie. "If you need to know who comes to the house you can come into my courtyard.

367

I have some real work that needs doing." They muttered something inaudible while shaking heads. "Go home! You are wasting your time." She moved decisively towards her own house and disappeared without looking back. The two remained silent but did not move.

Martha greeted Chloe with the story of her visit to Gaius, and it became immediately obvious to Chloe as to his intentions. "Did anyone come here?"

"Those idiots think that because I am crippled that I am also deaf. They saw Jacob leaving as we approached from the market road and made a big thing about telling Gaius. He could either have been making for the bottle workshop or Marcus' house. He would know something was very wrong if I was not here. I had a long talk with Gaius. He is looking for Christians to arrest. He needs to get the Romans' minds off his crimes."

Martha winced, "Getting carried on that table made my sores worse."

"Let me clean you up and then I'll go to find Jacob. The meal might be later tonight."

368

Jacob updated Judith on his disturbing day. He was apprised of the interruption to the day's work at the bottle workshop. He put Marcus' accounts in order as best he could without a report from the slaves that had fled the workshop. Eventually he mentally escaped from the stress of the day to his fulfilling work on the gospel. He turned to an insert sheet he had set aside "A steward was trusted with talents...." Jacob longed for his master's return, or at least for clarity on the future of Marcus' estate. His own stewardship was one of his best illustrations. As he was completing the parable he heard the women talking in the atrium, and recognised Chloe's voice.

"It won't be long before they come here," is what Chloe was saying as Jacob entered.

"My love you have to leave and find safety," said Judith, her eyes glistening with moisture as she turned to him.

"I can't imagine where we would go. Leaving would also make me look guilty." "Why don't you tell Casca that you have to go to Thyatira to trade again?"

369

There was a long pause as Jacob considered the possibility. He nodded. "I have to put the gospel in a safe place. If I am suspect they will come looking for evidence. I will put it in one of your bread baskets to take back to the farm."

"They might laugh at you doing women's work." Chloe and Judith giggled.

"Alright! You carry it back to the farm."

"We will leave together."

"I have to get back to Martha and start to prepare our meal." Chloe said, and put her arms round Judith who bent to give and receive kisses. Then it was Jacob's turn, and farewells were spoken. Then there was a glimpse of the evening sun, a deep red, on Chloe's face as she exited to the street. In a few moments, Jacob and Judith had their faces bathed with the sun a slightly deeper red. They turned their back to it and headed for the north gate.

Gaius' men were lighting up their brazier at the base of the arch that housed the gate. One of them turned as the movement in the corner of his eye indicated someone coming. His tapping on the back of his comrade and the body language as the four turned to face him was obvious to Jacob and Judith. They were waiting for him. These were not the mentally slow followers of Gaius that had encroached into Chloe's privacy earlier: these were the spearhead of any group that Gaius would have sent to armed conflict: they were the four that Sextus' force had confronted that morning.

"Whatever happens, you keep moving through the gate and take the gospel home to hide it," Jacob said quietly while still out of earshot. Carrying the basket on her left shoulder, Judith held Jacob's arm with her right hand. He knew all of the men in front of him from their frequent visits to Gaius' office. There had never been very much conversation, but they had always been civil. He greeted them on approach. The reply was nominal: they had other business to discuss.

"We need to take you to Gaius."

"Why?"

"Gaius will tell you. You are not going to resist are you?"

Judith was edging past trying to avoid of the attention of the four making the arrest. She was now deeply worried for her beloved

371

Jacob, but was very conscious of the incriminating evidence in her basket. Her bearing and movement must have given something away.

"Search them." There was no way out of the predicament. Between them there was only the basket as a container. And two of the men eyed it.

"Put it down."

"What is this?" The first searcher had come across the papyrus bulk but was unable to read. "I think we should take this with us." No-one would have expected anything but bread or other household goods. Whatever it was, it was out of place.

"It is the report of my stewardship."

"Well I think that might be evidence."

"Of what?"

"We are not here to discuss with you, Scribe. We are here to arrest you." The arresting officer was not about to confess to being unable to read.

"For what?" The reaction was swift and there was to be no discussion. One of the two behind him used the back of hand to hit Jacob across his left ear.

"Move! You know the way."

Judith, choking back tears and at a total loss what to do was ignored. She turned back, hoping to find Chloe. Jacob looked over his shoulder as he was marched away and their eyes met, and both found the deepest love and concern in those eyes. The gaze was broken as Jacob and his arrestors moved round the corner of a house. Judith sobbed uncontrollably as she walked away.

Dusk was closing in rapidly as Jacob was marched up the steps to see Gaius.

"We found them carrying this." The pile of papyrus was dropped heavily of Jacob's old desk.

"I'll arrange a trial for tomorrow." Gaius was decisive. He moved towards the document.

"For what?" Jacob was direct, but ignored.

"Lock him up." Two of the men that had brought him in prodded him towards the small cell block down a passage past the desk. It had last been used when holding the rioters that were crucified outside the north gate. Jacob stooped under the lintel and down the one step into the room. The door slammed and a bolt shot behind him. He was alone. There was a pall of dust hanging from the movement of air as the door swung and its reverberation as it banged on the small space. There was the smell of mould and a hint of dead rodent.

Jacob stood and prayed, not with any fluent words, but with a silent offering of the moment. He was powerless. Then his mind relived the moments of the last few minutes of his violated freedom. He came back to his presence in the cell and opened his eyes. It was not the total blackness he imagined.

He mind came back to his predicament: a trial in the morning. Whatever and whoever tried him, he would get a hearing before Casca if there was a death sentence. Whatever Jacob's supposed crime, Gaius would be merciless to any that had offended him. He may be going to join John, wherever that was.

Then he was curious why it was not totally dark. The building had been stressed like so many in the earthquake and its many aftershocks. He could see the fading daylight through one crack in the baked brickwork and beyond to the street behind the magistrate's building. Behind him, the door was not flush with its surrounds. It was fully two fingers' thickness further from the bottom of the door to the adjacent wall than it was at the top. He could see a finger-width of the middle of the bolt where it disappeared into masonry on one side and behind the door on the other. It was still flush against the lintel at the top and the step at the bottom. To the right of the door there was a crack of light on the side of the door carrying the hinges. Where the hinge bearers entered the right hand wall there was a crack down that masonry. At length, Jacob sat on the floor, his back next to the crack in the wall. His hand touched something on the floor. It was the remains of a predecessor's meal. It was blanched chicken bones. If Jacob was to eat that night, his food would need to be brought by Judith or one sent at her behest. He had often seen the food brought to inmates of the cells. The guards often took choice pieces themselves before passing on the remainder. No prisoner ever stayed long in these cells before their judgement and instant implementation of it. He held one of the bones.

375

It was from a chicken's lower leg. He tried to clear his mind completely, open to prayer and guidance.

He came round with a shock from what must have been one of his fits of re-living something. He could not fully remember the moment but it had had something to do with watching a crucifixion party leaving the city in Jerusalem during his childhood. The condemned man's face was of total resignation. His eyes were glazed. His pain from flogging was beyond his senses. For that man, death was going to be a sort of freedom.

Something in the prison was different. His hearing was sensitive to silence. There were no voices in the rooms outside. He was covered in dust. He tasted brick dust. There must have been an aftershock to the earthquake. It was lighter in the cell than earlier. Light was coming through the chink between the door and the wall. He was still holding the chicken bone. He walked to the door. Pieces of mortar and pellets of brick dropped from him. He spat to clear his mouth. He snorted to clear his nose.

He could see the bolt in the gap. The door was looser and rattled to his touch. With the chicken bone he tried to push the bolt back and there was enough purchase to move it a tiny amount. He tried the same action. There was movement of the bolt again.

His head was fuzzy. He tried to clear his thoughts. What was he going to do if he opened the door? He wanted no confrontation with the arresting force. Had they left when an earthquake threatened?

The bolt move again.

If he left the building where would he go? He could try to go to Thyatira but would the gates be being watched? There must be some confusion after another quake. He could go to Casca and beg his mercy. His service had been worthy he was sure. Gaius, on the other hand was somehow implicated in the death of those found among the vines, so the magistrate's credibility with the Romans was poor. He resolved, if he did escape, to go to the Romans. At least he would not then have to worry about getting out of the town gates.

The bolt moved sufficiently to release the door. He heard no voices in the entrance room in which he used to work and which guards would normally have been stationed when there was a prisoner. The light in the room was from a building fire lighting up the passageway. He could hear shouting from the streets. Some of the magistrate's building had collapsed. He closed the door behind him and re-shot the bolt. There was a crunch of rubble and dust under his foot as he moved. He edged forward seeing vaguely the unevenness before him. Once in his old working room he could see the open street where two columns and half of the front wall with part of the roof had collapsed into the room in a heap. The door to its left hung open. There was no sign of any guards. He wondered if they were under the masonry.

The dilemma struck him. Should he find Judith? Was she safe in the earthquake's consequences? His answer came as he moved down the steps. As he reached the street level he stood on a stone and turned his ankle and fell forward. As he rose, Judith was in front of him. She had run to see if he was safe.

After she had seen Jacob led away, she sought Chloe and her companions. She found them in Marcus' house. Between them they had carried Martha from Chloe's community house, evading Gaius' watch-keepers. There was no-one watching the rear door. At first Judith was inconsolable in her anxiety for Jacob. Chloe set about tasks that included making food to take to the prisoner. They were all about to go to the Magistrate's building when the earthquake struck. If anything it was stronger than that which had destroyed the Island. A roof collapsed

378

across the street. There were shrieks from nearby residents in panic. The only light on this stricken town was a rising last quarter moon. It was the Passover moon, thought Judith. With the dispersal of the church and their persecution they had not observed the Resurrection festival together. To her the power of the Lord was still very present though. The women knelt in the street. They could not keep their feet on the shaking ground. Walls were crashing down every few seconds. Those that could were staggering from their houses. Martha, sitting in Marcus' doorway, broke into a hymn singing of the Lord making a "memorial of his mighty deeds." Albeit with wavering voices on the heaving earth, some of the others women joined in.

It seemed that the shaking would keep going for ever. At last it eased and became still. The only noise was of cries for help from trapped citizens. Then came the rushing and shouting of those that had been uninjured as they called for those they were concerned to find. Forgetting the food intended for Jacob, Judith lifted her skirts and began to run towards the magistrate's building. She was weaving in and out of fallen masonry and had close encounters with other runners in the gloom but thankfully avoided collision. She had no concept of what she would find at the magistrate's building. From first sight it seemed

379

deserted. When she arrived she found a figure falling on the road. It was Jacob.

She held him.

"I don't know what happened," he muttered.

"There was an earthquake. How did you get out?"

"I mean I don't know what happened to me while the earthquake was happening. There was no-one in the building. I have to go to Casca." Bricks and stones and tiles made a small avalanche behind them.

"We can escape in this confusion."

"I cannot abandon my stewardship. I cannot betray Marcus. I have to find Casca. You have to find safety. Go and stay with Chloe until the baby comes. We will know what is happening to Marcus' property by then."

Judith was trying to interrupt. "If a tree has been burnt to ash will you still try to pick its fruit? Marcus is dead and they want to you dead. If Gaius wants you dead do you think Casca will save you? He backs him up. Just look at those who died after the riots." Judith was sounding desperate. "And Marcus is dead. Are you serving a dead master?"

"Yes, and so are you." After a second Judith realised the ambiguity. She wondered if Jacob had resolved to die for his faith.

"You don't have to die now. You have a family now. We could serve The Way somewhere else." Judith's voice was breaking and tears were welling. Jacob held her briefly, kissed her head and broke away.

"Pray for me and for the guidance and power of the Spirit. All may yet be well. I can't stay here though in case Gaius' men come back." Jacob turned and walked towards the barracks. Judith watched him disappear into the darkness and then wept uncontrollably.

At length, she turned back to towards Marcus' house. As she did, she met Chloe and two of her friends carrying the food. They held each other in a group hug. At first Chloe thought Jacob had died in the earthquake until Judith eventually sobbed her way through the exchange she had had.

"We pray all will be well," Chloe eventually breathed, and kissed Judith. They returned through the chaos to the two rooms in Marcus' house that had survived intact.

Chapter 37

Jacob arrived at the barracks to find that much of the Roman building work had survived with only a fallen perimeter wall. However, many of the roof tiles had been dislodged and a low mound of fallen tiles surrounded the buildings. There was no sentry as such, but soldiers were working in the courtyard in flickering torchlight. Among them Jacob could see men of the group that had accompanied the wine shipment with him. He made for Sextus.

"I have to see Casca."

Sextus was holding a torch for his troop. "Jacob, either you or this fucking earthquake are inconvenient, and probably both. This had better be good. Try me."

"Gaius arrested me and put me in his cell. He was going to try me tomorrow. I think he wants to blame me for the bodies in the vineyard."

"And you just walked out of the cell."

"The earthquake helped."

"I can't see the Procurator seeing you any time soon. Stand over there out of sight.

■■

Gaius felt satisfied that he had Jacob in his cell. He had the following morning mapped out for the trial and argument before the Procurator, the last word on capital punishment. He had a slave vulnerable in front of him, naked and bent over a table. He abused his slaves either when he felt frustrated and depressed when things were not going right, or when he felt self satisfied that he was being successful and the abuse was to give himself a reward. At other times he would abuse a slave because he was bored. This slave had marks on her rump that had not disappeared since his last assault on her.

The first jolt of the earthquake sent Gaius reeling and he fell chest first on a stool. The pain across his chest was searing. He had broken a rib. His breath was hard to catch. He was wheezing. The movement was violent and he remained on the floor. The most fortunate in his household was the slave gripping for safety to the table,

383

hitherto her place of torture but now a place of safety. Anything that could fall over was doing so. Roof tiles were to be heard crashing on the road outside. Household members were shouting in fear in other rooms. The flaming torch fell from its bracket on the wall, landed on the carpeting and the drapes of a seat and burst into flames. Despite seeing the danger, the violence of the quaking prevented coherent movement. Gaius shouted for help but all in the house, like him, were incapable of any action apart from staggering or crawling as best they could. The pain in his chest was excruciating, but he had to make his escape. The slave could equally sense the danger and lurched through the door. She had no intention of aiding Gaius. This, as for everyone in this visitation, was a matter of survival. Gaius made slow progress to the exit on all fours, still wheezing, but he was regaining his breath after the shock. Despite the crashing of tiles and house fitments, he made it to the street. The room he had left was now uncontrollably ablaze. Water containers were crashing over, even if anyone could keep their feet long enough to carry water to the fire.

Whatever else was happening around him, Gaius was aware of only one feeling and that was rage. This, for him, was the ultimate demonstration of the sorcery of his former scribe and a direct assault on his person and his property. At the top of his list of grievances at that

384

moment was his utter powerlessness to counteract the forces against him. He lay on the convulsing ground looking at the night sky, and the smoke from his house was now blotting out some of the stars. His prayer was to any god that would answer him in the affirmative and give him satisfaction for his rage. None was coming at that moment. The earth's convulsions continued with its horrific consequences for the buildings around him.

When the tremors ceased, Gaius was frustrated to find none of his slaves near him to order them to quell the fire now engulfing his roof, licking through the gaps where tiles had been. Given the distance from the water source at the end of his aqueduct, with a working group there would have been chance to save the building's integrity for restoration. He did not know that even could this force be engaged, the aqueduct had been fractured in the quake. He rose to his feet and headed for the magistrate's building picking his way through the fallen building materials by the light of his flaming home. He might, he thought, be able to assemble some of his posse to assist. Law and order would not be a problem instantly, but there could be disturbances in the morning with possible looting, if not a repeat of the riots of the earlier quake.

385

His panting arrival at his office gave him little hope. Breathing was agony. Two of his force, he was to discover later, those guarding his prisoner, had died in the collapse of one of his walls and were yet buried under the rubble. The others were dispersed searching for or rescuing their own families. He was too frightened to enter his office for fear of further collapse, and there was little he could do in the blackness of the interior. Alive or dead, he thought, Jacob was still in his cell; probably dead to see the destruction in front of him.

With no apparent members of his force available, Gaius resolved to head for the Roman barracks for support in law and order for the following day. As a deterrent to those who might risk good order, he resolved to ask Casca for the crucifixion of Jacob. He was a Christian after all, probably a sorcerer, and was the most likely cause of the gods' anger that brought the earthquake.

It was a difficult walk for Gaius. Through the dark streets he was picking his feet through scattered bricks and tiles. He was avoiding others finding their way in their concern for the consequences of the quake. Even on the more open road to the barracks there was a fallen wall and wandering or panicked animals. There were at least moving torches in the barracks that gave a hint of terrain in front of him.

386

The sentry point was unguarded. Soldiers worked with a will inside the barracks. There was much activity, and none of the barking orders that had been in evidence when Jacob arrived. Gaius approached the nearest squad, who were engaged in sorting and stacking bricks or tiles in the light of their superior's torch.

As he neared the group there was a shout. Gaius was not clear as to what was called but the working squad but the squad immediately looked for their weapons and the torchbearer had a drawn sword in his hand. They were facing the intruder.

"I am Gaius the Magistrate," called out the disquieted official, clearly disturbed to find weapons drawn against him. "I need to see the Procurator."

Sextus loomed from the dark and stood in front of Gaius too close for the latter's comfort. "I will find the Procurator for you Sir, but it may be some time before he can find opportunity to see you." Despite the respectful address, it was clear that Sextus was the authority. Sextus moved into the darkness again. The workforce returned to their tasks and Gaius was ignored. He became conscious of soldiers and slaves moving around him and became afraid of collision so moved to the edge of the parade square. He was out of range of the torch lights.

He stood for some minutes, until he saw another party of men coming round a distant building close to the Procurator's house. Hoping it was Casca he set off towards the light and was immediately startled by the figure in the darkness beside him.

"Greetings Gaius," said Jacob from a range of two steps. He had seen Gaius arrive, meet the soldiers and move uncertainly around the Roman enclosure. Jacob had been silent and patient. He had no wish for a confrontation before he was in the presence of Casca. However he had to stop the limited vision night sighted Gaius colliding with him

Gaius was immediately in shock. He had no evidence of Jacob ever being violent, but he was very threatened by the presence in his space. Jacob was, for Gaius, dead or trapped. The magistrates mind was racing in the supernatural world of Jacob the sorcerer and mover of earthquakes. Jacob was calmly awaiting the chance to meet the Procurator to demonstrate his innocence away from the corrupt judgement of the magistrate's office in the power of Gaius.

388

They were both saved further embarrassment or conversation by the arrival of the squad led by Casca. Sextus marched across to summon them. He marched back, stood before the procurator and saluted. The exchange between the Romans was out of earshot as they crossed the pavement, but Sextus was gesturing in their direction. The squad were disciplined. Off duty the men referred to Gaius as "Flatus Maximus." His town force was just "Flatus."

Casca was bound to take the ranking magistrate ahead of the steward in audience. Sextus marched to the magistrate. His was a military voice when he spoke. Jacob could expect no familiarity in these circumstances. He was told to wait where he was. Gaius was bidden to approach Casca. There were no buildings in which they could safely meet so the audience took place in the flickering torchlight in a square of soldiers. Jacob could hear voices but could not make out what was being said.

"Now Gaius," said Casca, "what is the condition of the town. Are there any law and order issues? You can see we have our problems but order would be our priority."

Gaius was bursting with another agenda but was obliged to answer. His was the responsibility for maintaining the peace and the Roman garrison was a reserve force. "The… there is much confusion," he stammered. My office is very damaged. I may have lost several of my men. There is a fire and much damage, but everyone seems to be looking after their families and dealing with their own damage. I see no disorder, Procurator."

"So why are you here?" Casca's tone was impatient.

I have…I had a prisoner. A criminal. I believe him to be a sorcerer and he caused this destruction through his god. He is there. Jacob, once my scribe. Now he is a steward."

"I know who Jacob is. I have oversight of him for Marcus' estate. This accusation is extreme. What is your proof?"

Gaius was lost for words for a few moments. His imaginings around the scene of the attack on the wine shipment was out of the reckoning. "He was in the prison when the earthquake came. He escaped unhurt from a locked cell."

"I was in a building when the quake came. I am unhurt. Am I a sorcerer? A quake damages doors and walls. If he caused the earthquake so that he could escape then why did he not run away instead of coming here? Why was he locked in your cell anyway? Not for causing earthquakes. That obviously came after you locked him up." There was a silence during which Casca took a pace forward into Gaius' space. The latter felt uncomfortable. Casca was annoyed at the delay in responding.

"Magistrate, in one simple sentence, why was Jacob your prisoner?"

"Bodies were found amongst his vines."

"I know that. He came to tell me that. I want to know how your men knew they were there. Sorcery did not kill them, and I don't see this steward killing anyone. He went to pieces when his wine shipment was attacked."

Gaius was floundering. "Jacob is a Christian," he blurted.

"That is a separate issue. Why did your men go to search his vines? How did you know there were bodies there?"

391

"I didn't. We were searching for missing men." Gaius had found a plausible answer and felt much relieved inside. Casca, however, was no fool and saw through the mental workings in front of him.

"Magistrate, I will examine the accused when you have gone. For now I need a town force of law and order after this destruction. Go and deal with it. This is not over. I will return to the matter of the murder victims you were looking for when there are less pressing matters. I am watching you. Go."

"I do not know if I have a force, Sir. My office is destroyed with men inside and there is much destruction in the town."

"Very well. I will send a force with you to keep the peace and prevent looting." He looked at Sextus, "Take ten men and escort the Magistrate for peacekeeping detail only."

Sextus saluted and began to bark orders to select a squad. They marched towards the town, Gaius could not keep up with the soldiers as they disappeared into the gloom. His breathing was laboured and the pain in his chest was searing as he breathed. The slow marching

392

force became silhouettes against their front torch and the low red and smoky sky of more than one fire in the town in front of him.

Back in the barracks there was silence for some time in the company left as the sound of marching receded. The soldiers were still in a square as for a court for the Procurator.

"Stand forward Steward."

Jacob moved into the centre of the square, the inward facing group and its soldiery lit by the flickering torches with the occasional reflected glint from a spear or a drawn sword.

"Did you hear the Magistrate's charges against you? What do you have to say?"

"There was no sorcery, Sir. The building was damaged and without guards. I walked out unchallenged to come here. If the true God wanted us destroyed then none of us would be alive here now." Jacob was surprised at his own calmness in the circumstances.

"Gaius called you a Christian. Are you?"

393

"I am a follower of The Way, Sir." Jacob was about to continue with an outline of his activities as a follower but Casca spoke again.

"The Emperor is the Lord, a God, worthy of worship. Do you deny that?"

"I obey the Emperor in his law and through his officers, Sir."

"That was not an answer to the question Steward. Who is your Lord? Christ or the Emperor?"

"On earth, the Emperor but in earth and heaven, supreme over all in the one supreme God." Jacob was surprised by the way the questioning had turned to his faith. He was distracted and yet unafraid, remembering Jesus before Pontius Pilate. He realised more fully the implications of what could happen to him. He was unafraid and filled with a surprising inner peace. The soldiery around him held no fear for him, but he had lost that twisted emotional knot that brought such panic and inner destruction of earlier meetings with Roman soldiers and authority. He knew he would not have another mental aberration. Casca was still pondering Jacob's last answer. He did not like the way he felt in himself that the answer was sufficient as such, but he was concerned that his own authority was in some way being challenged before his own force and in his own court by this servant of the suspect new religion. He needed more time to think but had to demonstrate decisiveness.

"Is there a secure room to hold this prisoner?"

"Yes Sir." A ranking soldier behind Jacob had stepped forward to attention.

"Then take him to it. We will continue at a more convenient time. Give him food and water. Dismissed. Let's get this mess cleaned up."

******

Two of the rooms in Marcus' house were serviceable albeit dusty from the fallen bricks in the courtyard. Judith, Chloe and her women, with Martha had spent many hours traversing the ruined streets with the distressed and injured to reach the door. The noise on route was of voices calling for family members, cries of help beside rubble that with varying degrees of certainty covered victims, and the moans of the injured. At least this time there was no Island structure to

395

collapse on hopeless and helpless humanity as in the earlier quake. Clearly even in the darkness there was not a house left undamaged. In the minds of the women there was hope that its victims would be recovered if they were under fallen masonry. There was the expectation that all would recover after healing and rebuilding. The buildings that had sustained the greatest damage were the larger structures of stone such as the Magistrates building, the Temples and the amphitheatre that had been under construction where several yards of a wall had fallen flat into the street. They had helped where they could. Their hands were abraded and their clothes were caked in dust and sweat. The only member of their group missing was Jacob. The group felt Judith's anguish particularly above the personal concern they had for Jacob, their friend and Deacon. They cleared dust as best they could, found bedding that was dust free and each found a place to attempt sleep resolving that nothing could be achieved until daylight.

Chapter 38

Marcus reached the brow of the hill amongst the street traders. He could see the two seas from this point: that he had just crossed behind him and the one before him over which was home. Corinth was all he had imagined: busy, colourful and cosmopolitan, arrayed with impressive buildings and under the canopy of its neighbouring mountain. He had a slight regret that he could not stay longer but was homesick for his vineyard and his family in the church, and keen to see how it had fared in his absence. He was also anxious about the rumours of earthquakes that had been reported in the region from returning soldiers who had been stationed in Ephesus.

He had paused beside a leatherwork shop and the smell brought back his bottle shop. He wondered about his faithful slaves in there with affection.

He looked again over the glinting sea behind him. He thanked God for the blessings the trip had brought him: reconciliation to his wife and closeness to his son. He had a new son he had claimed his own, Severus, and arrangements had been made to bring them to live with him later. He had even found an accommodation with his father after so many years. He clasped his bag to him with its precious senatorial documentation for Casca and the town authorities. He was to be appointed Magistrate until the corruption surrounding that office

397

could be investigated and elections held again. Greek democracy was to be suspended and Roman authority imposed.

Above all he thanked God for his Baptism, still fresh in his emotions with the mental picture of emerging wet and with the bright emergence into the sounds of air and a cheering church. He could now greet Onesimus, Jacob and the church family in Chloe's house as a brother in Christ. Yes Chloe, that lovely affectionate saint who first provided him with a family when he was so distant from all that felt homely. For all its attractions, Corinth would have to wait for another excursion, maybe with Octavia and Livius. He walked again towards the ship he assumed was his transport home.

Chapter 39

"The Emperor's law is clear. I have no choice steward." Casca had asked Jacob three times in uncompromising terms and no matter how diplomatically Jacob claimed loyalty to the Emperor, he would not call him Lord above the Lord Jesus. He stood condemned to be crucified. The allegations of sorcery and the other myths surrounding what Christians did as stated by the Magistrate had been dismissed, but Domitian's law on his divine pre-eminence could not be set aside.

398

"Take him away. He is to be locked up." The last order was to Anthony who was guarding the prisoner.

Anthony stood to attention and saluted. Gently but firmly he grasped Jacob by the back of the arm and turned him towards the door. The door was opened by the guard standing outside who could hear the proceedings within. Anthony released his grasp once they were through the door and approaching the descent to the courtyard.

"I can't save you Jacob." Anthony had great affection for his friend. "I'm sure your Jesus would understand if you said what the Procurator needed to hear." Jacob's face was pale and his expression slightly distant. He had a death sentence on him and he was still in shock.

At the bottom of the stairs Anthony's comment had sunk in and he was able to formulate a reply. "Right after Domitian stands beside the throne of God for denying Him, then I would be next."

There was a long pause as the two moved towards the cells.

"Doria did not die when the Island fell. She is a Christian as well. Don't betray her."

399

The anguish that showed on Anthony's face matched that on hearing that Doria had perished in the Island. "Where is she?"

"I hope she made it to Thyatira. She is training to be a seamstress. You know what happens to runaway slaves." There was another pause until they reached the cell door.

"Can you tell Judith what is happening to me please?"

"Where is she?"

"I think she is still in Marcus' house."

Anthony nodded, his mind already on his erstwhile lover. For all the bravado and boasting in the barracks, Anthony had only been physical with one woman in his life, and she, until a few minutes before, had died in the cataclysmic collapse of the Island building. Now she seemed to be as remote in Thyatira as she had been under the rubble. Unless there was another caravan to guard, and he remained a soldier he was tied to his military masters.

Jacob returned to his cell to lie down in silence, as he had done for what seemed endless hours. He had lost track of time apart from the distant awareness of the difference between darkness and light

400

somewhere at the end of the labyrinth of storeroom buildings in which his cell was located. At least he was receiving two meals a day, partly supplied, unbeknown to him, from the gifts left at the gate of the fort brought by Judith's friends under her roof. He laid quietly on the floor, the empty emotional feeling in his stomach compensated by his prayers. There was in all the answers to his prayers a silence. It was the one certainty in all his fear for the future: silence in this cell.

Chapter 40

As the qualified seamstress and senior member of the group. Hikane was the first across Obadiah's threshold clutching the papyrus from Jacob. Doria, Rebecca, Agathon and Aethon remained with the beasts of burden awaiting instructions. All were utterly weary and desperate for a positive response from hoped for benefactor and potential investor. It was late afternoon. Obadiah, even if he was not to invest in their future, would at least be obligated to give hospitality to these tired and needy travellers.

When Hikane shown to Obadiah's presence, he was quick to open Jacob's letter. Jacob was emphatic on the need for accommodation for these economic migrants not least because of their

home buildings due to the earthquake. As steward, he was also made a good case for a partnership with Chloe and with Marcus' successor in the business venture under Hikane's skills. Agathon was put at Obadiah's service until such times as further arrangements were made when Marcus' estate was settled. Obadiah was shocked to hear of Marcus' possible death at sea.

He was soon enthused about the joint venture with Chloe's women for a clothes manufacture and gave two of his many rooms to work and residence for thee women. Agathon and Aethon were put to work with his transport animals. The tired travellers were soon reassured of a secure future, as far as that was possible for Christians in Domitian's "divine" world.

Gaius and his surviving force commandeered the arena for his new headquarters. Gladiators' preparation rooms made decent offices and quarters, while the cells used to victims of violent sports made perfect places for incarceration of criminals. The population were unlikely to riot after their recent memories, and most were heavily engaged with rebuilding, not least because most living space had been damaged. The magistrate's building would take too much labour to

402

render useable for the foreseeable future given the demand for construction skills.

Gaius still felt rancorous towards Marcus, his household and staff, and believed his home to be a refuge for Christians but felt warned off by Casca's words in such a way as to make an intrusion off limits. The Roman soldiers allotted to his force made him uneasy. He felt himself being policed rather that him leading the policing. The tension between Gaius's men and the Romans made everyone uneasy given their standoff in the vines.

Jacob at first welcomed the silence of his prison but grew more restless and anxious. If only he could believe Martha's words and he could see Marcus return. On the second day he was summoned to see Casca. From his dark confinement he had no idea of time. The sunlight glared and he shaded his eyes as he reached and crossed the parade ground. Casca had a room restored for his administration. He passed under the round arch one the ground floor and faced the seated Roman leader.

"Steward, you have been faithful to your master. It gives me no pleasure to pass a sentence of death on you. This is your last

403

opportunity to avoid a charge of treason. All you have to do is burn a pinch of incense before the Emperor's image and worship him as Lord. How you worship your own chosen God after that will not be questioned. Do you agree to this judgement?"

Jacob was silent for a moment as the import of this question sank in. "Sir, many of the Emperor's proclaimed themselves gods. As gods they did not either prevent their deaths or enable them to rise from the dead. I have a God who raised my Lord from the dead. I honour the Emperor as my lawful leader and you as his servant here. I am not a traitor."

"Your crucifixion will be in the morning. After nightfall there will be no going back. You guard will be within earshot if you change your mind before then." Casca returned his eyes to a clay tablet in his hand. Jacob could feel the presence of the soldier behind him. He did not know him, though he thought he recognised the faces of most of the force in the barracks.

"Before you go, steward, your master did not die. I have a message here that he is on his way from Rome. I hope you are still alive to greet him. Guard! Return this man to his cell."

Jacob's mind was in confusion as he walked weakly to his cell. There was a little joy in his thoughts to know that Marcus was returning. If only he could arrive quickly: but even his return would not remove the sentence unless Jacob betrayed his Lord Jesus. Marcus giving support might cause his own demise as a baptised and practising member of The Way.

Jacob was facing certain pain. He had seen many people crucified. Hopefully one of his guards would despatch him quickly. If only one of his soldier acquaintances could see to the execution. But then, what of Judith? What of her unborn child? Marcus would surely take her into his home again along with her child. He had to get a message to her. Still in the daylight before the improvised cell block, he addressed the soldier, "Please can I see Sextus or Anthony? I need my wife to know what is happening."

"You are not a slave? You have a wife? I will be relieved soon. I will let them know."

The cool of the cell block was a marginal physical relief from the heat, but the emotional turmoil this time was not calmed by the silence of the cell when the door closed. His prayer seemed to intensify the silence. Silence always seemed to be the answer to his prayers. His mind fell on his own account of Jesus in the garden awaiting arrest. The disciples fell asleep, ran away and denied him. He pleaded with the Lord that he in turn would not fall short of true discipleship. But what of the pain of the cross? What of his wife's pain? Judith would see him. He thought of Phoebe and the terrible grief she must have had seeing one of her children on a cross. Then he thought of Jesus and his mother under His cross. It was hard to tell if this was a comfort, but it helped his resolve to keep faith with his Lord.

The passage of time was hard to estimate, but eventually the door was opened to Sextus alongside the previous guard's relief. His face was stern. "I have my work to do tomorrow. If I did not do it I would be joining you. My detail is your crucifixion. You don't have to do this."

"If you were a traitor to your Lord you would take the punishment. I am not going to be a traitor to mine. I am not a traitor to Domitian either. Please let Judith know if you can."

Sextus nodded sternly. "I'll do what I can." The door closed. Jacob pondered what Sextus meant: did he mean letting Judith know, or did he mean something about the crucifixion?

Chapter 41

Marcus reflected on his meeting with the church in Corinth, formerly of so much of interest to the late disciple Paul. His intent to return home was tempered by his new enthusiasm for the welfare of the church and its communications. He brought news from Rome and he was keen to update the Corinthians on Jacob's new document. That, surely must be completed now.

He stood in the prow of the bireme, facing home. There was a breeze in his face and he had a feeling of wellbeing. At last he could rid the community of Gaius' excesses and corruption. He had plans. Casca was to give him his new force to ensure law-keeping. He pictured the magistrate's office under his administration. Jacob and Judith would well administer his estates until Octavia arrived.

He looked forward to his new role in the church as a baptised member. He could curb the excesses of those who would persecute its worshippers.

407

The officers of the ship were respectful of his new rank. He was requested to join them for food rations. He had found his sea legs and walked between the rowers to the stern. They would be docking by late afternoon, he was informed. He could see the land on the horizon.

********** **********

Judith intended to be strong for Jacob's sake as she watched the crucifixion force arrive. That morning she had been sick from her pregnancy. She was churning emotionally. She had not been able to eat for more than two days.

As expected, Jacob was carrying the cross piece from which he was to hang. Gaius and his force, supplemented by the Roman soldiers allocated to him lined the final part of the road to the dockside crucifixion site. Here was to be a warning to all travellers of the local enforcement of justice. Judith and her supporters, including Chloe and Phoebe could see the front soldiers. Anthony was the foremost spear bearer.

Judith was watching Jacob's demeanour of resignation. He still had dignity. At least they had not stripped him yet, or beaten him. Their eyes met. Her resolve collapsed and she ran towards her husband.

408

She had no idea what she would do when she reached him. Gaius' force moved to intercept her. The Romans in Gaius' group stood unmoved to attention. What violent intent the local Greek police intended was never to be discovered. Anthony's spear levelled to bar the Greeks' advance. A sharp glance showed Anthony's expression. It warned them not to move further. Judith reached Jacob and the marching party without order stopped as one. Nobody spoke. There were no sobs. Tearful eyes were streaming from each of the couple to blur their vision, but both knew the greater love was of the Lord. Neither were going to step back from this pain, both emotional, and in Jacob's case additionally, physically.

The moment did not last long. Anthony firmly held Judith's shoulder and she retreated for the party to march slowly on.

Much as Gaius wanted the humiliation of his erstwhile scribe there was no baying crowd. There was no spitting. A few bystanders watched in silence. In that community Jacob was popular and respected.

409

Out of earshot of Jacob who was now on the ground beside the lapping sea of the port, Judith sobbed on Chloe's shoulder. Arms of women surrounded her. She could not watch the hoisting of the victim.

Above Jacob was the daubed sign of "Christian." Anthony looked sombre. He had seen many crucifixions before but this was the first where he had a personal relationship with the criminal. He looked up at Jacob with understanding. Through the extreme discomfort, Jacob was aware of the eyes below him. Anthony nodded. It reminded him of the nod Sextus gave him before leaving the cell the previous night. The force that had come from the barracks, their work done, ordered themselves for the march back.

Gaius' force remained. The Romans were somewhat aware of the relationship of some of the soldiers with Jacob. They had noted the lack of taunting and humiliation that usually accompanied crucifixion for the personal entertainment of the executioners. Only Gaius seemed willing to taunt the man on the cross. "Don't you wish you had taken the Jewess for your slave now? I could have saved you."

Jacob bore the excruciating pain of raising himself on his feet to draw enough breath to reply, "Then I would be dead under your

death trap at the island. You should be here you murdering criminal."
He paused to recover from the exhaustion of speaking. He drew enough
breath to go on. "But no cross would be strong enough to carry your
weight."

Gaius raged inside. His locals on the force tried to keep
straight faces. The Romans were less controlled. Gaius squealed in his
falsetto, "Stand to attention!" The three Romans ignored him and
unspeaking, as one began to walk away up the hill and back to the
town. Each of them met Jacob's eye with the same nod of respect given
by Anthony.

Gaius and his remaining two officers, the same that had
watched Chloe's house remained unspeaking under the cross. Gaius
had nothing left to say. His taunt had caused his own humiliation. He
was not going to risk further loss of face. Jacob continued labouring to
breathe. His arms and legs were already weary from bearing his weight.
The small lath against which he bore his weight cut into his heels. The
other lath and means of support cut into his bare buttocks. His prayer
was not coherent. It went no further than, "Lord, behold!" At least there
were no nails. He was conscious of where his Lord had been before
him. He bore three hours that Passover. Jacob had heard of victims

411

lasting two weeks before the merciful release of death. And would they then break his legs?

Gaius and his minions shambled off to Jacob's right, out of range of his sight. They were sitting on the rocks at the end of the path from which the jetty projected. Jacob was left alone, staring out to sea. There was no ship. Most vessels arrived round the headland. When one was coming from Athens or Corinth, or coasting from the north, it was only minutes from landing when it became visible.

"Out of the sea I called. 'Lord hear me!'"

Jesus had used words of the psalmist, "Lord, why have you abandoned me?"

Apart from the sea there was silence. No voice was carried along from Gaius' group, not that there would be lengthy conversations forthcoming. There was no familiarity between Gaius and his force. Judith hoped there would be no guards around later that day. The heat of noon had passed. Jacob would be desperately thirsty by now. She clutched the leather cup with its precious contents. If she could just find one moment alone, she could wet he beloved's lips at least, if not enable him to drink. No-one must see her. She was in terrible danger of

412

prosecution if caught. Neither the Romans nor Gaius would be merciful.

There was no-one in sight. She arrived under the cross. Jacob was aware of her movement. He was aware of the danger. With his eyes and facial gesture he tried to warn of the force to his left and breathed, "Gaius." It was too late. Gaius had moved into sight. No crime had taken place but he did not find technicality a problem. Here was a woman assisting a crucified man.

"Arrest her!" Gaius had his chance for vengeance. The two minions raced up to Judith and immediately manhandled her, even though there was no attempt to resist arrest. The leather cup dropped and its water briefly pooled and sank into the trodden earth.

She looked up to Jacob. "See you with the Lord my love." Her arm was then twisted up her back while the other minion took the opportunity to squeeze one of her breasts painfully. She had no further chance to look to Jacob.

Gaius arrived under the cross. He had a smirk as he looked up at Jacob. He drew breath to say something taunting, but Jacob endured the pain of drawing breath to speak first. "You have never known love

413

have you Gaius? I am the happier man." He smiled through the pain as if with a joyful memory. Then he looked out to sea. Gaius verbally had nowhere else of go and he shambled off up the path towards the arena to vent his anger on his new prisoner.

The sun moved on. He heard soldiers talking and moving towards the shore. They were not marching. At last Anthony and Sextus appeared before him, Anthony still with his spear. Sextus spoke. "Forgive us Jacob. You do not deserve this. May your God take you to himself."

Jacob drew breath to answer with, "Bless you."

He managed to say it before Anthony's spear sharply and quickly penetrated under his ribcage and though the heart. That pain was mercifully short. The sound of the sea faded rapidly for him and Jacob was no longer conscious of any sensation, especially the multiple agonies of his cross.

The two soldiers had obtained the consent of Casca. No-one from the barracks who knew Jacob thought he was criminal enough for the agony of having his legs broken.

414

Chapter 42

The bireme rounded the headland. The homesick Marcus was on the prow. He had dreamed of this moment for some weeks. He was in haste to deal with formalities at the barracks with Casca before heading to his household and a joyful re-union. The town looked familiar but the cross on the distant quayside jarred slightly with his mood. Yes, criminals had been executed there before, usually for piracy, but it was exceptional. The approach to the sound of the oars, hitherto giving anticipation its rhythm, unfortunately now had an optical focus of death. Even at that maximum distance, there was a body visible on the cross.

As the rowers moved the boat into the evening shadow of the headland, it was clear whose body was on the cross. Confused emotions ran through Marcus, but that to the fore was anger. There was a large measure of grief, but a salutary warning of how he had to present his faith commitment. He could read the charge above the body.

At last the port oars were withdrawn and the boat ground alongside. Docking formalities completed, Marcus stood on land again, and walked to the cross. His allocated guards joined him with his credentials, ready to present to the procurator. The few possessions he had brought from Rome were in the possession of a slave, and he had given instruction as to the house for their delivery while en route. Marcus now had some foreboding as to the condition of his home and property. Had there been an attack on the property of Christians? Had it extended to his?

Marcus and his escort set out to the barracks, catching the discarded cup as he turned. He picked it up and recognised its workmanship.

He was shocked to see the devastation evident from the earthquakes. Some work was still being done to repair buildings, but the streets were largely deserted. A distant cheer from the arena explained the absence of evening crowds. He passed the magistrate's building, one of the few colonnaded buildings under normal circumstances, clearly unusable in its present condition. Rendering it useable had to be a priority.

Casca appeared to be ready for him. The formalities of his taking up office were brief. The procurator made it clear the deposing of Gaius was not a moment too soon, and Marcus was apprised of the

416

evidence of the corruption. A search of his properties would no doubt bring more. Disarming, dismissing and arresting Gaius' force had to be immediate. The arena would be their location, as well as where Gaius would be. A force of soldiers was put at Marcus' disposal. Seeing his home would have to wait. This change of political oversight would have to be swift and emphatic.

The unfinished business was heavy on Marcus' mind. "Why was my steward crucified?"

"He left me no choice. I gave him opportunity to acknowledge the Emperor's status as a god and he refused. I even gave him the rest of the day to recant his treason. I was merciful enough to end his suffering quickly. I know he was a good steward, and I am sorry for the loss of your friend. I now hand the responsibility for rooting out those who deny the Emperor's divinity to you Magistrate."

Almost as an afterthought, Casca added, "When the barracks are repaired sufficiently, you can have all the labour available to restore the Magistrate's building, and restore your home. I'm sure your present residence is worthy of your status. And Marcus," the tone became informal, "I hope we can be friends as you were with my predecessor.

417

He was very complimentary about you and your previous service to Rome."

Marcus nodded with an expression of grace. He had much to do before darkness fell, and the sun was changing to an evening yellow. "Thank-you, Casca." He avoided the temptation to salute as he would have done in an earlier phase of his life, but his turning away from a superior was still military.

Chapter 43.

Knowing the military qualities of Gaius' force, Marcus had little fear of resistance. Sextus had seen some of them faced with real soldiers in the vines after they discovered the bodies. This was not going to be difficult. Gaius had paid for most of the entertainment himself, he had been told. It seemed to be in Gaius' interest to be popular with the masses. This seemed to be his payback for tolerating the commonly held opinion, often with direct experience, that he was corrupt.

Two of the force at Marcus' disposal were sent round the opposite side of the arena from the barracks. They did not want the guards on the outside gates warning those inside the arena that a

418

Roman force was approaching, for whatever reason they might suspect. Swiftly, an order of "Drop your weapon!" was obeyed in all confrontations. The disarmed men were ordered to sit on the ground in a group, being guarded. The distractions of the games inside meant that there was no communication with the remaining few of Gaius' force. Knowing the arena's layout, the positioning of his remaining guards was fairly obvious to the Romans. Entering both from the gladiator's entrance and the front gate, the soldiers moved quickly. Marcus and his two soldiers ran up the steps to the president's box where they knew they would find Gaius. How well guarded he would be was not known. The one guard with him was out of his eye-line and watching the arena. The forceful hand over his mouth and the drawn sword in his face ensured silence. Marcus took the guard's weapon and one of Marcus' soldiers escorted him away down the staircase to join his disarmed comrades. They would all be incarcerated for the night and interviewed in the morning. Gaius' property would be searched.

Only Gaius was left. He was reclining in the place of honour behind a curtain beyond the guard and overseeing the entertainment as it reached its climax. Marcus moved alongside the prone president. The remaining soldier moved to the other side. Gaius gave a start as he realised the identity of his visitor, and then, complacent, relaxed. He

419

continued his previous position peering over his three times folded corporation to the entertainment in the arena.

"I hereby relieve you of your position as magistrate," stated Marcus baldly.

Gaius smirked. "On whose authority?"

"The Emperor, Senate, and now the Procurator here. You may inspect the authority now in the hands of the Procurator."

Gaius was unconvinced, suspecting a hoax and a reprisal from Marcus for the loss of his steward. "Guard!" There was a brief movement from Gaius' left hand. "Guard!" he shrilled more vehemently.

Gaius was distracted by movement from the arena. Satisfied the soldier on the other side of Gaius was equal to any sudden movement or threat, Marcus looked for the first time at the scene about to be enacted for the crowd. There was a naked, bleeding and bruised woman spread-eagled in the centre, each limb roped to a different horse.

420

The woman screamed, "Lord, forgive them." Marcus for the first time recognised Judith.

The scream startled the horses and prematurely began the movement that would otherwise have been signalled by Gaius from his vantage point. Gaius again had a realisation, this time the previous connection of the victim with Marcus. There was no going back. The horses in panic lurched and wrenched the ropes. There was a visible noise of Judith's hip joint being dislocated and another bone broken. A major artery was torn open and a massive jet of blood sprayed the sand. Her pain was short lived as she went unconscious with pain and blood loss.

Marcus went through a range of emotions in a very short time, but very quickly they all converged on extreme rage.

"She asked for her god to forgive. Do you think he will?" goaded Gaius, as he fed himself a handful of snack food with his right hand. Marcus knew the left held a weapon.

"He may," replied Marcus with a steely controlled voice, "but I don't think I can."

421

The food sprayed from Gaius' mouth. It was followed by a sprayed vomit of blood. He looked confused at his source of pain and saw the hilt and handle of the sword in Marcus' hand, the sword previously carried by Gaius' erstwhile guard. The blade had completely entered the prone belly from above the hip to enter the chest cavity. Gaius tried to raise the dagger in his left hand but he had lost the ability to do so and was losing consciousness. There was a metallic sound as it fell to the stone paving. He gagged again, gave a throaty death rattle, and died.

Chloe, in Marcus' house with her remaining women and Phoebe were worried about the late return of Judith. At last they resolved to leave the house to look for her, aiming first to see if she was under Jacob's cross. As they passed the road down to the port they could see the cross, and the motionless Jacob, but the bireme with its attendant activity. They heard the distant uproar of the crowd from the arena and headed in that direction. As they reached the entrance they found the seated men of Gaius' force with their attendant Roman guards.

At that very moment Marcus exited the arena into their path. The recognition was instant, with cries of joy from the women. Then a murmur of consternation at the sight of the blood on Marcus' tunic.

"Are you alright?" Chloe uttered, standing back from the gore.

"I am fine. This is Gaius all over me. He couldn't control himself. I am sorry to say that Judith has died in the arena for her Lord."

He called one of the soldiers. "Take these women to the gladiators' gate. Commandeer two of the attendants and a stretcher. Take the body of the woman from the centre of the arena and take it with these women to my house. They will prepare it for burial. Then take those same men with another stretcher and recover the body from the cross in the port. Take it to the barracks and await instructions." The tearful women left Marcus to his responsibilities and followed the appointed soldier.

In the oil lamps of the Procurator's office, with his soldier witness present, Marcus reported the death of Gaius. Yes, he was armed, and no, he made no concession to his successor. Arrangements were made for Marcus to return for the interview process of Gaius'

423

men, who were to remain separated to avoid conferring and manufacturing evidence. The bodies of Jacob and Judith were to be buried together in the late Urbanus' olive grove in the morning. Marcus would meet the force at its entrance. Marcus had asked Phoebe's consent. After further consultation Casca conceded that Marcus should be allowed to go home and see to his household and estate. He was granted a Roman guard to patrol his street.

He entered his house alone. The residual damage to his home was a shock to him. He could hear women's voices and traced them to their source and the light across his courtyard. The re-union with Chloe, her household and his household with him was emotional. The report on the events of the previous weeks went on well into the night.

Messengers would be sent to Thyatira and Ephesus. The Christians would need to be discreet, even secretive, but at least they now had a measure of protection from open persecution. Marcus resolved to place an image of the Emperor by his door. He would also insist the church meeting in either his, or Chloe's house would pray for the Emperor. At the end of a long and eventful day he slept, images of Jacob and Judith and the dead Gaius delaying his eventual slumber.

424

Chapter 44

Having ascertained the whereabouts of the former church leaders in Ephesus and the escapees to Thyatira Marcus composed suitably cryptic messages to be given to envoys to invite their return. His own slaves continued the repair of his home. Chloe and her women returned to theirs relieved that it was not being watched. Marcus continued the arrangements for the burial of his former devoted staff. Casca was helpful in this regard.

Phoebe and her family were honoured to have Judith and Jacob buried in their family burial area at the end of the olive grove. It was moving and very surprising to see Jacob's body carried on his own old bed borne by Sextus and Anthony. Judith's body had been carried earlier by Chloe and her women wrapped in unbleached material she had supplied. In the absence of clergy, Chloe recited several psalms before the burial, and they resolved that when the church came together there would be a more worthy worship memorial for them.

425

The missive sent to Ephesus, to Onesimus, included, of course, the news of the death of Jacob and Judith. In practical terms, Marcus now needed a new steward for his estate and a scribe for his office as magistrate, both roles hitherto fulfilled by Jacob. The letter asked Onesimus for help in finding a successor. In those days of risk to Christians, the words were couched in terms that implied, but not overtly that such a role would be consistent with the role of scribe for the church, if not an office of its clergy.

Marcus' new police force was initially ten of Casca's choosing from the barracks, but Casca, knowing the history of previous relationships included Sextus and Anthony in that force.

The interrogation of Gaius' former staff soon revealed the extent of the corruption, and all were blaming others for their participation in it. It was, however impossible to find the actual culprit for the death of Fortunatus and his conspirators for the attack on the wine convoy. All the fingers were being pointed at the dead, especially Gaius. Given Gaius bulk and likely fighting ability, he would not have been proactive in any conflict involving swords. The final judgement relieved no-one in Gaius former force. The most likely risks to future security in the community were sent to join the rowers in the Roman

426

biremes, and the rest obliged to join the building force labourers the magistrate required for the rebuilding of the community after the earthquakes. Bodies still had to be recovered from the Island ruin and that site cleared for future community purposes. The water supply and aqueducts were working in a much reduced capacity. There was much work to do, and Marcus' engineering experience was in demand.

A search of Fortunatus' properties eventually realised the discovery of evidence linking him to the earlier wine theft. Accusations from some of Gaius' force linked that assault on the train to Thyatira to a combination of forces made up of both Gaius and Fortunatus. The subsequent murders in Marcus' vineyard were an attempt to avoid the implication of Gaius in criminality while giving Gaius superiority in his power grab. Further volunteered information with subsequent searches linked Gaius and Fortunatus to receiving and profiting from stolen goods from piracy at sea.

As the labourers removed the fallen stones from the wrecked magistrate's building, Marcus was keen to recover any documentation. Jacob's church work on the life of Jesus eventually came to light. Marcus was keen to save it. Thankfully it was little damaged. None of

427

the labourers was literate, so there was no concern for accusation of Marcus keeping a Christian and therefore treasonable work.

There was much rejoicing at the return of the former exiles to Thyatira, though breaking the news to Agathon of his mother's death was a touching moment. By con-incidence, Anthony was guarding Marcus' house as Doria lifted a bundle from the ass she had led. Their eyes met. There was a smile of recognition. The smile stayed on Anthony's face for some time after Doria had carried her bundle into the house.

The church met in Chloe's house on the first day of the third week after Marcus' return when much of the repair work to the community and its homes was nearing completion. For the first time, some of Jacob's work on the life of Jesus was read aloud. Marcus, unusually, was tearful as he read from the scroll, "You will be handed over for execution and people of the world will hate you for your adherence to me." It was a much depleted group of worshippers, but most had tears, if not sobs in a hiatus that followed. In the absence of a Bishop there was no bread and wine. It would have been Marcus' first reception of the Communion in his home church had Onesimus been present.

428

When Onesimus returned some weeks later he brought with him a young deacon named Ignatius. They stayed with Marcus until accommodation could be located and made habitable. Pudens did not return. His health was failing and the journey from Ephesus was not possible.

Chapter 45

Several days after Onesimus' return, Marcus was entering his house to find the Bishop musing on the statue in the entrance porch. His comment was not unlike that of Jacob in those remote days of his first entry as a guest, and Marcus gave a very similar reply. "It is a fine piece of sculpture, but is only stone, so is no god."

"I think it gives the wrong impression for a follower of The Way" noted Onesimus.

"Given the present climate I think it gives exactly the right impression." Marcus was sharp to his spiritual superior for the first time ever. Marcus became more animated "I also have an image of Diocletian outside the door. Do you think I worship him as a god as well? I serve him as an officer of his law, but I will indulge the self-deluded narcissist until, like other men, he dies. I have no expectation

429

of his resurrection. And if I am challenged to give the same oath as Jacob, I will pay lip service to that fantasist to keep my life and serve the true God who I am sure will forgive me, even if you cannot."

Onesimus, unruffled, gently drew breath to reply but Marcus, provoked again to anger at the loss of his friend and steward and the former devoted Judith went on, "If the option is for us all to queue up for crucifixion, or in my case, beheading, where will be the proclamation of the Kingdom of God for the future?"

Onesimus did not try to respond this time. He reached up to put his hand on his friend's shoulder. Who would know, when the time came, what the response would be if challenged to deny the Lord Jesus, or at least put him on a par with a god of this world when the option was to die for the faith? Marcus' position as the man responsible for the rooting out of traitors to the god Emperor while being one of that number claiming Christ as Lord was, on the surface, untenable. Meanwhile, the report going back to Rome of two Christians being brutally executed seemed to satisfy the authorities of the observation of the Emperor cult in Casca's jurisdiction.

Ignatius publicly became Marcus' scribe as magistrate and privately his steward. Secretly, for the duration of the persecution, he was Onesimus' deacon and scribe for the church. His capabilities and demeanour were such that all expected him to be a bishop one day.

In due course, Jacob's document was copied faithfully several times, and Marcus, in the course of going to Rome to bring his wife and sons home deposited the new Gospel in the church in Corinth and Rome, where it was received with acclaim. Coming from Marcus in his baptismal name of Matthew, so the title was ascribed to the document in that name.

The soldiery attached to Marcus' police became permanently stationed in the town, and were eventually homed there separately from the barracks. Doria and Anthony set up home together, and in due course married. Both were baptised and became members of the church.

Agathon, in training by Marcus to be his steward. eventually was taught to read and write by Ignatius. At his baptism at the Passover two years later, as Agathon rose from the water, Onesimus laid his hands on the newly baptised and ordered, "Receive the Holy Spirit."

431

Looking at the scar on his forehead, The Bishop traced his finger over that scar and said, "I sign you with the sign of the cross. You are now a returned slave to the true Master."

The reading in that worship was from Jacob's, now the Gospel of Matthew's writing, and his Jacob's original hand. Baptise people everywhere in the Name of the Father, and of the Son and of the Holy Spirit, and obey all I have commanded. And I assure you, I am with you for ever, to the end of the ages."

Marcus hugged the young man afterwards. "Your mother would be proud of you." Octavia joined them her toddling son beside her and then clinging to her leg. Livius joined what seemed to be a group hug.

"Marcus you are truly blessed." The voice of Onesimus moved over them like balm.

Chapter 46. Epilogue.

Some ten years after the events of this story, Domitian was assassinated and the senate spent some energy decrying the man as a cruel tyrant. History has rewritten the narrative to show he may have been the administrator that set the economy and structure of the Roman Empire so that it could flourish under his successors. The next recorded persecution of Christians was to be found in letters from Pliny to the Emperor Trajan recording the torture of Christians to research the truth of their faith and loyalty. There were greater persecutions in the next centuries, and the church itself was torn by the issues of those of faith denying the Lordship of Christ in the face of possible torture or execution. One certain fact is the uncertain and nameless number of those professing the Christian faith who lived in a challenging culture who had a vision of a better life in the world if the values of the Kingdom of God, as lived and proclaimed by their Lord Jesus Christ. These are those we remember as The Saints, facing difficult choices in dangerous times, but with a vision for the better world433 still described as "The Kingdom of God."

Printed in Great Britain
by Amazon